# Praise for *Fool Me Once*

'I adore Karly Lane's books—t[hey are the perfect way to spend] time curled up on the couch wi[th ... Karly's books have such] compelling characters and relati[onships that I keep coming back] for it.' —Noveltea Corner

'With its appealing characters, easy pace and happy ending, I found *Fool Me Once* to be another engaging and satisfying rural romance novel.' —Book'd Out

'*Fool Me Once* is a guaranteed perfect light read ... Karly Lane has woven a delicious tale of lust, love, betrayal, consequences and chasing dreams, which as time passes often need to be reconsidered.' —Blue Wolf Reviews

'Karly Lane's affinity for the land shines through in her stories ... *Fool Me Once* is a feel-good story not to be missed.' —The Burgeoning Bookshelf

# Praise for *Someone Like You*

'Karly Lane's latest book is must-read ... there's plenty to enjoy in this sweet, rural read.' —*Gold Coast Bulletin/Cairns Post*

'The chemistry sizzled off the page ... I love this story and would recommend this one to anyone who loves some humour with their romance.' —Beauty and Lace

'Within an authentic country setting, Karly's trademark humour knits together a fabulous story about fresh beginnings and new love. A snapshot of Australia's colonial history is interwoven throughout the narrative with both truth and sensitivity ... Karly's novels are always full and rounded; reading one is like stepping into a new community for the duration and being welcomed in with open arms ... a heart-warming read that will have you flipping the pages long into the night.' —Theresa Smith Writes

## Praise for *Return to Stringybark Creek*

'Captivating, entertaining and most enjoyable, this return visit with the Callahans encourages the understanding that sometimes there are, even from the darkest of times, huge positives to be discovered.' —Blue Wolf Reviews

'Lane has added additional depth to this story that highlights the plight of Australian farmers and farming communities who are under strain . . . I'm grateful for the calm and considered way Lane has approached the topic. The Callahans have become a favourite book family of mine . . . they define family and friendship and it's been a real pleasure to read their stories.' —Noveltea Corner

'Karly Lane creates likeable, warm characters as she twists and turns her story . . . an entertaining read with an intriguing love story set against the challenges of farming and its stresses.' —*The Weekly Times*

## Praise for *Mr Right Now*

'To say that I've been waiting for the sequel to *The Wrong Callahan* might be understating just how excited I've been to read this book! Karly Lane has a wonderful way of creating a sense of place; and the characters leap off the page. These are books I know I can fall into time and time again and still be transported.' —Noveltea Corner

'*Mr Right Now* is another delightful read from one of my favourite authors, Karly Lane . . . Lane's stories have depth and explore many themes that are relevant to relationships in all forms, exploring father/son relationships and the old-ways versus the new-ways, farming accidents, diversity on the land, droughts, storms, community support, family and friendships . . . I simply can't wait for book 3.' —Beauty and Lace

Karly Lane lives on the mid north coast of New South Wales. Proud mum to four children and wife of one very patient mechanic, she is lucky enough to spend her day doing the two things she loves most—being a mum and writing stories set in beautiful rural Australia.

**Also by Karly Lane**
*North Star*
*Morgan's Law*
*Bridie's Choice*
*Poppy's Dilemma*
*Gemma's Bluff*
*Tallowood Bound*
*Second Chance Town*
*Third Time Lucky*
*If Wishes Were Horses*
*Six Ways to Sunday*
*Someone Like You*
*The Wrong Callahan*
*Mr Right Now*
*Return to Stringybark Creek*
*Fool Me Once*

# KARLY LANE

## Something Like This

ALLEN&UNWIN
SYDNEY·MELBOURNE·AUCKLAND·LONDON

First published in 2020

Copyright © Karly Lane 2020

All rights reserved. No part of this book may be reproduced or transmitted in any form or by any means, electronic or mechanical, including photocopying, recording or by any information storage and retrieval system, without prior permission in writing from the publisher. The Australian *Copyright Act 1968* (the Act) allows a maximum of one chapter or 10 per cent of this book, whichever is the greater, to be photocopied by any educational institution for its educational purposes provided that the educational institution (or body that administers it) has given a remuneration notice to the Copyright Agency (Australia) under the Act.

Allen & Unwin
83 Alexander Street
Crows Nest NSW 2065
Australia
Phone: (61 2) 8425 0100
Email: info@allenandunwin.com
Web: www.allenandunwin.com

 A catalogue record for this book is available from the National Library of Australia

ISBN 978 1 76052 925 3

Set in 12.2/18.4 pt Sabon LT Pro by Bookhouse, Sydney
Printed and bound in Australia by Griffin Press, part of Ovato

10 9 8 7 6 5 4 3 2 1

 The paper in this book is FSC® certified. FSC® promotes environmentally responsible, socially beneficial and economically viable management of the world's forests.

*For Guy Fawkes Bonza Girl, Guy Fawkes Romani, Guy Fawkes Dunvegan Lass 'Gypsy', and Guy Fawkes Dunvegan Lad 'Billy'*

A wild, unhandled lot they are,
Of every shape and breed.
They venture out 'neath moon and star,
Along the flats to feed.

But when the dawn makes pink the sky
And steals along the plain,
The Brumby horses turn and fly
Towards the hills again.

'Brumby's Run', Banjo Paterson

# One

Jason Weaver stood out on the verandah, cradling his coffee cup in his hand as he watched the sun slowly poke its head above the horizon. There was a crispness in the air, a signal that winter was on its way, but it wasn't as cold as other places he'd been, and he liked that sharp slap to the face from an early-morning rise. It reminded him that he was still alive.

He'd never heard of the township of Ben Tirran before he'd stumbled upon the house and land in an online real-estate search. Nestled in the New England mountains, it was a world away from the Hawkesbury region where he'd grown up.

He loved the bushland that surrounded his new home. Thick eucalypt forests full of brush box, Sydney blue gum and tallow-wood stood towering over the gullies and mountains that he looked out on from his back yard. Jason breathed in a lungful of clean mountain air as he rested his cup on the huge round strainer post that supported the fence. He let his gaze follow the high ridges that rolled, like a set of waves, one hill after another as far as the eye could see. His property overlooked a valley, the farmland of paddocks like a patchwork in varying shades of green and brown as it unfolded over the hills into the distance.

Jason had arrived just two days earlier, and the place could only be described as a fixer-upper, but that was okay because that's what he'd been looking for. It wasn't a cutesy little farmhouse with wide verandahs; it was more of a boxy, tired-looking dwelling that had been added to over the years by previous owners—none seemingly particular about improving the aesthetics. Despite that, the old girl had good bones and would come up a treat with a little tender loving care. He could already see the finished product in his mind.

As a builder, Jason was more than capable of constructing a new house from scratch, but he didn't want something new. New houses lacked character. He wanted something rustic; something he could put a bit of his own personality into. And most of all, he wanted peace and quiet.

It had been a rough transition from his army days. He'd had a lot to adjust to: coming back home, fitting into the civilian world again and adjusting to life with a disability. That had been the hardest challenge. It wasn't only that he'd lost part of his leg, it was that somewhere along the way he'd lost a part of what had made him . . . *him*. The army had given him purpose and stability. He'd planned on it being his career, and then one day he'd woken up in a hospital bed with half a leg missing. At thirty-two years old, he suddenly had no idea what he was going to do with the rest of his life.

He'd been lost for a long time after returning home from the Middle East—trying to work out where he fitted in. He wasn't particularly pleasant to be around for the first six months, but he was lucky to have a mum who refused to let him wallow in drink and self-pity for too long, and friends and a community who supported him when he started up his own handyman business.

He'd grown up in Lochway. All Jason's childhood memories were filled with the small town, but after his mother had passed away from a long illness, he knew there wasn't anything left for him there. He needed something new. A place he could put his own stamp on, and get away from the memories and constant reminders of the life he hadn't even realised he'd wanted until he couldn't have it.

Jason tipped the last mouthful of coffee down his throat and turned away from the view. There would be plenty of time to sit around and head down memory lane. Now, he had a house to rebuild.

∽

Tilly Hollis rested her arm across the long neck of the horse that was nudging impatiently through the bucket of feed at her feet. 'Anyone would think you're starving,' she said, shaking her head. 'Nothing could be further from the truth, could it, boy?' Her old brumby, Denny, who technically hadn't been a brumby for almost fifteen years, ate on, oblivious to her gentle mocking.

Denny was her star—he was the horse she taught beginner riders on and used in demonstrations. He loved kids and would stand as docile as a statue while they climbed about on his back. He'd been seven when he was caught wild in the Guy Fawkes National Park, and was the first horse she had ever trained. Tilly had bought him when she'd first moved to Toowoomba, and then when she had returned to the family farm, Brumby Creek, of course he had come too. David used to joke that he came second to a horse in their marriage. In all fairness, Denny *had* been there first, and Tilly *had* warned David about what he was getting himself into. A familiar pang of grief touched her lightly at the thought. It wasn't as painful now, not like it had been for the first year or so, but it was still there, lurking in the shadows. She gently pushed the sadness away and breathed deeply against the horse's neck.

Denny was a buckskin; he had a creamy tan coat, with dark legs and mane, the same colouring as the iconic horse from *The Man from Snowy River*—Tilly's favourite movie of all time.

That film had shaped her life, from her love of horses to her very name. She blamed her mother for the latter, but it was her Pop who had instilled the passion for brumbies. It was family folklore that her mother's side of the family were related to Banjo Paterson, the great Australian poet, and though no one had gone back that far in their family history to prove it, her Pop took great pride in the Paterson name.

Her mother, growing up with the Paterson surname and family pride, had fallen in love with the movie inspired by Banjo's famous poem. She had named Matilda after the main character's young mother from the story; Tilly's older sister was named Jessica after the lead character, and her brother was named Jim. Tilly hadn't thought it strange until she'd got older and realised that perhaps her family's obsession went a little too far, with their cats being named Mrs Bailey and Rosemary, and their dogs Spur and Harrison.

Her mother never thought it a problem. 'There's nothing wrong with being quirky and passionate about something, Tilly,' she'd said on more than one occasion. If you looked up quirky and passionate in the dictionary, there was probably a photo of her mother there—possibly her sister as well.

With a reluctant last pat of her trusty steed, Tilly trudged back up the hill to the house. She wished she had time to just hang with the horses. Maybe if she won the lotto, but in the meantime in order to keep her horses fed and her bills paid, she had a day job.

The cafe wasn't exactly her dream job, but it helped put food on the table while allowing her time to build up her business. She was a veterinary nurse by trade and would still have been doing that if there'd been a local vet close enough to make it practical. But the truth was that Tilly had grown weary of the job she'd once loved. Her passion lay in horses—it always had—and now her dream to build up an equine therapy business to one day become her main revenue earner was getting closer.

∞

'Morning,' Tilly called as she walked in through the back door of the cafe.

Allie glanced up from her chopping board and gave her a bright smile. 'Morning, Tilly.'

Tilly loved her workmates. Allie, the chef, was a single mum who had moved back to Ben Tirran a year ago with her three teenage sons after a divorce. It was hard to imagine that she was old enough to be the mother of teenagers. She always had a smile on her face and her long dark hair was usually pulled back in a ponytail, giving her a youthful appearance. Tilly knew Allie had married quite young and then had her first two children. She didn't like to talk about her second marriage, which had recently ended, but Tilly knew from things she had said over the past twelve months that Allie felt a little ashamed that she had two failed marriages and two different fathers for her three children. It didn't seem to matter that Tilly always pointed out it wasn't a big deal; it remained a touchy subject.

'Morning, Paul,' Tilly said as she put her handbag away and picked up her notepad and pen.

'Mornin'.' Paul was the least likely person you could imagine owning a cafe. His surname was Searle; Searle by name and surly by nature was how he was known. But the Cafe-*in*ated was his pride and joy. Coffee was not only his business, it was his passion. He had an intense dislike for the yuppie modern barista—the 'man-bun–wearin' hipster freaks givin' the coffee industry a bad name'. You would no sooner see a man-bun on Paul than a pink tutu on a construction worker. But he did make the best coffee Tilly had ever tasted.

'Morning, girls,' a bouncy blonde greeted them cheerily as she burst through the back door a few minutes later wearing the cafe uniform. Today Josie's T-shirt read: *May your coffee be strong and your Monday be short.* For a grump, their boss had a very weird sense of humour, which he took very seriously when it came to sourcing their coffee-related T-shirt slogans.

'Morning, Pauly,' Josie added as he walked from the front of the shop to stand in the doorway.

'You're late,' he said, mid-scowl. 'Again.'

'No, I'm not. Look,' she replied, holding her wrist up in front of the big man's face.

Paul pointed at the clock on the wall. 'We go off that time. You're late.'

'Oh, come on, five minutes. If that. It takes time to get this pretty. Beauty doesn't just happen like magic, you know,' Josie pouted, crossing her arms over her ample chest.

Tilly and Allie exchanged glances. Josie used her feminine wiles on men all the time, and much to Tilly's disbelief, it usually worked. Paul was no exception; it seemed Josie's heaving breasts were even too much for Surly Searle to fight.

'Set your watch to that,' he said, throwing a nod at the wall clock before turning back to the front of the store—but not before Tilly caught a creeping redness begin to make its way up the back of his neck.

'I will. I promise,' Josie cooed after him.

'Really?' Tilly said, sending the other girl a dry glance.

'What?' Josie shrugged.

'One day he's not going to be blinded by those boobs and then what are you going to do?'

'We both know that day will never come, *Matilda*,' Josie said sweetly, before sashaying from the kitchen.

Sometimes Tilly wished she could dislike the woman, but she was actually quite likeable. It was hard to understand—usually the Josies of the world were very annoying. Tilly couldn't think of anything worse than acting helpless just to attract the attention of a man, and yet Josie did it on a daily basis. At twenty, she was younger than the other two women, and Tilly suspected most of her behaviour came from sheer boredom. Tilly and Allie had been encouraging her to find a job out of town, somewhere with more opportunities than Ben Tirran. Tilly was a firm believer in broadening one's horizons, and if anyone needed their horizons broadened, it was Josie.

'Morning, Tilly dear,' the older woman seated at the window said as she came over.

'Good morning, Vera. It's nice to see you up and about.'

'I wanted to thank you for dropping my groceries off to me the other day. You're a good girl,' she said, patting Tilly's hand.

'That's okay, I have to drive past on my way home anyway.'

Tilly smiled. Vera Loveday had been a dear friend of her grandmother's and had been a godsend during her mother's illness, often staying with her so Tilly could come in to work.

Vera gave a small, somewhat annoyed sniff. 'It saved a visit from my son anyway—he's still trying to talk me into selling the house.'

Tilly knew Vera's family were worried about her living alone in the house she and her husband had bought as newlyweds almost sixty years ago. She was getting on and had recently had a small operation, but as far as Tilly could tell she seemed to be capable enough. She came into the cafe at least twice a week to meet up with friends and was still an active bowler. She drove herself around wherever she needed to go and even took her own bins out each week. It seemed a bit unfair that her son and daughter-in-law continued to hound her about giving up her independence as often as they did.

'It's no trouble, Vera. Honestly. You make sure you call me anytime you want me to do it again.'

'I should be fine, thanks, sweetheart. But it's always good to know there are people about who I can rely on if I need them.'

'Always, you know that. Now what can I get you today?' As Tilly took the order out the back, she smiled a little sadly, remembering how kind so many people had been when she'd needed help with her mother. There were a lot of good folk in this town and she valued the close-knit community more than they'd ever know.

Tilly heard the door of the cafe open and glanced up, noting with a touch of surprise that she didn't know the man who was walking in. She watched him move across to a table in the far back of the cafe, absently observing he had a limp, but waited until he was settled before she approached him to take his order.

'Good morning,' Tilly said pleasantly.

'I'll have a coffee and a bacon-and-egg roll,' the newcomer said.

'Please,' Tilly tacked on dryly. Rude people annoyed her, but she hated even more that she'd wasted a perfectly cheery 'good morning' on this particular one.

'What?' The man looked up at her with a slight crease between his eyes.

'You forgot to say please,' she said, taking the menu from him.

'Please,' he replied a little stiltedly, a somewhat guarded frown on his face.

'Not a problem. I'll have that brought out to you as soon as possible.' She plastered on an extra wide smile just for him, before turning away from the table.

'Who's the new bloke?' Paul asked, craning his neck for a better look out into the cafe.

'I have no idea. He's not exactly the chatty kind.'

'Send Josie out, she'll get the info out of him,' Paul said with a grunt, before getting busy with the order Tilly gave him.

'I should,' she said with a hint of malicious glee. He looked like the kind of man who would welcome a bubbly blonde chattering away in his ear first thing in the morning . . . not.

At this time of the morning the cafe was frequented mostly by locals dropping in for their morning coffee, and Tilly saw them darting quick glances over at the nearby table, talking quietly, more than likely trying to work out who the stranger was.

When Paul had finished making the coffee, Tilly carried it across, placing it carefully on the table before him. 'There you go. Your roll won't be long.'

'Thanks,' he said, almost reluctantly, but when Tilly looked at him, she noticed that he wasn't wearing the petulant expression she was expecting. In fact, she was rather surprised by the level look he gave her, his hazel eyes watching her curiously.

'You're welcome.' She moved away from the table, slightly confused. What on earth was that? He was a jerk a few minutes ago, and now he was turning those smouldering eyes on her. She wasn't even sure she wanted to admit they *were* smouldering . . . Clearly, she needed some quality horse time to realign her whatever-the-hell that was out of kilter.

Horses could fix anything—well, if not fix, at least help break down barriers, which could lead to ways to fix things. That's what Healing Hooves was going to do. Tilly had volunteered in a horses-for-therapy centre when she was younger and had seen first-hand the difference animals could make. Having horses in her life had certainly helped her work through her own grief over the past two years.

It had always been her and David's dream to create such a place, right here in Ben Tirran on her grandparents' property. She wanted to make a difference to the world.

'Order up,' Paul called, snapping her from thoughts of horses and her wish that she could be home with them right now.

Tilly braced herself as she made her way to the stranger sitting alone and placed his food in front of him. 'Enjoy.'

'Thank you,' he said, and this time there was less hesitation in his voice.

Tilly smiled to herself as she walked away. She had done her good deed for the day—given a grump a lesson in manners and hopefully turned his day around.

The door opened and the cafe began to fill with a busload of elderly residents from a nursing home on a day out from the coast, arriving ready for morning tea. She was kept busy taking orders and helping with seating arrangements, and when she glanced up later, she found the table at the back empty. Tilly told herself it was fine that he hadn't said goodbye. Why would she even care? He was probably some guy passing through, who she would never see again. It happened every day, people came and went. Well, maybe not every day—this was Ben Tirran, after all. She had far more important things to think about, though, like trying to remember what was on the shopping list she'd left on her kitchen bench. She was pretty sure there wasn't even milk left in the fridge to have on cereal for dinner tonight.

# Two

Jason dodged another pothole and cursed as he was jostled around in the cab of his four-wheel drive. He'd been on some pretty ordinary roads in his time, but this one, which switched from bitumen to dirt for the last few kilometres to his new house, was up there with some of the worst he'd ever come across. Well, bar the ones in Afghanistan maybe . . . Nothing was as bad as those roads.

There were a lot of things he was having to get used to around here. For instance, Jason now knew that he needed to allow an extra twenty minutes if he went into the post office due to the fact that the woman who ran it, Deborah, liked to fill him in on the history of just about every building in town.

It had started the first time he'd gone in, when he'd innocently asked if she'd known the family who had owned his property. About fifteen minutes into the conversation, and with an apologetic look at the line of people waiting behind him, he'd regretted asking. He hadn't even really cared—he'd just been trying to make conversation.

And if he was having anything delivered, he had to check not the post office but the produce store, which he had discovered was the only place courier services dropped deliveries for anyone in the area. Jason found this out after spending two hours trying to locate a lost parcel—on the phone between the courier company and the business he bought it from, because apparently it had been delivered somewhere. It was only when he'd gone into the post office a second time and got a snooty rebuke from Deborah reiterating that it was most certainly *not* in her post office, that she suggested he check at the produce store. He'd been driving all over town and abusing customer-service people all day and she'd left it until five minutes to five to tell him about the produce store!

Still, as his tyre hit another pothole, he pondered the idea that maybe a crappy road was a small price to pay for the isolation and peace he had out here. Not many people would be willing to drive down this road just to see him. He really did sound like a grumpy old bastard, he thought absently, and gave a reluctant snort at the blunt reprimand the shapely brunette at the cafe had given him earlier. Jason hadn't realised he'd stopped using manners. His mother would have been horrified. They'd never been big on ceremony back home, but they had been big on manners. His mother had drilled them into him as a kid growing up, and the army had given him a refresher course during basic training. He wasn't sure when he'd stopped using them automatically. Admittedly, Jason hadn't been much of a Mary Bloody Sunshine over the past few years—there hadn't been a lot to be happy about—but he was trying. He'd come a long way since his darkest days when he'd first come home. Miss Sassy Mouth at the cafe clearly thought he still had a long way to go.

Jason frowned. The last thing he needed at the moment was another woman problem. He'd come here to escape the last one—he wasn't keen on putting himself through that particular kind of balls-in-a-grinder fun any time soon.

He'd come here for a quiet life, but he supposed there were worse things to spend his time thinking about than that backside in those jeans and that slightly too tight T-shirt she'd been wearing with *You had me at coffee* scrawled across the front.

Calling into the cafe for breakfast had been a spur-of-the-moment thing after he'd collected the supplies he'd needed. He had food at home but the smells floating out the door as he'd walked back to his car had been too much of a pull. He was only human, after all, and the combination of bacon and coffee was enough to tempt a vegan to the dark side.

Jason got busy unloading the timber and hardware paraphernalia he'd bought, determined to get a solid day's work in on his place today. The old farmhouse was built sometime back in the early 1940s. Its semi-enclosed front verandah was in need of a facelift and he had plans to open it up to bring more natural light into the front of the house. The two side verandahs had also been enclosed at some point and turned into bedrooms, and he planned to extend a verandah from the front the entire way around the house until it reached the back, where he had a large deck with staggered heights sprawling down into the back yard.

The yard contained an old chook pen, long since abandoned and left unused to rust away and fall down, and a few scraggly fruit trees in desperate need of attention. A previous owner had obviously once lovingly tended the garden, but it had been left to go wild in the years since the old place had been abandoned. As far as back yards went, it was pretty rough, but his eyes saw what it could be with a bit of time and care.

It reminded him of his childhood home—his grandparents' house. He remembered watching his grandmother over the years as she tended her gardens and orchard, picking the fruit and preserving it faithfully. Eventually, his mother had taken over the preserving. Jason missed the bittersweet tang of the preserved peaches he always put on his cereal for breakfast as a kid. Standing now in his new home, he smiled at the memory; he hadn't given it a second thought over the years, until now.

The renovations didn't stop at the outdoors. He had extensive plans for the kitchen and bathroom: gutting them and putting in updated versions of both. He didn't mind that the project was going to take a while, he had the time. Jason had bought this place with the money from the sale of his mother's farm down in the Hawkesbury area, and he had a nice nest egg from his army days and payouts. He wasn't in a rush.

Jason didn't need a lot of money to get by, and if he did start to run low, he could always work. He was a builder by trade, having worked for his dad when he left school early before joining the army, and he'd been working as a handyman until recently, building up a sizeable business in Lochway. He'd left the company to be worked by a young bloke he hired before leaving, and still drew a tidy income from that as a sideline. But for now, he was just looking to work on his own place and enjoy the pride and sense of accomplishment he always got from creating something with his hands. It didn't matter if it was a whole building or a new fence—Jason felt the same joy in any finished product he'd played a part in.

He loved the sound of driving a nail home, straight and true into a fresh piece of timber. The sun was warm on his back, and as he measured and worked his way steadily through laying the boards in position on the first part of the back deck, Jason's thoughts drifted to the woman in the cafe. It was nothing, he told himself again and again throughout the day. It was normal that his mind would drift to something more interesting than banging nails into a piece of timber.

When he worked on his own, there was always plenty of thinking time—sometimes too much—but Jason preferred to work alone than with a radio blaring and some talkative bastard yapping on all day. In the silence between hammering, he could hear the birds up in the trees and the buzz of insects in what was left of the garden. It was one of the things he'd missed for too long while living in a war zone. There'd been days back then when he could barely remember what it was like to hear only a breeze in the trees or a bird chirping. It was something he'd vowed never to take for granted again and he looked forward to spending time in the garden.

This house reminded him of himself: a bit rough and neglected, but with solid foundations. Jason was a work in progress, Hayley would have said. He gave a small twist of his lips at that. It didn't hurt as much as it used to when he thought about her. It was more of a dull throb nowadays. Hayley had given him the tiniest glimpse of what a normal life could be. What a future could look like, when he'd never been game to think about one before.

With the help of a good woman, a man could find his way back from the brink of pretty much anything. He'd had hopes that finding Hayley had been the start of something great, only she'd fallen in love with someone else—his childhood mate. He'd really wanted to hate Luke, but deep down he'd known those two belonged together. Jason thought he would be able to handle seeing them as a couple, but Lochway was a small place and there was just no avoiding someone in a town that tiny. So, he left.

He wasn't ready to take on a relationship—hell, he'd barely got himself sorted out. Besides, who'd want damaged goods like him? He may have come to terms with losing half a leg—it wasn't like he had much choice—but he didn't expect a woman to be with a man who had a disability, when she could find one who had all his limbs. He was just a worn-out soldier-cum-tradie.

Jason was relieved that he didn't have to play the whole dating game like he'd once done. Nope. He was a confirmed bachelor and that was fine by him. While all his other mates were dealing with divorce, and kids who were about to go through their teenage years, he was going to be sitting back on his new deck, drinking a beer and taking in the mountains and sunset. He wiped his brow with his forearm and stretched his neck. Yep, he had a far better deal in life.

∽

Tilly watched the young gelding circle the yard, admiring the floaty gait as it lifted its feet daintily in a smooth, clean stride. Rommie was her latest trainee; he'd arrived a little over three months ago, unhandled, fresh off the park. She'd always tried to name her horses after something that was linked to their heritage breed. Rommie was officially named Guy Fawkes Romani, after the Battle of Romani which the Australian Light Horse had been involved in during World War One.

They were all unhandled, as in essence all brumbies were wild horses. Horses that lived in a mob, running free, never really encountering humans in the vast wildness of the national park. While Tilly loved nothing more than to watch these magnificent animals run wild, they had begun to overpopulate the park and needed to be controlled.

Tilly's grandfather had caught wild horses all his life, before they became part of the current trapping program. He, like his father and grandfather before him, had lived his life in remote, hostile country only accessible by horse or foot, and had always caught and trained his horses from the wild stock roaming the countryside.

Tilly had been gathering her small herd and working with them, preparing them for the next stage of her plan, to be her therapy animals. She'd put a lot of time and energy into her horses and knew that they could make an enormous difference to people's lives one day. In particular, troubled teens.

Pets in therapy had a long history, and the scientific evidence backed it up—animals aided in human emotional recovery from mental and physical health conditions. Horses in particular were extremely useful as therapy animals. There was something spiritual about the peace a horse could bring to a person's soul. To look into their huge brown eyes and see nothing but calm and serenity could bring a tranquillity rarely felt. Tilly's program would include working with horses to build trust and confidence. These particular horses developed special bonds with their handlers, and the reward of gaining a wild animal's trust was priceless. For a person with a traumatic past, developing that bond with an animal was often the thing that managed to open the door to more progressive help, building self-confidence and bridging the isolation that was a huge issue for people who had suffered traumatic experiences.

It was horses that had helped Tilly heal from the emotional rollercoaster her own life had been a little over two years ago. Losing her husband unexpectedly and then her mother's death so close on its heels had just about brought her to her knees, and without her horses and her dream to create the Healing Hooves Horse Therapy program, she wouldn't have been able to drag herself back up again.

It wasn't the future some would associate with a city-born kid—she wasn't sure it was something she'd ever thought she'd be doing either—but here she was.

She'd left school and found a job, working for a woman whose business focused on horses, providing horse-riding lessons as well as therapy for the disabled and emotionally troubled. Sue had been a trained psychologist and had devoted her life to her horse therapy institute.

Tilly had loved working with the animals; it was pretty much her dream job, but after a few years she realised there wasn't any real ability to progress, and being a stablehand wasn't going to pay her bills for much longer. Sue had done her best to encourage Tilly to go to university and study psychology, but university and study weren't things she was particularly interested in. Tilly admired Sue immensely, but in some ways, she was a little intimidated by the older woman. Sue was so . . . *smart*. The woman had more letters after her name than Tilly could remember, earned over many, many years of study. It wasn't a path Tilly could envisage for herself.

It wasn't until the vet who cared for Sue's horses suggested Tilly apply for a vet-nurse traineeship opening at his practice, that Tilly had taken the plunge and discovered she actually enjoyed the job.

She'd worked her way up through the ranks of the small city practice, but her real passion was working with larger animals, horses in particular. When her mother met a man and moved to Toowoomba, Tilly realised the potential such a place held. She applied for a position at a veterinary clinic, and two days later the practice manager called her with a job offer. Tilly didn't have to think twice before accepting and moving inland with her mother.

Though her mother's budding relationship hadn't worked out, Tilly met David.

She hadn't really given too much thought to the whole falling-in-love thing. Up until that point, she'd been totally consumed with work. Her parents' unstable relationship before her father's death had given her little idea of what the foundations of a steady, reliable relationship between two adults should look like, but when a tall, gentle giant of a policeman dropped in an injured dog he'd found, she figured out what all the fuss was about.

The dog was in poor condition, undernourished and neglected. He had, at best, multiple broken bones that would need surgery. The vet told David it looked like he would need to be put down. The dog had no microchip, and even if the owner was found, it seemed highly doubtful they would be willing to pay for surgery. At that point David stepped in and offered to pay the bill.

The vet had tried to talk him out of it, but David was unmovable.

'This dog is at least fifteen years old,' the vet told him. 'The operation to save his leg will cost upwards of three thousand dollars. It's a lot of money to spend on an animal who at the most might only have a handful of years left.'

'I'm good for it, Doc,' David had replied, with a smile for Tilly. 'Just do what needs to be done.'

They'd gone ahead and operated and the tough little dog had pulled through.

David had won her heart then and there, but it had taken another week for him to ask her out. After that first date, they became inseparable. They loved the same kind of movies and he didn't run a mile when she told him about the history of her name and her mother's fanatical love of *The Man from Snowy River*. A month after Tilly and David met, they moved in together. The scruffy little terrier, whom David called Pluto, made a full recovery after the few thousand dollars' worth of surgery, and spent the last few years of his life being loved and pampered.

David had a huge heart and dedicated a large portion of his time to the local Police–Citizens Youth Club. Nothing frustrated him more than watching kids head down the wrong path. His pet hate was drugs and the destruction they wreaked on families and young people, and he did everything he could to give kids an escape through sport and other programs he had helped set up through the PCYC.

In the back of Tilly's mind a plan had begun to niggle. She could see a program similar to Sue's working in this kind of environment. There was a need in the community for something that could reach troubled teens before it was too late for them to turn back from a life destined to end in jail time, or worse.

Life had been good. Life was predictable—which was also good. Tilly liked predictability. Her job was perfect—she was working with horses on a regular basis in the practice and loved the reconnection with the animals.

A year later she and David married, and her mother left Toowoomba as a new romance blossomed elsewhere.

For three years, Tilly and David had the ideal marriage. She settled into the life of a policeman's wife and counted her blessings every day to have found a man who loved and supported her the way David did. She loved her job at the vet practice, but in the back of her mind, a new dream was taking shape.

She became involved in David's youth work at the PCYC in her spare time, and together they planned the beginning of a program to turn problem teenagers' lives around with the help of therapy horses. They bought her grandparents' old property and were in the process of starting their venture when tragedy struck.

One evening in the carpark of the PCYC, David had intervened in a fight between some boys he'd been coaching in basketball and an older man—a known drug dealer in town—when he'd been fatally stabbed.

She would never forget opening the door to David's boss, Colin. At first she'd thought he was there to pick up David for work, having only just got home herself, and had called out to David over her shoulder to let him know Colin was there. But the look on the older man's face when she'd turned back sent a wave of unease through her.

'I'm so sorry, Tilly,' was all he'd said, and she instantly knew her whole world was about to fall apart.

At age twenty-eight, Tilly suddenly found herself a widow.

The first few weeks had been a blur. There had been so much to organise and so many decisions to make. Her mum had come to stay with her and help out where she could, but the gap David had left was too huge to fill. Tilly found herself unable to find joy and excitement in anything the way she had when he was alive—she even stopped visiting Denny—until her mum, at her wits' end, bundled her into the car and drove her out to visit her horse.

Once they got there, for a long time Tilly couldn't get out of the car. When she did, Denny gave a loud nicker, calling to her over the fence. As Tilly reached out and touched him, the horse leaned into her and she wrapped her arms around his neck, burying her face into his soft coat as the tears began to fall, followed by huge sobs that racked her body. Once the floodgates opened, there seemed no way to stop them, but Denny just stood there and let her cry.

After that, things slowly began to improve. She still had a hole inside her that felt empty and gaping, but she could at least begin to function once more. Each day she was a step ahead of where she'd been the day before.

Eventually, Tilly made the decision to plough on with her and David's original plan to move back to Ben Tirran.

Without David, Toowoomba held nothing but sad memories. So, she put the house up for sale and packed away her old life.

Selling the Toowoomba house was supposed to have been the start of a new chapter with her husband. They should have been embarking on a new business venture, but instead she was moving on alone.

The first year without David had been a nightmare—one long, unending nightmare. Then, only six months later, when Tilly's grief was still raw and with her plans in turmoil, her mother had found out she was in the advanced stages of breast cancer.

It felt as though everything in her life was slowly being torn away from her. She'd already lost so much. Her father had died in a truck accident when she was still at school. Tilly remembered her mother sitting on the edge of the lounge as the police officers broke the news. 'I knew it was going to happen,' her mother had said numbly. 'I always knew he'd die in that bloody truck.' She'd hated him being a truck driver. It had been the centre of pretty much every fight they'd ever had. They'd argue over money—how much it would cost when it broke down. How long he'd be away on jobs. She went into hysterics each time a truck driver was killed on the news. Her father had lost plenty of mates over the years, and her mother constantly worried about him when he drove. It seemed she'd been right to worry, but it didn't make his death any easier to accept.

The death of her father had brought about the slow burning destruction of their family. He hadn't always been at home, but once he was gone, it was like the glue that had held them all together had suddenly disappeared.

Their family became a bunch of strangers living in the same house. Everyone just kept their heads down and tried to avoid saying or doing anything that might upset their mother. Everyone except Jim.

Tilly's heart still clenched when she recalled that horrific time. It still sometimes didn't feel real. Her brother had been so young—he'd had his whole life ahead of him and in one reckless, teenage moment of stupidity, he was gone. The carnage left behind for Tilly, her mother and her sister to pick up had been just as awful as what was left on the road after his car accident. She could still feel the numbness and grief. The years may have passed, but the memories were still painful.

And then her mother's diagnosis. It was too much.

Some days Tilly had felt like staying in bed and hiding there forever, but she didn't have that luxury. Her mother needed her and so, instead, she spent hours sitting in hospital waiting rooms and ferrying her to and from treatments and appointments; then towards the end, long hours by her bedside.

Looking back, it was all a painful blur.

David had been gone almost three years now. Sometimes it seemed like a lifetime and other times it didn't seem very long ago at all. She'd almost missed the first anniversary of his death. It was only when his workmates sent flowers and messages that she remembered what day it was. It was surreal. How could it have been a year since she'd lost him?

A year since she'd kissed him goodbye that morning when he'd gone off to work? A year since she'd sat in that cold hospital room and wept, feeling empty and more alone than she'd ever felt in her life.

The second anniversary, Tilly was better prepared for. She had watched the dates on the calendar slowly tick over as it drew closer. Colin and his wife sent flowers and a beautiful card, but only a couple of his friends sent text messages. Next year there probably wouldn't be any. People moved on and she understood that, but it felt as though he were fading from everyone's memory far too quickly.

David had been her best friend, and their shared passion for the kids-at-risk program had made it seem like destiny had drawn them together. That's why it felt like such a betrayal. Why had fate bothered to bring them together, just to take him away so soon? What was the point?

Tilly walked into the cafe's kitchen and heard voices, spotting the man in the fluoro yellow-and-blue hi-vis work shirt who stood inside the back door, tapping details into his palm-held device.

'Hi, Tommy.'

'Hey, Tilly,' he said, giving her a swift smile before turning his attention back to Allie as he handed over the device for her to sign for the delivery. 'So, how you been, Allie?'

Allie scrawled her signature and smiled at Tommy. 'Fine. I've been working late shifts for the last week.'

'Yeah. I know. I haven't seen you around.'

'Well, I'm back on mornings this week.'

Tilly watched as Allie handed the device back to him. He didn't seem in any hurry to leave.

'How're the boys?'

'Good. So far this week no trips to the hospital.' With three boys, there was always someone doing something that required a visit to the emergency ward.

'That's good. We can't afford to have anyone away for Saturday's game.'

'They'll be there,' Allie assured him.

'You coming to watch?' Tommy asked, lifting the two small boxes onto the countertop.

'Yeah, after work.'

'Great. I guess I'll see you there, then,' he said, giving her a brief wave as he backed out the doorway.

'You know Tommy has a thing for you, right?' Tilly said as she watched Allie open the new delivery of coffee beans.

'He's just being friendly.'

'He never hangs around to flirt with me.'

'Tommy is the kids' footy coach. He's not flirting.'

'He's flirting,' Tilly said dryly.

She saw Allie's face turn red. 'Like I'd take that seriously.'

'Why not?'

'Because, I don't know. He's just not the kind of guy you take seriously.'

Tilly could see Allie was getting flustered, but this only intrigued her more. 'He seems nice enough.' She judged him to be in his forties. He was attractive; he'd had a haircut recently and had a bit of a five o'clock shadow going on.

'He is. It's just . . . I was warned by a few of the other mums at footy a while back that he's a bit of a ladies' man. I think there was talk of him cheating on his first wife. He's had a few marriages. I don't know, I didn't want to go into it too much. I don't need that kind of trouble in my life. I just want the boys to finish school and have some stability for a while.'

'There could be something in it,' Tilly conceded, 'but I'd make up my own mind about someone before I trusted local gossip. Especially around here. Some people in this town have far too much time on their hands and love a good drama.'

'I haven't let it change my mind. I just don't think it's a good idea right now.'

'Tilly!' Paul's booming voice reached her, warning of customers out the front. Paul didn't do customer service. He just made the coffee.

'Coming,' she called back. Allie turned away and went back to preparing the next order, adding salad to two plates, and Tilly let the subject drop. If there was one thing she hated, it was gossip—she had grown up surrounded by it—but she didn't want to push Allie.

She remembered coming home for her brother's funeral. Tilly had volunteered to go into town to get a few things on the shopping list, just to escape the oppressive sadness that hung over her grandparents' house in the lead-up to the funeral. Her mother hadn't left her bed or stopped crying, and Tilly just wanted a few minutes away from it all to clear her head. She'd been trying to be strong around her mum, but it was exhausting. While she was adding things to her trolley in the supermarket, she overheard some women discussing her brother.

'I heard he was on drugs, and goodness only knows what else he would have been doing. Fancy that. At sixteen?'

'What kind of mother lets their child run around in that kind of company?' another said with a disgusted huff.

'Well, we *are* talking about Corrine Paterson,' the first woman added, and Tilly detected a smirk in her tone that made her blood boil.

'Poor Dulcie, how she managed to have a daughter like Corrine, I have no idea. The Patersons are such lovely people too.'

There were a few murmurs of agreement, and then: 'I still remember when she ran off to the city and married that man—he used to beat her, you know. And she's been dragging those poor kids all over the countryside! None of them had a hope in hell of leading a normal life with a mother like that.'

Tilly was shaking as she stood frozen behind the display shelf in the supermarket, unable to believe what she was hearing. How dare these people talk about her mother that way. They didn't know her . . . they didn't know anything.

She didn't tell anyone what she had overheard when she got home, but the shock stayed with her. Her mother wasn't a bad mother—she just had an unhappy marriage, and her father had never beaten any of them.

Her mother had had a wild reputation in high school and was never one to particularly care what people thought about her—perfect fodder for the gossip mill.

Being a single mother, raising three kids and having to deal with the death of their father, only then to lose her son—that would make anyone more than a little depressed. She had a right to want to hide away from the rest of the world for a while.

Tilly didn't know who those women were that day, but she had never forgiven them for the way they had made her feel. Even today, she was wary of who she trusted in town.

When she returned to Ben Tirran after David's death, it had started again. Some of it was just natural curiosity, but there were a few times she'd overheard talk of her mother and vague mentions of, 'Wasn't there a brother who died tragically or something?'

It amazed her that despite the fact she hadn't openly talked to anyone about her private life, it became widely known she had recently lost her husband. Discovering that was bad enough, but to hear conjecture about how he died was another level of gossip altogether. Everything from a car accident to getting mixed up in a drug bust gone wrong had been passed about town.

Her mother had just shaken her head and given her a hug. 'Welcome to small-town living, baby,' she'd said dryly. 'The good news is, if you ever don't know what you're doing, there's sure to be someone else who will.' How true that was.

Tilly hoped she managed to hide her surprise as she glanced up at the man who was walking into the cafe. It was Mr Uptight from a few days earlier. Maybe he hadn't just been passing through after all. She waited for him to sit at the back table once again before heading over to take his order. 'Morning. What can I get you?'

'Bacon-and-egg roll and a strong coffee,' he said, reading from the menu before looking up and adding, 'please,' pointedly, but it was softened by the slightly wry twist of his lips.

Tilly smiled, genuinely. Mornings at work were not her favourite time of day—she would much rather spend it with her horses, but right now she didn't mind being here. There was something about this man that, despite her best attempts to ignore it, intrigued her. There was a strange vibe about him. A *keep away* kind of feel. He was clearly a private guy who didn't seem to be much of a talker. She wasn't sure why she liked that—maybe it reminded her of her brumbies and the way they put up such a fight at first to keep everyone at arm's length.

She was used to picking up on subtle signs with horses. They didn't talk much either, but if you knew what to look for, they did. A twitch of an ear. The widening of an eye. A movement of the head. It was much the same with this stranger. His body language told her a lot. He was a loner. He liked personal space, which was evident in the way he always chose the furthest table from the rest of the cafe's patrons.

He was also very observant. She watched him covertly from behind the coffee machine. He may have looked like he was minding his own business, but there was something about the alert tilt of his head that suggested he was aware of everything around him and ready to react if necessary. He had a coiled energy, something she had come to recognise, working with wild horses.

'Here you go,' she said, placing the plate and coffee in front of him a few minutes later.

'Thank you,' he said as he leaned back and let her set them on the table.

'Enjoy.'

'I will. The last couple have been great.'

'Couple? I've only seen you in here once.'

'I came in yesterday. You weren't working.'

'No, I don't work Tuesdays,' Tilly said, wondering if she was imagining the tone in his voice. Maybe it was her imagination, but it almost had an accusation to it. But that would be silly. 'So, you're not a tourist, then, I take it,' she said, against her better judgement. She should just leave the man to his breakfast and move on.

'Nope. I just moved to town.'

Ben Tirran was a great little place, despite the gossiping locals. The old abattoir had closed down twenty-five years ago, leaving agriculture as the main industry and most of the jobs on family properties. But then the mines had opened up just outside of town and the place began to flourish. New people arrived and brought their families with them, and the population had been steadily growing ever since. The town, though, had managed to hold on to its country charm.

'I was looking for somewhere quiet.'

'Well, you came to the right place.' She smiled. 'You don't get much quieter than Ben Tirran.'

'Good.'

She waited for him to add something else, but when he didn't she realised the conversation had shut down. 'I'll leave you to it, then.'

'Josie won't be too impressed,' Paul said in his gruff, gravelly voice as she walked past.

'Why?' Tilly asked, frowning.

'She tried for ages to get that bloke to talk and all she got was a grunt or two. You must have the magic touch.'

'Whatever,' Tilly scoffed, annoyed that she could feel a blush creeping up her neck.

'So, what did ya get out of him? Who is he?'

'I don't know. I just took him his order.'

'Seemed to be talkin' an awful long time not to get any info.'

'He's just moved here, okay? That's all I know.'

Paul gave a reply that was somewhere between a grunt and a huff as he turned away to see to a timer going off. She glanced over at the far table and saw the man in question looking her way. She averted her gaze, getting busy clearing away dirty dishes left on the front counter.

So, Josie had been trying to chat up the new guy? She frowned a little at the tick of irritation the thought caused. Why would she care? Josie always chatted up men and it had never bothered her before. Tilly frowned as she thought about it. Before David, she looked at men, sure, but she'd always been too busy to really care about having or not having a boyfriend. Then she'd met David and everything just felt right. But since losing him, it simply hadn't entered her mind to think of another man being part of her life, even for a date. Her heart just wasn't in it. It was impossible to even contemplate anyone taking David's place.

And she still couldn't.

'Thanks for that.'

Tilly gave a small start at the voice from behind her, turning to find Mr Bacon-and-Egg-Roll-Strong-Coffee. 'You all done, then?' she asked, taking a small step sideways to head for the front counter. She caught the faint whiff of sawdust as she moved past him, storing that little piece of evidence away to think about later. She tallied his order and he handed over a credit card. Tilly glanced down at the name written across the front. *J. Weaver.*

'Would you like to tap or insert?' she asked.

For a moment he looked confused—maybe even a little shocked—before working out she was talking about his payment method.

'Ah, sure. Tap is fine,' he said awkwardly and she bit back a grin. He was obviously old school. No fear of him ever coming in and using his phone or a watch to pay for his purchases. Not that they had a lot of people up here who did so. She handed him back his card and held up the eftpos machine.

As he tapped his card she let her gaze run across him. His caramel-brown hair was cut close to his head. His skin, she noted absently, was tanned, like someone who worked outdoors a lot. His hands were large and tough looking—the skin stained with dirt in the crevices but clean otherwise. So, he wasn't an office worker, she surmised. She smiled briefly when the machine announced that it had accepted payment, before ripping off the docket and handing it to him. 'There you go. Have a good day.'

'Yeah. You too,' he said, holding her look as he slid the faded leather wallet into his back pocket.

Tilly found herself swallowing past a suddenly dry throat as her gaze automatically followed the action, running down his white T-shirt and across his jeans, and quite liking the view. *Very nice indeed.*

'Sorry?'

Tilly's head shot up in alarm. 'Sorry?'

'You said something?'

'No, I didn't.' *Did I?*

'Okay. Well, I'll see you later, then.'

'Yep. Bye.' She bit back the groan that threatened, and turned away from watching his departure; the last thing she needed was for him to turn around and catch her staring at his butt. Although it *was* a rather nicely shaped butt, she conceded, thinking about it later as she wiped down tables.

# Three

Jason climbed in his car and shut the door. He sat quietly for a minute, rubbing his leg distractedly—he'd pushed himself too hard yesterday and was now paying the price. He stared through the windscreen as he replayed the morning's encounter. *So, what the hell was that?* It wasn't as though he hadn't expected to see the woman. He'd found out the day before that she worked every day except Tuesday and Thursday. *Tilly.* The other waitress had told him that was her name. What he hadn't expected was the stir of excitement he'd experienced the minute he'd walked into the cafe today and spotted her.

So much for the big experiment. Ever since the day he'd met her Jason hadn't been able to stop his mind coming back to her as he worked, but he'd convinced himself it was an overreaction, that his mind was playing tricks on him. She wasn't anything special—the only reason she continued to distract him was because he hadn't allowed himself to think about any woman since Hayley.

He'd decided to go back to the cafe to prove it. So, off he'd gone yesterday, ready to feel absolutely nothing once he saw her again—well, nothing but relief that he'd blown her all out of proportion. But instead, he'd walked into the cafe and a curvy blonde bombshell had sauntered across to him with a come-hither smile, tossing her long hair over her shoulder and jutting out a shapely hip as she took his order.

It hadn't been the woman he was looking for. He'd left feeling disappointed, but he had found out her name—Tilly—and when she worked. Still, if his theory had been right, then wouldn't the sexy blonde have given him heart palpitations as well? Okay, so admittedly she looked far too young for his liking, but shouldn't he have felt at least a small twinge of something?

Never one to give up easily, Jason had come back today, when he knew Tilly would be working, and prepared himself all over again. Today as he'd walked through the door his gaze found her immediately and he felt something go still in his chest. *Just be cool,* he'd told himself firmly. He waited for her to come over and felt his hands begin to sweat. *Sweat!* Jason couldn't remember the last time that had happened. Maybe when he'd been dared to kiss Karla Simpson in year five, but not since then . . . until now.

Okay, so as far as experiments went this one hadn't worked out the way he'd hoped. It was supposed to prove he'd been imagining Tilly to be something different to what she really was, but here he was, feeling as though he'd been stunned all over again. Today her T-shirt read: *It's not procrastinating if you're drinking coffee, it's procaffinating.*

She'd been every bit as hot as he'd remembered. And it wasn't just that—hell, the blonde from yesterday had been hot too, but she didn't make his heart thud against his chest like it was trying to fight its way out of his bloody body the way it just had when Tilly did nothing more than smile at him.

This was not good.

He hadn't been lying, they really did make the best bacon-and-egg rolls and coffee. Damn it. He didn't want to stop coming here now that he'd found it. But was he seriously going to put himself through this every time he wanted a coffee while he was in town?

Jason started the car and put it into gear. He would just stay away from town, only come in when it was absolutely necessary. That's what he would do. In time this thing would all fade away and he'd be wondering what the hell he'd been thinking.

Tilly smiled as a familiar couple walked into the cafe early the next morning. In their green work shirts with the Heritage Horse Association logo, dusty boots and no-fuss jeans, the couple projected an air of down-to-earth, hard-working country folk. They achieved a look that couldn't be copied by any fancy country-apparel catalogue.

*Something Like This*

Tilly often chuckled to herself whenever any of the nearby university crowd happened through town on their way to the coast. No matter how hard they tried, they could never look as country as the locals. Their boots were too clean and free of scuff marks. Their shirts still had the creases in them from the manufacturer. Their jeans were brand name and worn for looks, not practicality.

'Hi, Janice. Morning, Ted,' Tilly greeted them as she reached their table. She swore they hadn't aged at all since she was a kid.

'Morning, Tilly. We've got fresh horses in,' Janice announced.

Tilly glanced up quickly from her note pad. 'Anything interesting?'

'Maybe,' the older woman hedged with a poker face that finally slipped to reveal a wide grin. 'I reckon there's a few possibilities in there for you.'

Tilly had been waiting for a new batch of horses to come into the holding yards. She knew the association had been expecting word that the national park had trapped more horses, and it looked like they finally had.

'That's fantastic.' It was like Christmas for Tilly when they had new horses in. She never knew what would turn up. The brumbies had been bred up over generations with a wide variety of breeds introduced to strengthen certain characteristics: from bays with white blazes from their Clydesdale genetics to buckskins and palominos handed down from prominent Australian stock horse breeds.

Over the years, horses from the park had been caught and conscripted into various wars—her Pop had been an avid military history buff and rode his brumbies in many local Anzac Day parades—and Tilly loved the history attached to these beautiful animals. She shared her Pop's belief that they should be recognised for the heritage value they had provided for Australia. It was a sore point in other places across the country, and throughout the world for that matter, where wild horses occupied vast areas of national park land. The brumbies were a feral animal introduced to Australia, but unlike other feral animals the horses had been vital to the building of a new nation. Without them, farming, travel and even war efforts wouldn't have been possible.

These were the horses she intended to stock her herd with. Although they had heritage significance and were a rightful breed of their own, she couldn't help but love the term brumby, despite the fact a lot of people still associated the word with being feral. The romanticism of the name had been instilled in Tilly from a young age, along with the family obsession with *The Man from Snowy River* and all things early Australian history.

It didn't matter what they were called, to Tilly they were the link to creating her dream. She wanted to showcase these horses, to prove how valuable they were and to make sure they were never culled as they had been before. These horses were unlike all others. Yes, any horse could be used effectively in a rehabilitation role, but the fact that brumbies had never had human contact before they were captured gave them a unique quality. Their wildness—their almost magical purity—had a profound effect on everyone they came into contact with.

The thought of seeing some new arrivals sent a ripple of excitement through her. 'Is it all right if I come up on the weekend for a look?'

'Yeah, that'll be fine. We should be done assessing by then.'

For the rest of the morning, Tilly found her thoughts wandering. She'd been living within the restrictions of a very tight budget for the past five years, and while she was used to making do with the bare essentials and going without many of life's little luxuries that most people didn't think twice about, such as extra-soft toilet paper and name-brand grocery products, she was grateful now that she had saved so diligently. She had money put aside for buying the horses she would need for her new business and she was determined to spend it wisely.

That's why Tilly was so picky. The horses she chose had to have a certain extra quality about them—a quiet, sensible disposition, and a kind eye. After all, these horses would help to give some pretty damaged people a chance at a happier life. They had to be even more special than the average brumby.

∽

Ebor was such a funny town; more a village, really. It appeared in the middle of nowhere and had always been a resting place for weary travellers who had either just travelled across the New England region or survived the twisting, narrow road up Dorrigo Mountain from the coast. It was quaint with all the charm of a long-forgotten era. The drive from Ben Tirran to Ebor took about forty minutes, and like Ben Tirran it was surrounded by national park.

Tilly loved the property where the holding yards were located. Three hundred acres of the most beautiful country ever created. It was cold in winter—actually, it was cold for most of the year—but she didn't mind that when the place was so breathtakingly picturesque. The mountains and gorges, along with the rugged, unforgiving terrain of the area, made this the perfect home for wild horses. The vast majority of the surrounding national park was only accessible by horse, foot or helicopter.

Some of the most spectacular waterfalls were located around this area as well, including Wollomombi, Dangar, Crystal Shower Falls, and Tilly's favourite, where the Guy Fawkes River plunged a hundred metres over two waterfalls at Ebor Falls.

She parked her car and headed over to the large cluster of enclosures that were interlinked in an impressive maze of stock yards. The horses were divided into mares and foals, of which there were many, as well as young colts and older bachelor stallions.

She made her way towards the closest yards and folded her arms over the metal rail, watching the mob of young bachelor colts as they moved to the furthest side away from her. Tilly loved the older colts. There was something about them—she had a soft spot for the mares and foals too, but these guys were characters. They weren't much different to a bunch of teenage humans with all their swagger and cockiness on show. For the most part, though, they were brave in a crowd, but happy to keep as much distance between them and her as they could. All except one. The chestnut.

The others were dark, their coats varying from black to dark brown, but the stallion Tilly guessed to be about four years old was a deep red chestnut. He was magnificent. Sunlight filtered down between the tall gum trees surrounding the yards and caught the red in his coat, making his lighter, strawberry-coloured mane gleam. He'd taken a step forward, away from the rest of the mob, and faced Tilly almost defiantly.

'Well, aren't you a brave boy,' Tilly murmured softly, causing his ear to flicker towards the sound.

'See anything you like?'

Tilly turned her head as Janice came up beside her, before looking back at the horse in the centre of the yard.

'Yep.'

'I can't work out if he's got personality or attitude,' Janice said dryly, taking up a position beside her at the railing.

'Maybe it's a bit of both.' Tilly grinned.

'I reckon so.'

Tilly eyed the colt thoughtfully. Her plan had been to buy some mares with either young foals at foot or in foal so she could boost her stock numbers for future program rotations, but there was just something about this guy that drew her to him. Had her grandfather been standing here with her now, he would have said to walk away and think it over. He was a born horseman. If he'd ever decided to take up poker, she reckoned he would have been one of the best. No one had a better straight face than her Pop.

People had often told her she was a lot like him. Her mother and sister took more after her grandmother. Gran had always been cooking or sewing or knitting, and much to her eternal dismay, Tilly hadn't enjoyed any of those things. She'd always wanted be out with her Pop and the horses rather than stuck inside learning to sew.

She'd watched him buy many things over the years, everything from a car to a horse, and he'd always walked away at first. 'Never let a salesman see how eager you are,' he'd warned her once. 'Always keep them waiting.' Tilly hadn't been too sure why this was so important, but her Pop had always had a distrust of two things in life: banks and salesmen. It was probably a hand-me-down from previous generations, but she was surprised by how many times in her own life this advice had served her well. Sometimes you needed to walk away before making a big decision, just to make sure it was something you really wanted and not an impulse buy.

'What about mares? Anything interesting?' she asked Janice.

Janice gave a knowing grin before nodding her head. 'You're a chip off the old block,' she said as they walked around the outside of the yards towards a larger group of mares and foals.

'I can only hope to be as great as he was,' Tilly said, clearing her throat.

'Your grandfather was a good horseman,' Janice agreed, 'but he was an even better man. He'd be real proud of you, Tilly, and all you've accomplished so far.'

Tilly felt her eyes go gritty and blinked quickly. She still missed both her grandparents and, nowadays, even more so. What she wouldn't give to have her Pop here with her as she launched her dream. He would have been such a great sounding board for all her doubts. He was like a walking encyclopaedia when it came to horses, and she wished she'd been able to sit down with him and draw out every ounce of that knowledge before he died. Now it was too late. So many of those precious things were lost forever.

Tilly looked over the mob before her and immediately spotted two possible candidates. 'The tall bay,' she said, pointing to the centre of the group where a large brown horse with black lower legs jostled for position to be the furthest away from the weird two-legged creatures watching them from behind the fence.

'Yeah, she's a good sort. Only young. We reckon about two years old and she's in foal.'

'And the bay with the white stripe,' Tilly said, eyeing the smaller mare critically. She had a very young filly foal with her, maybe only two or three weeks old, Tilly thought.

'Yep, both good choices.'

Tilly trusted Janice's opinion without doubt. She admired the woman's dedication to the horses they rehomed. The association was made up of tireless volunteers, who cared about the welfare of these magnificent creatures and never again wanted to see the wholesale slaughter of horses in the national parks that were full of so much beauty. The association was entirely self-funded, relying on money from donations, memberships and the sale of horses to feed and pay for the upkeep of the property, so Tilly knew with each animal she bought, she was helping the future of the program.

'Righto,' Tilly said, pushing away from the rail. 'I'll take them.'

'Great. I'll sort out the paperwork,' Janice said, moving away.

'You better add the chestnut stallion too,' Tilly added.

Janice looked at Tilly for a moment, lifting an eyebrow. 'You sure you want that one? If he's going to be one of the trainees' horses, he might have a bit more spirit than you want. Could be a bit of a handful?'

'I'm not sure I'll use him for the trainees,' Tilly said, glancing over at the big horse. She knew she had to be savvy with her budget and not let her heart rule her head, but she couldn't shake the feeling that this horse needed to come home with her. Janice was right—he was a little older than the other colts in his yard, making him a young stallion, and even a novice could tell he had a bit too much spirit about him for a first-time horse trainer, but even so . . . she knew he had a place with her. She could figure out where and in what capacity later. Tilly's ultimate aim was to work the horses she had to riding school level. She trusted the ones she already had with her life, and was more than willing to vouch for their temperaments, but it took a lot of training and time to get horses from this stage—fresh off the park—to being quiet enough to use for riding lessons with kids. Still, she'd choose to do it with these horses over any others because she knew how special they were.

'Anything else?' Janice asked.

'I think that'll do for now,' she told the other woman with a grin. The stallion hadn't been on her shopping list today, but there he was. Tilly still had time to buy more horses before her business opened and so far she'd been very careful with her choices. She continued watching the horses in the yards while Janice filled out the paperwork, and by the time she'd finished chatting to a few of the other volunteers she knew and headed back to the car to bring the horse float up, she was satisfied with her buys and eager to get them home. It had been such a long haul getting to this point, but finally, there was light up ahead and Tilly's dream was almost within reach.

# Four

The next few weeks were a constant turntable of work–sleep–wake–repeat. The weather had turned nasty, raining almost nonstop for the past three days. There was a special kind of hell reserved for days working with horses in the rain and mud. Not a great deal of work got done, which was annoying in itself when Tilly was just beginning to see some real progress in her young stallion, who was now a gelding. A week later, with his wound healing nicely, she had just started working him in earnest.

She always bit back a sigh when people assumed training a brumby was the same as training any other unbroken horse. It wasn't. Most domestic horses had been born and raised around people. They grew up being touched and rubbed and handled. But with a brumby it took incredible patience and a lot of work just to get a hand on them.

Tilly and her new gelding had started to make progress, but now that they'd had a forced break in training due to the weather, she knew that she would have to revisit a few steps before they got back to where they'd been.

As she came around a large sweeping bend on her way home from her shift at the cafe, Tilly found a white ute parked on the shoulder of the road with its bonnet up. She didn't recognise the vehicle, but she pulled in behind it and opened her door, grateful for the break in the heavy rain as she got out to see if anyone needed help.

As she approached the set of jean-clad thighs that belonged to whoever had their head behind the open bonnet, she had a strange feeling. Then the man straightened and she came face to face with Mr J. Weaver.

'Hi,' she said after a brief, surprised silence.

'Hi.'

'I didn't know it was you,' she finally blurted.

He lifted an eyebrow at that. 'Or you wouldn't have stopped?'

'No,' she said quickly, 'I just meant, I wasn't expecting you to be . . . never mind. Do you need a hand?'

'Is that what you do when you're not working at the cafe? You're a mechanic?' he asked, pushing back to lean one elbow on the engine bay, seemingly to make himself comfortable for a chat.

'Nope. When I said a hand, I meant I can lend you a phone to call someone like roadside service.'

'Ah, pity. I could use a mechanic.' He shrugged. 'Thanks anyway, I've got a phone,' he said, bringing out his mobile from a pocket and holding it up. 'I don't actually need roadside service, I know what's wrong, but the part I need to fix it is at home.'

'Oh. Well, do you need a lift?'

'Actually, that would be really good. If you're sure? The road's not great out this way.'

Tilly gave a small grunt. 'Tell me about it. It's okay, my old girl's used to it.'

She led the way back to her older-model four-wheel drive after she waited for him to put his bonnet down and lock the doors. If she hadn't already known he wasn't from around here, she would have figured it out then. No one out this way locked their cars.

'This isn't the kind of vehicle I would have imagined you driving,' he commented as she hoisted herself up into the driver's seat.

She looked across at him, amused. 'What did you imagine me driving?'

'I don't know. Something a bit more . . . girly,' he finally admitted.

'I should kick you back out and make you walk into town for that remark,' she said dryly. 'But you've got a sore leg, so I'll let you off.'

'A sore leg?'

'I've noticed you limping the last few times you've come into the cafe,' she said, looking over her shoulder and in the side mirror as she prepared to pull out onto the dirt road. 'So, where's home? Where am I taking you?'

'Rhones Creek Road. About another five k's along.' Tilly gave him a sharp glance and he sent her a hesitant one back. 'Do you know it?'

'Whereabouts on Rhones Creek Road?'

'Three twenty-one.'

'*You* bought the old Browning place?'

'Yep.'

Tilly continued to stare at him. They were practically neighbours. Give or take a few kilometres of road.

'Is there a problem?'

'No,' she said, shaking herself from her stupor. 'I just hadn't expected you to be living . . . there.'

'Why? What's wrong with it?'

'Nothing,' Tilly said quickly. 'I mean, it's been pretty rundown for a while now. I don't think anyone's actually lived in the house for a few years. The land was agisted for a while. I didn't realise it'd been sold.'

'You know a fair bit about it.'

'I live just up the road from you,' she said, and almost chuckled as she saw his eyes widen.

'Yeah?'

'Yeah. Pretty observant, aren't I? I didn't even know anyone had moved in and I drive past it every day.'

'Well, in all fairness, I haven't really advertised the fact I'm there. And you can't exactly see the house from the road.'

That was true. Nothing had looked different about the place. The gate was still closed whenever she'd driven past, and the driveway was just as washed out and neglected as it had always been. But she experienced a funny, fluttery feeling now when she thought that he'd been right there all this time. So close she could have practically run into him at any point over the past few weeks and hadn't even known it.

'Well, there you go,' she said, before re-checking her mirrors and pulling out onto the road.

'There you go,' he echoed, turning to look out his window.

They drove in silence for a while, Tilly concentrating on the wet road, dodging the deceptively deep potholes now full of water scattered in front of them.

'I just realised I don't know your name,' Tilly said, more to fill the silence than anything else.

'Jason. Weaver,' he added stiltedly.

'Tilly. Hollis,' she added with a twitch of her lips as she mimicked him.

'So, how long have you lived out here?'

'The farm used to be my grandparents' when I was a kid, so I've kind of been out here on and off most of my life. But I bought the place and moved back here from Toowoomba almost three years ago.'

'That's a big move.'

'Yeah, I guess.'

'What made you want to move to this place?'

'I'm planning on opening an equine therapy centre and I could only ever picture it out here.'

Jason seemed to ponder her words for a moment. 'Why equine therapy?'

'I used to volunteer at a centre when I was a kid back in Sydney, and I like the idea of helping people. I've always believed in the healing power of horses—they've got me through some pretty terrible things in my life.'

'I've heard about animal therapy, but I'm not sure I believe in it myself,' Jason said.

'Why not?'

'I don't know.' He shrugged. 'I think there're some pretty dark places people can fall into, and I can't see how brushing a horse is going to fix it.'

'It's more than brushing a horse,' she said a little defensively. What the hell did this guy know about anything?

'Hey, I'm not trying to rain on your parade or anything, I'm just not sure I buy it.'

'Well, I've seen some pretty remarkable changes in the people I've worked with and I know for a fact it can make a difference.'

They drove in silence for a few moments before he spoke again. 'I didn't mean to sound like a jerk. I've been told in the past that I can sometimes come across that way. I think my social skills are still a bit rusty.'

As far as apologies went, this one lacked pretty much everything an apology needed, and yet she somehow knew that for this man, that was probably as close as you were ever likely to get to one. 'Why are your social skills rusty? Where have you been?' Tilly asked.

Jason didn't turn to look at her. 'I was out of the country for a while.'

*Well, this is like pulling teeth.* 'Travelling?'

'I was in the army.'

*Oh.* 'How long have you been back for?'

'Going on four years.'

'Were you sick of army life when you got back?' she asked. 'Is that why you got out?' He glanced across at her quickly and she noticed his wary expression. 'Sorry,' she said. 'Too nosy?'

'No,' he said, looking back through the front windscreen. 'I took a hit from an IED and ended up coming home on a hospital flight.'

'That doesn't sound ideal,' Tilly said weakly. Oh well, she was in too far now not to keep ploughing on. 'An IED is like a bomb, isn't it?'

'Yeah. Improvised Explosive Device. They make them with whatever they can scrounge up and set them in places they know the military will be patrolling.'

'That would have been terrifying.'

'It wasn't fun.'

'Were you very badly hurt?'

She took her eyes briefly from the road when he hesitated, and saw his jaw clench a little.

'There were others a lot worse off than I was.'

Tilly heard the steely edge beneath his tone and knew it was time to back off. She was picking up all kinds of body-language signals, just like in her horses, and these were saying very clearly, *I'm not comfortable and I don't want to talk about this anymore.*

His turn-off came up and she almost let out a sigh of relief when she spotted it.

'Thanks for the lift. I'll see you around,' Jason said, moving to close the door as he got out.

'Hang on,' she said quickly. 'I can wait for you to grab the part and drop you at your car.'

'Nah, it'll be okay. I'll go back later.'

'But I'm here now. It'll save you going back lat—'

'I'm fine. Thanks for the lift,' he said, cutting her off firmly and shutting the door.

Tilly stared after his retreating back, her mouth still open in protest. She abruptly closed it and gave a soft, incredulous grunt before putting the car in reverse and heading back down his rough old driveway. *Well, that was weird. And rude.* By the time she reached the road she'd worked herself into a bad mood that lingered the rest of the way home.

Jason walked up the front steps, noting the creak of the old timber planks beneath his work boots. That was on his list of jobs—replacing the faded, almost silver weathered timber boards. It was too dangerous to leave them much longer. The last thing he needed was to put his foot through one. He frowned. Knowing his luck it would be his only good foot.

He closed the door behind him and tossed his car keys on the kitchen table, taking a beer from the fridge on his way out to the back verandah and easing down into a chair. The view of the mountains before him felt like a balm for his bad mood. After a few minutes he tipped his head back and closed his eyes. He'd acted like a jerk again. He knew he had. He'd heard himself, but he couldn't do anything to stop it. It wasn't Tilly's fault. He wasn't angry. He was just trying hard not to fall back into a place he didn't want to be in. This was why he kept to himself. That way he didn't have to answer difficult questions.

Jason swore softly and took a long drink of his beer. It wasn't that her questions were especially difficult. Christ, it was just normal, everyday conversation, with questions people tended to ask someone they'd just met. What do you do? Where have you been? What happened to your leg? It was a logical question. He had a limp. Most people thought he would have a mildly humorous story to go with it, like he'd fallen down the pub staircase or broken it playing football. There was never a good way to soften the real answer, that it had been blown off by a bomb in the Middle East.

He'd thought he'd got over it by now—not *over it* over it, but over the whole waiting for the horrified look on the person's face once they found out the truth. Jason hated that bit. He supposed it was because he seemed almost normal, except for a bit of a hitch in his step when he was dressed in his usual work clothes. That's why it always came as such a shock. Maybe if he just met new people for the first time in shorts, there wouldn't be this awkward need to address the issue of his fake leg at some stage down the track. Jason had never quite mastered the technique of bringing up the fact he was an amputee at the very first meeting. Shaking someone's hand and saying, 'Hey, nice to meet you, the name's Jason and I'm missing half a leg. Nice weather we're having,' just didn't sound right.

Deep down he knew there were still some psychological issues he'd left undealt with that only added to his whole neurosis. He still felt like half a man. Maybe he always would. Jason downed a long slug of beer and put the can down on the table beside his chair with a little more force than was needed. He'd spent a long time proving to himself that he could still do everything anyone else could, and then worked hard to make sure he could do it better. He'd started his own business because he couldn't bear thinking about approaching some boss and trying to convince them that he was still able-bodied enough to be a hard worker.

Eventually, he could do everything as well, if not better, than other men in his trade and he prided himself on making sure he did the job not only as quickly, but to perfection. The army had taught him that. Discipline was a bitch to learn—they pretty much had to break you down in order for you to be taught, but once you had it, you had it for life. No matter what you went on to do—be it making your bed in the morning or building a shed—with enough discipline, it would be done and done well.

The thing was, he had no problem with his ability when it came to work, but when it came to his personal life—and in particular, women—he was nowhere near as confident.

He tossed the empty beer can in the oil drum he'd been using for a bin and listened to the satisfying *thunk*. Why the hell had he insisted on going back to that bloody cafe?

*Should have left well enough alone.*

The first rule of working with horses was that you didn't take your bad mood into the yard with you. She should have listened.

Arriving home, Tilly had gone straight down to the paddock and brought up Red. She needed to do something constructive to take her mind off whatever the hell had just happened back at the old Browning place. As soon as she started working, she realised nothing was going right. Red refused to respond to everything she tried, which in turn only made her frustration levels peak.

When the horse refused to hook up with her after she'd tried running him for a third time, Tilly finally snapped. 'What's wrong with you today?'

Across the round yard from her the horse tossed its head and stepped sideways.

*It's not him.* Tilly almost swore the words came from somewhere around her, but she knew it was just a trick of her imagination. The voice even sounded like her grandfather's. *You're the one with the problem.*

Tilly gave a sigh. 'I know,' she said wearily. Horses picked up on your mood. Her grandfather had taught her that from day one. 'I'm sorry, boy,' she said, lowering her tone soothingly as she looked away from the young horse. Almost immediately she saw him quieten his feet. Breathing out slowly, she continued to relax. 'It's just been a really weird day,' she said, taking a seat on the large stump she used as a mounting block. 'I don't know what I said to this guy, but one minute he seemed happy and talkative, and the next he'd turned as prickly as a damn pear.' Maybe she had been too nosy, but he'd started talking about getting hurt first. She'd just asked what happened.

What was his deal, anyway? At the cafe it was almost as though he wanted to strike up conversation, and again in the car, he was trying to be friendly . . . and then he wasn't.

After a few moments a movement caused Tilly to look up and she held her breath as the gelding took a tentative step forward. They'd been working together for a few weeks now, and she was finding this boy to be a bit of a tough nut to crack. He had a kind eye and beautiful formation, but she wasn't making the progress she'd been expecting. He continued to be skittish and wasn't responding as quickly as she'd hoped. Tilly knew that he was special, though, and she desperately wanted to break through the current barrier between them, but with horses, particularly these wild horses, patience was key. You couldn't force or rush anything. The payoff, however, was more than worth it. Once you earned their trust, you got it for life.

She knew if David were here right now, he'd be smiling that knowing grin of his—the one he always had when she'd vent about something, and by the end of it, would have worked out a solution. He knew sometimes she just needed to talk through a problem. He'd known her so well.

Tilly let her gaze follow the long sleek face of the horse. His big brown eyes were still wary, but there was a curiosity now that hadn't been there for the first few weeks.

This one small step was a huge deal, and Tilly forgot all her earlier grumbles. Suddenly, she was filled with optimism. She settled back and smiled. It didn't matter what else was going on in her life, horses always knew how to bring her back to focus on what was important.

Rowdy laughter came from the centre table where four women sat for their weekly coffee catch-up. They'd been coming to the cafe for the past few months and were great for business. Most of the women's husbands were working with the mines, which accounted for their money-to-burn attitude. They usually had two coffees each and made good use of the brunch specials, the sessions often dragging out for two hours or more. Despite this, Tilly found them annoying. She knew two of the faces from when she'd gone to school here briefly. They were a couple of years younger than her but they'd made her life miserable on the bus back then. Shelly and Veronica. Tilly didn't know the other two, but remembering those names stirred up unpleasant memories. She'd been ten when she'd first met them and Jim had been eight. Jess had already started high school and took a different bus. The girls had teased Jim mercilessly every day about the fact he couldn't read well or write properly, and she'd sat beside him, at recess and lunch and every day on the bus, being his big-sister protector. Shelly still had those beady little piggy eyes she'd had back then.

Tilly knew that it shouldn't bother her anymore. They'd been kids, but it was hard to shake her dislike. She didn't even really know them. Allie, on the other hand, did.

'Your friends are back,' Tilly said, preparing her friend for a big order.

'They're not exactly my friends. I just know them from the kids' school,' she said, taking the order slip from Tilly and scanning it.

'How was football the other day?'

Allie sent her a swift glance, before shrugging nonchalantly. 'It was fine.'

'See anyone special there?' Tilly asked innocently.

'No one in particular.'

'Uh-huh.' Tilly smirked.

'Would you stop?' Allie grumbled. 'There is nothing going on between me and Tommy. He's my kids' coach and that's all.'

'If you say so.'

'I do,' Allie said firmly.

'Okay, fine. Whatever. I just think it's a shame you're not giving him a chance. It'd do you good to have some company and fun.'

'Look who's talking. I don't see you putting yourself out there.'

'Because I have a business to set up.'

'And I have kids and a terrible track record with men.'

'You have awesome kids,' Tilly said, with a smile at her friend. 'And you're doing a great job at raising them to be respectful young men. I just worry that you're punishing yourself over something that's not your fault. You didn't do anything wrong.'

'I don't know, Tilly,' Allie said quietly. 'Sometimes I think I rushed into each of my marriages for the wrong reasons, and it's my kids who are paying the price now. I just can't risk making any more mistakes.'

'Your kids are lucky to have you. You haven't done anything to hurt them.'

Allie looked at Tilly with a brief, knowing look, before giving a faint shake of her head. 'You'll understand one day when you have kids. Mother's guilt seems to always be hovering.'

Another wave of loud laughter cut through the cafe and Tilly sighed, glancing out through the kitchen to the table of women. There wasn't any self-blame going on out there. Earlier when she'd walked past, she'd overheard one of the women explaining how she'd just come back from a shopping spree in Tamworth, and after her husband complained about how much money she'd spent, she told him that a divorce settlement would cost him more.

Tilly sighed again. No wonder she preferred horses to people.

# Five

Tilly eased into the saddle and concentrated on keeping her body relaxed. She had a number of horses at various stages of training and she'd been working steadily with this one, Sheeba, for the last few months and had just started under saddle. Tilly was impressed with the young mare's gentle nature and happy she was such a quick learner. This was only her third ride and already she was handling it like a seasoned pro. With a quick click of her tongue, Tilly set out at a walk in a wide circle in the middle of the large sand-floored arena she used for riding lessons. It had been the first and most expensive item on her list in preparation for launching Healing Hooves Horse Therapy. The covered arena would mean she could run her current riding lessons rain, hail or shine, and also move the Healing Hooves program in here should bad weather suddenly make an appearance. It'd been the best investment she'd ever made.

After a few circles, Tilly gave a little kiss sound that Sheeba was trained to recognise as the signal to move into a trot and then effortlessly transitioned into her gentle, loping canter. Tilly practised switching from one gait to another for a few circles, then put the little bay mare through a series of other movements—backing her up as well as stopping and starting with verbal commands.

'Good girl, Sheeba,' Tilly praised, bending down to rub the mare's neck affectionately. She looked up as she heard a car pull into the driveway, and frowned slightly as she recognised her visitor.

'Hi,' Jason said as he approached, and she could tell by the way he avoided her gaze that he wasn't as calm as his easy greeting would imply.

'Hello. Got your car running?'

'Yeah.' He turned his head to glance over his shoulder, still avoiding her eye. 'Good as new.'

'Well, that's good.' If he wanted to pretend they hadn't left on a weird note, then she'd just play along. Tilly urged Sheeba towards the gate and dismounted, dropping lightly from the saddle onto the sand floor and leading the horse out of the arena towards the tack shed.

'I, ah—' he cleared his throat, walking along beside her '—just wanted to drop in and thank you,' he said. 'For the lift the other day.'

'No worries.' Tilly tied Sheeba to a post and began removing her saddle.

*Something Like This*

'It would have been a long walk,' he said, with a brief glance her way before fixing his eyes back on the horse.

'Well, I was hardly going to leave someone stranded on the side of the road.' She carried the saddle to its rack and returned to remove the bridle, replacing it with a halter to click a lead rope onto.

'You make a habit of picking up strangers, then?' he asked, turning to look at her with a slight frown.

'You weren't a stranger.' His attitude started to prickle.

'Near enough. You shouldn't trust people so blindly.'

'Blindly?'

'Just because I'd been into the cafe a few times doesn't mean you know me.'

'Good to know. Next time I'll just drive past,' she snapped. 'I've got things to do.'

'Look,' Jason said, running a hand through his short hair irritably, before blowing out a sharp breath, 'I'm sorry. That came out wrong. I told you my social skills were a bit rusty.'

Tilly wasn't sure that being an overbearing, condescending jerk could be blamed on rusty social skills.

'I just meant that I could have been anyone. I'd hate to think of you putting yourself at risk.'

'I'd like to think I'm not a complete moron. I'm usually pretty good at reading people and I didn't think you'd be a risk. I'm beginning to question my judgement now, though,' she said, moving past him to walk Sheeba back to a nearby yard, all the while hoping he would take the hint and leave.

He didn't.

'All I'm trying to say . . . albeit, badly,' Jason said with a wince, 'is that while you think you know me, you don't know all that much.'

'Oh, I don't know . . . I'm starting to figure out a few things,' she said through gritted teeth.

'My limp,' he continued, ignoring her tone, 'isn't from a sore leg.'

This caught her attention and she eyed him with reluctant curiosity.

'I don't have a leg. Well. Lower leg,' he amended, leaning down to tug his pants up to reveal a stainless-steel prosthetic leg. 'That's why I limp. That's why you shouldn't assume that you can know everything about someone you just met. And why you should be careful who you pick up on the side of the road,' he said stiffly.

'What's missing a leg got to do with anything? Were you planning to beat me to death with it or something?'

For a moment he stared at her, his mouth slightly open in disbelief before a stern, straight line replaced it. 'It's not the leg. I'm pointing out that even though you said you thought you knew me, you didn't even know about this,' he said, gesturing towards his leg.

'So what? Even if I knew you had a missing leg, I still would have stopped. I knew you from the cafe.'

'Forget it,' he said, turning away.

Tilly gave a short huff. 'Wait a minute,' she said irritably as she trailed after him.

'I should mind my own business,' he said, holding a hand up.

'Is that why you came here today? To lecture me?'

'No. I came to apologise.'

'That's strange, because I didn't hear any apology. All I heard was you treating me like some kind of idiot because I stopped to help out a neighbour.'

'You didn't know I was a neighbour at the time,' he pointed out, leaning against the side of his car.

'That's beside the point.'

'Okay, then.' Jason's sarcasm was not missed.

'The point is, out here we stop and help. I don't know why you're making such a big deal about it.'

'Do you watch the news at all?'

'Oh, for goodness sake,' she muttered, at peak exasperation level. 'Fine. Non-apology accepted.' Tilly didn't wait for a reply as she marched back to her horse.

Jason clenched his jaw the whole way down the driveway. That had not gone the way he'd planned. At all. He dodged a large pothole in the road and muttered under his breath. All he'd been trying to do was point out that her trusting nature could very well have got her into trouble. He could have been an axe murder for all Tilly knew.

Still, had she not stopped and given him a lift, his day would have been much worse. So, there was that.

When he'd caught sight of her riding, he'd pulled the car to a stop, watching her as she'd gracefully cantered the brown horse in a large circle. He'd never really taken much notice of anyone riding before—but watching Tilly, he'd been mesmerised by the way horse and woman moved almost as one. He'd been reluctant to interrupt, but as she'd slowed down and then seemed to be wrapping the session up, he'd realised his car had been idling in the driveway and he didn't want her to notice him sitting there spying on her.

Why the hell couldn't he stop finding any excuse to see this woman? Yeah, she was good-looking, but even from their first encounter she was pretty bloody annoying—calling him out for not saying please and thank you. Opinionated women had never been his type before. Admittedly, his type had been pretty limited for a long while now. He wasn't even sure he *had* a type. But he was fairly certain that there had to be women around who were a lot less prickly. The blonde woman from the cafe crossed his mind briefly, but he instantly dismissed her. She wouldn't hold his interest the way Tilly did. Buggered if he knew why, though.

When Jason pulled into his driveway he forced himself to release a long breath. He didn't want to go through another few days with this eating at him the way it had been. With a reluctant groan he headed back the way he'd just come.

Tilly was in the centre of the yard holding a long stick, slowly turning as a young horse, different to the one she had just been riding, ran in a circle around her, kicking up sand as it went.

Jason pulled up again and saw Tilly turn to shade her eyes against the last of the afternoon sun and then straighten as he strode towards her. He didn't give her a chance to open her mouth, instead he started talking before he'd even reached her.

'I'm sorry, all right? I didn't mean to come here and lecture you. I don't think you're an idiot.'

When she went to cut in, he held up a hand. 'Just let me say what I came here to say the first time.'

Tilly closed her mouth and folded her arms across her chest warily.

'I wanted to explain about the other day. The way we left things . . . I don't talk much about what happened. I guess it kind of caught me off guard. My leg . . .' Jason made the mistake of looking up and saw her watching him, and it threw him off again. He was almost hoping he would see unease or maybe discomfort so he could just put an end to this weird attraction he was feeling. But no, she was standing there, patiently waiting for him to speak as if the fact he'd revealed he had half a leg missing hadn't even registered. 'I wasn't expecting to tell you all that the other day.'

In the silence that followed, he saw her twist her lips slightly. 'I was probably being a little too nosy,' she conceded with a shrug. 'I didn't mean to back you into a corner.'

'Wasn't your fault. I'm just not used to the whole . . . conversation thing.'

Tilly gave a small chuckle. 'No kidding.'

'I'm making an effort,' he said, and realised it'd come out sounding a tad more defensive than he'd intended.

'Well, I suppose I can make allowances.'

'Good,' he said, shuffling a little. Now that he'd got that off his chest, he wasn't sure where to go from here. A low nicker from the centre of the ring drew his attention. 'What were you doing . . . with the horse?' he asked, nodding at the animal standing to one side, looking much calmer than it had been when he'd first arrived.

'We were having an attitude adjustment,' Tilly said dryly, following his gaze to rest on the horse. 'This guy decided he didn't really want to listen today, so we did a bit of lunging.'

He lifted an eyebrow, waiting for her to continue.

'In the wild, the lead mare will run a misbehaving or new horse out of the mob until it decides to do as it's told, then she'll invite it back in once it's showing respect again. This bloke just needed a bit of a refresher course on who's the boss, didn't you, mate?' she said, turning back to the animal, who looked a little more docile and was no longer tossing its head around.

'So, this therapy thing of yours, with the horses. How does it work?' Jason asked.

'Look at you go, making conversation,' she said, sending him a grin then giving an offhand shrug. 'It's basically about taking a group of people who need something and using a measured exposure to horses to help them find focus and meaning. I'm starting with troubled teens, but as I develop the program I'm hoping to open it up to lots of other different areas.

'Then I'd like to set up other non-therapy related things, such as trail riding and pack saddling for overnight camps to add to the business. We have some of the most spectacular national parks in the world, just right for showing off to tourists and locals. It's an untapped market.'

After a brief pause, Jason frowned slightly. 'But how, exactly, do the horses help troubled kids?'

'Gaining the trust of a five-hundred-kilo wild animal gives a person quite the confidence boost,' Tilly said dryly, before adding seriously, 'There's a sense of accomplishment. They've met this animal that starts out running away from them and refuses to be handled, and over time, with patience and persistence, they develop a bond. The horses allow them to take themselves out of their own problems for a while and focus on something else, and then when they see what they've accomplished, they realise just how far they've actually come.'

'So, are the kids actually breaking in the horses?'

'God no,' she said with a horrified look. 'They're simply initiating contact. Depending on the horse, sometimes that'll happen fast and they might get as far as haltering and leading, maybe being able to groom it, although the programs are only short ones, so I'm not expecting to get further than just a touch or two, although that's usually more than enough to make some pretty impressive changes in a kid . . . or anyone, for that matter.'

'Are you able to continue buying new horses in with each new group? Won't you end up with too many?'

'I won't need to use unhandled horses with every group. I just like to use them for troubled kids, because they really do see the results so dramatically. I think they see something of themselves in the horses—the trust issues and whatnot—but it'll depend on what kind of groups I get. These horses will go on to be trained to be ridden eventually and can always be used for groundwork skills. I've got my stable of rideable horses for the riding school side of things, and I'm looking to increase the numbers with some of these once they're trained and I've put some miles on them with regular riding.'

Jason was impressed. His gaze moved across to a big red horse further over. 'How come you don't just breed your own instead of buying them in?'

'Because I want to support the rehoming program. I've got a few mares who've come already in foal, but it doesn't make sense to breed them while there're still so many to rehome in the park.'

He liked her honest, open attitude to the whole thing. Tilly's passion for her horses and the program lit up her face and momentarily distracted him.

'I have to take Red his hay, if you want to come down and have a look,' Tilly said, crossing to pick up a couple of slices of the hay from the larger bale by her feet.

'Here, let me,' Jason said, making to take the hay from her, but stood back when she sent him a look.

'Thanks, but I can manage.'

Maybe he was even rustier than he'd first suspected. Clearly it was the wrong move to offer any kind of gallantry. Not that he'd ever been accused of being the gallant kind before. Jason walked beside her as she headed towards the other yards and tried to stay out of her way as she unlocked the gate and slowly eased inside. The horse watched her warily, his feet moving slightly as Tilly closed the gate, without taking her eyes from the animal standing across from her.

Immediately, the animal sprang into action and ran, his backside crashing into the fence panels during the panic, banging the metal, which only seemed to freak the horse out more. Jason was half ready to leap the fence and grab Tilly, but instead of looking terrified, she was moving towards the crazed horse appearing to be calm but focused.

'There's a good man,' she said, in a low gentle tone that made Jason wish she were talking to him.

He watched as she eased closer, and the horse stopped, his eyes fixed on her, although he didn't look any less at ease as his nostrils flared and his ears twitched. Tilly slowly broke off a section of the hay and lowered it to the ground, then took a small step back. After a few moments the animal tentatively stepped forward and gingerly nibbled at the hay. 'Good fella,' Tilly crooned, before slowly leaving the yard.

'How long have you had this one?' he asked when she came to stand beside him.

'Only a couple of weeks.'

'The others seem a bit quieter. Is that normal?'

'They're all different, like people, I guess. The foals tend to be easier to win over—they're like little kids, naturally inquisitive. The mums are usually a little more wary, but once they get the hang of regular feed and feel safe with some basic handling, they settle fairly quickly. This guy, though—he's going to be a bit of a challenge, I think.'

'Will he be handled by beginners?' The thought of anyone without any horse-handling experience getting in the pen with this thing was more than a little alarming.

'No.'

'I thought the whole point was to get these unbroken ones in to work with the kids?'

'Yeah. Well, I had a weak moment. I don't know what this guy's purpose is, but I guess we'll find out sooner or later. For now, I just need to get him settled and start handling him.'

'Have you ever had one you couldn't tame?'

'Not yet,' Tilly said, shooting Jason a swift grin. 'They really aren't that hard to quieten. When they're captured it's more that they don't understand the concept of being contained in a yard. In the bush they don't have things that run horizontal like yard rails—they're used to swerving in and out of trees and saplings—so it's a bit of a shock to come across fences. But they figure it out soon enough, and once you start feeding them and they sense you're no threat, they actually quieten down quite a lot. Once you earn their trust you've got a friend for life.'

They stood and watched the horse eat his hay, and although he seemed intent on his meal, Jason was fairly certain he was very aware of exactly where they were and what they were doing, and the slightest movement would set him off again. Jason walked away from the yard with a new respect for the woman by his side. He'd been in more than his fair share of sticky situations over the years in hostile countries, but he wasn't sure he'd have the guts to get inside a yard with that horse the way she just did. Jason couldn't decide if she was incredibly brave or just plain crazy.

# Six

Tilly lay in her bath that evening, her eyes closed as she listened to the soothing Celtic music playing on her phone. This was her one guilty pleasure. After being on her feet all day at the cafe and then coming home to work and feed the horses, a hot bath was her reward. It gave her time to reflect on the day and unwind. Tonight, though, she was finding it really hard to relax, despite the candles and the bubbles and the music. The afternoon visit kept playing over in her mind.

Tilly had been on edge since the disastrous afternoon she'd dropped him home. She knew that talking about his previous life in the army had contributed to him shutting down the conversation the way he did, and she felt bad about digging up old memories for him. But until today, she hadn't known exactly what had caused the abrupt halt to the conversation that afternoon.

Jason hadn't given Tilly time to react to his unexpected revelation today and now, with hindsight, she could see he was clearly uneasy about the whole thing. She felt like a bit of a dill when she thought back to her offhand comments about noticing his limp. Tilly swished the water absently with her fingers as the sound of soft harps and flutes floated in the steam-filled bathroom around her. She sighed. How was she supposed to know he'd lost a leg? He'd been wearing work pants or jeans every time she'd seen him, and his limp wasn't all that noticeable. She'd been shocked when he'd jerked his pants up to show his prosthetic leg—as any sane person would have been, quite frankly, but he'd barely given her a chance to respond. He'd got her hackles up by taking on that condescending tone about picking up strangers, and they'd somewhat brushed over the fact he had just revealed he'd lost half a leg.

Now, Tilly still wasn't sure what she would have said about it even if he had given her time. She'd been too annoyed with the way the conversation was going to bother wasting any sympathy on him, but that didn't mean she didn't have compassion. It had to make life difficult to work in a labour-intensive trade like building. The fact that Jason was able to said a lot for the guy's character. No one would blame him if he'd decided that working was too hard and sat around feeling sorry for himself all day—but that's not what he was doing.

Still, the afternoon hadn't been a complete waste. Tilly was glad they'd had the opportunity to clear the air. She just wished it didn't matter to her so much. This guy was occupying way too many of her thoughts lately.

She wasn't supposed to be dealing with something like this yet. It wasn't clear when a new man was scheduled to fit in with her plan as it hadn't been in the *Widow's Handbook for Beginners.* Tilly wished there *was* some kind of magical book with all the answers so she could figure out how she was supposed to feel and what she was supposed to do. She knew there was a whole shelf in the bookstore dedicated to self-help tomes of wisdom. She'd made herself go in there once and leafed through a couple, but found them a bit too clinical. The advice to get out and socialise was great, unless of course you were the carer for your sick mother—not that she'd felt like socialising all that much when David had been alive either. Nope, Tilly just wanted a book that told her all the decisions she'd made on her own were the right ones and that everything would turn out fine. But so far she hadn't found a book that did that.

The only thing she'd been focusing on was getting her horse therapy program up and running. Part of her felt like she was betraying David by even thinking about Jason in any way other than as a customer from the cafe, and yet another part of her was clearly interested, judging by the way her stomach always ended up in knots when she saw him. *Why him?* The thought made her frown deepen. Sure, he wasn't bad on the eyes. If you liked the stubble-jawed, rugged type. Jason was in pretty good shape. He was like most of the men around here—farmers whose lifestyle and living gave them all the workout they needed. His personality wasn't exactly a drawcard, though that had improved. He'd started out of the silent-bordering-on-surly kind, but he'd started to warm up. Maybe it was just that in Jason she sensed someone who had been dealt some of life's crueller cards and come out the other side.

Well, whatever it was, maybe taking a step back would be a good idea to see if it calmed down. She was probably overanalysing everything, making it a bigger deal than it really was. There was no reason Tilly needed to see Jason outside of work, so it shouldn't be too hard to avoid any further encounters. Surely it was just a passing thing . . . she would just lie low and everything would get back on track.

∽

Tilly carried a pile of dirty plates out to the cafe kitchen and put them on the sink. She glanced up at Allie and saw her frowning into the sudsy water.

'What's wrong?'

'Oh, nothing. Tommy was just here,' she said, looking over to where a stack of mail lay on the bench.

Normally Tilly would tease her, but this morning Allie didn't look in the mood. 'What happened?'

'He asked me out.'

Tilly tried not to look as surprised as she felt. 'What did you say?'

'I said I didn't think it would be a good idea.'

'Oh.'

'Don't you give me that look. I already feel bad that Tommy looked at me like a wounded puppy.'

'I'm the last person who should be giving advice here, so all I'm going to say is this: If you like the man, you really should give it a go. I know you're thinking of your kids, but you have the right to be happy. Life's too short.'

'I just don't think I can trust him,' Allie said with a sigh. 'Believe me, the irony is not lost on me here—I've got two marriages behind me and I know how that sounds to people, but . . .'

'But what?'

'I was at the football on the weekend and Tommy was there. The same women who warned me before felt it was their "duty" to fill me in on his past. He cheated on his first wife to marry his second wife, and then she left him, apparently because he had a, quote, "roaming eye".'

'Were these women friends of either of his ex-wives, by any chance?' Tilly asked pointedly, already having a feeling she knew who the women were.

'Maybe, I don't know. But even so . . .'

'I'm not vouching for the guy—honestly, I don't know much about him at all—but what I do know is this town, and the harm gossip can do to a person's reputation. Talk to him about it, Allie, before you make up your mind based on what those women have told you.'

She saw Allie ease off her vicious scrubbing as she considered Tilly's words. 'Yeah. Maybe. I'll think about it.'

Tilly left the kitchen to take out an order, but there was a heaviness hanging over her. It was none of her business, she knew, but she'd seen the way Allie lit up each day when the deliveries arrived. What if this was her friend's shot at happiness and she let it go by, based on rumours?

∞

A few days later, Tilly crossed the street, her arms weighed down with grocery bags as she looked up and recognised the white delivery van.

'Hello, Tommy,' she said, stepping up onto the kerb as he hefted a box onto his shoulder.

'Hi, Tilly.'

Allie hadn't mentioned turning down Tommy's date again and Tilly hadn't brought it up with her. She hadn't intended to stop and chat, but when she heard Tommy call out as she moved past, Tilly stopped and turned back.

'Look, this is a bit awkward. I wouldn't normally do this but the thing is . . .' He shifted the box onto his other shoulder. 'Has Allie mentioned anything to you about me?'

She saw him wince and bit the inside of her lip as she considered her answer.

'I know, I sound like some primary-school kid,' he said, shifting his weight a little. 'I thought things between us were kinda moving in a good direction and then all of a sudden she just . . . I don't know, clammed up. Did I do something?'

'She hasn't really said much,' Tilly hedged, not wanting to get into the middle of anything.

'That's okay. I shouldn't have asked. That wasn't fair,' he said, turning to walk away.

He looked so uncomfortable and embarrassed that she instantly relented. 'Tommy, wait.' Tilly gave a small sigh. 'I think she's had certain people in her ear.'

'What people?'

'I don't know for sure. I think she's been hearing about past . . . relationships.'

He looked at her blankly for a moment before his eyes hardened slightly. 'Oh, I get it. The whole cheating thing again,' he said bitterly.

'I don't know any of the details, all I know is she's just wary about any kind of new relationship.'

'How do I fight that kind of crap though, Tilly?' he asked almost pleadingly. 'It was all so long ago, but it just keeps following me around. The fact there're two sides to every story doesn't even seem to matter. Why let facts stand in the way of some juicy gossip?'

'Maybe if you tried to explain your side of the story to her?'

'What's the point?' His shoulders slumped.

'The point is, she's only heard one side.'

'I think she's already made up her mind.'

'You should give her more credit than that. She's got every reason to be careful, she has kids, but she's also got a past of her own and I think she'd have an open mind if you explained it.'

'Either way I come off as a jerk. I *did* cheat on my first wife, but it's not as clear cut as that. The gossips don't care, they don't mention that I was a twenty-year-old bloke working two jobs to support a couple of kids and a wife with undiagnosed mental health issues; stuff no one ever prepares you for. Life was a living hell there for a while. I'm not making excuses, I could probably have done a lot of things differently . . . or better, you know?' Tommy said, searching her eyes. 'But I was young and stupid. Then I thought I'd found someone I could have a life with, and I did. We were together for a long time before things went bad. It wasn't my decision to end that marriage, but apparently I got what I deserved, if you listen to the general consensus around here. Whatever,' he said with a low growl. 'I was used to people talking behind my back by then. But clearly things have been boring in my love life if all they do is keep dragging up my past. It's been years since I was in a serious relationship, and that's only because I'd given up trusting my own judgement where women were concerned. I thought both times I'd found the person I was going to grow old with, only for it to blow up in my face. Until I met Allie. Christ, Tilly, I wasn't even game to think about asking her out until now. It's taken me twelve months to work up the courage to ask her.'

Tilly felt for the guy. No one had a right to sit and speculate about someone else's relationship—it was easy to assign blame when you hadn't lived in that person's shoes. Relationships were messy, and everyone was human. It was a shame people couldn't just worry about themselves and leave everyone else alone.

'Talk to her, Tommy. Tell her everything you told me. I think she'll understand. Allie deserves to hear the other side of the story so she can make up her own mind.'

'Yeah. I guess. Sorry. I didn't mean to unload all that on you.' Tommy sent her a brief, almost embarrassed smile. 'I better keep going.'

Tilly watched him with a thoughtful frown as he walked away. She hoped he would try again with Allie. Now more than ever Tilly believed her friend needed to have all the facts.

Her phone was going off on the counter when Tilly stepped out of the shower after finishing with the horses that afternoon. She frowned as she read the name on the screen. 'Hi, Jess,' she said, trying to keep her tone neutral, wishing that her nerves didn't instantly feel on edge whenever her older sister called.

'Where were you? I've tried calling three times.'

'I was in the shower, sorry. I didn't hear the phone.' And it didn't look like this conversation was going to be any different to their usual kind. 'What's up?'

'I'm thinking about heading out there for a visit.'

'Out *here*?'

'It's been a while since we caught up, and it's not like you'll come to me, is it?'

Tilly realised she was grinding her teeth and made a conscious effort to stop. 'Where are you? Last time we spoke you were about to head off to India for a few months.'

'I *was* over there. Now I'm back. I'm in between shows, so I figured I'd come for a visit.'

Jess was a talented fashion designer and had worked hard for years to build a very successful brand. Tilly admired her sister's designs but they weren't her style. Tilly preferred the basics—jeans, T-shirts and boots—but she'd learned to keep her mouth shut, because it never took much to set her sister off on a very long and very boring lecture about the styles and disciplines of the fashion industry.

They were so different that Tilly seriously wondered if they really shared the same parents. Jess took after their mother, who loved sewing and fashion, though not to Jessica's extent. Even though Tilly didn't particularly care for fashion, she'd always admired her mother's sometimes eclectic style. She could throw together an outfit of the oddest combinations, and yet never looked like a two-year-old playing dress-up, the way that Tilly feared she would if she'd ever tried.

Her mother had always been too cool for fashion. She'd never blindly followed the trends. Tilly loved going through her grandparents' old albums to find the photos of her mother as a teenager. They always made her smile. The one she loved the most was of her mother's high school formal. Gathered together in a group photo with her classmates, her mother had been like a bird of paradise sticking out in a dry, dusty paddock of corn stubble. While the other girls were dressed in expensive store-bought dresses of silk and taffeta that somehow managed to all look similar, her mother had made her own. She'd detested all the dresses she and Gran had found in the bigger stores of Tamworth and Armidale, so instead she'd found a discarded wedding dress at a local op shop and taken it home to pull apart and redesign. Her friends all thought she was crazy, but she'd just smiled and told them to wait and see. For months had she hand-sewed the elaborate flowers with sequins and threaded small pearl beads onto the skirt that flounced out in a cloud of soft tulle around her—complete with an elegant sweeping train. She had looked like a real-life Cinderella and there was no way anyone would believe that she'd taken a five-dollar op shop dress and turned it into a one-of-a-kind evening gown that would easily be worth hundreds from a bridal store.

She hadn't gone to university to study design the way Jess had. She'd married young and soon had three kids to care for, and whatever hopes she may have had to turn her creativity into a career fizzled out early on. Her parents' romance had been a whirlwind and as full of drama as any TV soap opera. Her mother was the rebellious daughter and her father was the kid from the wrong side of the tracks. It had all the makings of a trashy eighties love song, except suddenly finding themselves teenage parents and the idea of living on love quickly lost its shine. But they eventually pulled themselves together; her father finding work in the trucking industry while her mother worked as a seamstress from home when they were growing up, doing alterations and small commissions. Occasionally her mother would be asked to design a bridal dress. She was in her element then and over the years built up an enviable reputation, booked out for months in advance. She could have opened her own shop, but she didn't seem to have the business drive to pursue that kind of thing, choosing instead to work from her sewing room at home.

'Tilly? Are you listening?'

'Sorry. What was that?' Tilly forced her focus back to the present.

'I'm planning on coming out tomorrow. Will you be home?'

'I'm working until three.' *Tomorrow!* Tilly mentally ran through a list of things she would need to do between now and then.

'I won't get there until late afternoon.'

'Okay, then,' Tilly said, glad that her sister couldn't actually see her. She was pretty sure there would be no way to disguise the dread she was feeling.

'See you then.'

Tilly was left to listen to the abrupt silence in her ear. Her sister never was one for a long goodbye.

*Great.*

She sighed, instantly feeling bad. It shouldn't be this hard. Sisters were supposed to be close once they were adults; at least that's what she'd always heard. Only, for the Paterson women it hadn't really happened. Maybe they just weren't considered grown-ups yet.

Tilly had assumed that after their mother had died, their relationship would become stronger. After all, they were all that was left of their family, with both parents and a brother gone. But their mother's death had seemed to only widen the gap.

Tilly gave a long sigh. They needed to fix things. They had both lost so much over the years that it made Tilly sad to realise her sister was almost a stranger. Maybe this was Jess making the first move? Her spirits lifted a little at the thought.

# Seven

The next morning Tilly rushed in through the back door of the cafe, grabbing her order pad as she moved out to the front. She gave Paul a brief glance and shook her head. 'I know. I know. I'm late. It's been a crazy morning.'

'I wasn't going to say a thing,' he said, continuing with the coffee he was making.

'Hey!' Josie said. 'How come when I'm late I get read the riot act and when Tilly is it's okay?'

'Because unlike you, she doesn't think ten minutes' late is the acceptable norm.'

'Goody two shoes,' Josie muttered under her breath as Tilly hurried past. Despite her flustered start to the day, she did have time to give the younger woman a smug smile as Allie chuckled quietly behind her.

She'd fed the horses in record time so she could clean the house and make up the spare bed before she left for work. For anyone else she wouldn't have worried about the state of her place, but Jessica had never quite mastered the habit of keeping her thoughts to herself, or off her face. The last time she came to the house Tilly had felt her sister's disapproving gaze everywhere. 'Why don't you redecorate? Wallpaper went out of fashion thirty years ago.'

It didn't seem to register with Jess that not everyone had a house redesign account with surplus cash hanging around. All Tilly's money went into building up her business and her horses. She wished she didn't always get so anxious about her sister's visits, but no matter how hard she tried to force it from her mind, she'd tossed and turned all night. It was almost a godsend to have to come into work, where she'd be kept so busy that she wouldn't be able to obsess about it for at least part of the day.

The door opened, and Tilly's welcoming smile teetered a little. *You had to go and tempt fate, didn't you?*

It was the first time she'd seen Jason since the apology-that-wasn't-an-apology visit. He hadn't been into the cafe during her shifts and she'd wondered if things would be a little strained when she eventually did see him again. *Just play it cool. He's like any other customer . . . Wow, I never knew rolled-up sleeves on a guy could look so hot.* 'Oh, for goodness sake.'

'Sorry?' Jason said as he came level with her.

'Nothing. Hi. How are you?' She smiled brightly at him. 'Take a seat. Are you having the usual?' Tilly knew she was rambling, but she didn't care. *Get the order and get out of there!* was what her self-preservation was screaming at her like a drill sergeant.

'That would be great. Thanks,' he said, sitting down at what she now considered his table.

Tilly put in his order with Paul and went back out to clear a nearby table.

'How've you been?' Jason asked.

Tilly glanced up from stacking the tray. 'Fine. Busy. You?'

'Yeah. Same. Busy. You know,' he said, waving a hand dismissively.

This was new. He had never initiated a conversation before. Maybe this was why he didn't try to make small talk—because he clearly sucked at it. Tilly took pity on him and straightened up after she'd finished gathering the dirty dishes. 'How are the renovations going?'

He looked up and seemed relieved at the question. One he could answer, apparently. 'Yeah. Good. I finished the decking. I'm about to knock out the back wall and put in new glass doors.'

'That sounds like a pretty major undertaking.'

'It'll be a bit breezy for a while, which is why I wanted to get it done before winter. I wasn't too keen on having black plastic as my only barrier between inside and out in the cold.'

'God no. I hope you get it done in time. You'll freeze.'

'She'll be apples,' he said with a smile, and Tilly couldn't help but smile back.

'My Pop used to say that. All the time.' It was strange how something so seemingly inconsequential could take you back to your childhood in the blink of an eye.

'So did mine,' Jason said with a surprised look.

'I haven't heard anyone say that in years. It's nice.' Tilly's throat felt tight and she realised she'd been holding his gaze a fraction too long. 'I'll just go and check on your order,' she said quickly.

Tilly was always surrounded by memories of her grandparents. Sometimes when she walked up the street, when she wasn't rushing about, she could almost picture her Gran walking beside her, dressed up even just to go into town to shop for groceries. Other times, it was a smell—like wattle floating on a warm breeze, or the smell of leather—that reminded her of her Pop.

She wouldn't change it, though. There were a lot of people in town who remembered the Patersons and often brought them up in conversation. Most of the stories Tilly had already heard, but occasionally someone would tell her something new and it was like peeling back the layers of her grandparents to reveal them as people in their own right—Dulcie and Toby Paterson—not just her Gran and Pop. The stories were getting fewer and farther between as more of their generation passed away. With news of each funeral, Tilly felt the loss of her grandparents even more intensely.

When she first moved back with her mother, the reminder of them had helped her feel not so alone. Old family friends had rallied around her once word spread about her mother's illness, and it was a godsend to have so many people step forward, simply out of respect for the memory of her grandparents who had always helped others.

Tilly knew that her mum felt bad about needing her support so soon after losing David, no matter how many times Tilly reassured her. It was both a blessing and a curse—well, more of a curse, because she was losing her mum, and the fact it was so soon after her husband made her feel like she'd been in one continuous cycle of mourning. The blessing came from the time she got to spend with her mum. Life had taken Tilly, Jess and their mum in separate directions after Tilly left home, and apart from the few months they both lived in Toowoomba, get-togethers had been sporadic over the years. So, Tilly had treasured those final few months together. They had talked more than they ever had before and each had discovered a new side to the other—for Tilly, it was learning more about her mother as a person. They would stay up late and chat about things Tilly had never spoken about with her mum: boyfriends and school crushes, sneaking out to parties and watching movies just to drool over the hunky lead man. It was like having a new friend and learning everything about them for the first time, and as sad as it was that they'd only had a little bit of time, it had meant the world to Tilly.

But there were other memories of those days that weren't so good. She fought hard not to think about them too often, but her sister's phone call had stirred up those feelings again. Jess hadn't come home to see their mother in those final months. She'd had a huge show in New York at the time. Their mother had understood—it would have been madness to back out of such a once-in-a-lifetime, career-defining moment and she had always played down how ill she was when Jess called. But Tilly couldn't bring herself to play along. She could understand her sister's drive and passion for her art, but not to the extent of putting it before something so important.

Tilly placed the order in front of Jason and turned to leave.

'Hey.'

She stopped and looked back. Had she messed up his order? Surely not. He had the same thing every time.

'Are you okay?'

His question surprised her, and she hesitated before answering. 'I'm fine.'

'You just seem a bit distracted.'

'Sorry. I've got a visitor coming today and I've been a bit preoccupied, running around getting organised.'

Jason gave a bit of a grimace. 'At least I'm safe from people visiting while I'm pulling down walls.'

'There's method to your madness.' She grinned and felt that little tug of awareness at the twitch of his lips. She really wished she didn't find the guy so damn attractive. It would make concentrating on her job a lot easier.

'Is there anything I can help with? I mean, if you're stuck at work all day, I don't mind stopping in at your place on the way home if you need something done.'

Tilly wondered if she looked as surprised as she felt by his offer. 'Ah, no. I think I'm okay. But thanks for the offer.'

'No worries. It's not like I'm on a schedule or anything. Yell if you need a hand with anything.'

'Thanks,' she said, and realised that again she was holding his eye just a little too long and dropped it quickly. 'I'd better get back to work before Paul sacks me.'

∽

Jason watched her walk away. Distracted by her last words. *I wouldn't mind sacking her.* He blinked away the image that popped into his head and picked up his roll, forcing his mind away from the lurid, very unneighbourly thoughts he was having. He wasn't sure of the reception he'd get this morning. He thought things ended on an okay note last time, but he still didn't know exactly where he stood with this woman.

Her T-shirt gave him his usual morning chuckle. *I don't need an inspirational quote. I need coffee!* He was pretty sure he came here as much for those as he did for the food and caffeine.

As he ate, he pondered who her visitor might be. An old friend, maybe? She seemed kind of distracted for it to be a friend. Surely most people were a little more excited about the idea of an old friend coming to visit than she sounded. He watched her as she moved around the cafe, delivering orders and clearing tables. It was a small space but it was almost always busy. The blonde caught his eye a few times as she took the long way around to a couple of older ladies who'd just walked in, passing by his table and sending him a smile that he'd have to be blind not to read as downright sultry.

She wore the same uniform as Tilly, but with the slogan *OCD: Obsessive Coffee Disorder* stretched across her ridiculously tight T-shirt—her breasts were practically spilling out. Jason heard his uptight Sunday School teacher's voice in his head and groaned. Maybe he was already turning into that grouchy old bachelor he always told himself he'd most likely become one day.

When had a decent set of boobs ever been a turn-off?

He switched his gaze across to Tilly as she leaned down to place two heavy plates of food in front of the people sitting nearby and he swallowed hard, the bacon-and-egg roll going down his throat like a mouthful of concrete. Catching the slight swell of her breasts as she leaned forward sent a spear of white-hot fire through his groin. It was just a glimpse of cleavage, a hint of skin, but it made him shift uncomfortably in his seat. It was safe to say that clearly not all boobs were an apparent turn-off and for this he was somewhat relieved.

He'd been trying not to think about Tilly—he knew it would be asking for trouble—but the harder he tried *not* to think about her, the more often he found her sneaking into his mind. Did he really want to go down this route again?

In all fairness, his recent heartache hadn't actually ever been *a thing*. He'd simply thought he'd had a shot at something, but it wasn't to be. She'd chosen someone else. It still stung a bit, though. This was different, and that was why it felt dangerous. This time, he got the feeling that maybe Tilly was more than a little interested in him. But then, just when he'd convinced himself to maybe test the waters a little, she pulled back, becoming distracted and distant. Did he want to rock the boat? What they had at the moment was safe and he looked forward to seeing her when he came into the cafe, but what if he asked her out and she said no? Coming in here would be awkward. Did he really want to risk losing the friendly banter and the best bacon-and-egg roll he'd had in years?

∞

Tilly gave a short sigh as she spotted the fancy Audi parked at the front of the house. She shut off her engine and took a calming breath before opening her door and heading inside.

She followed the trail of luggage—a draped coat on the back of the lounge and a pair of blood-red shoes with a lethal stiletto heel kicked off near a groaning suitcase—to discover her sister sitting out on the back verandah sipping from a wine glass.

'Finally. I thought you'd never get home,' Jess said, and as usual the hint of an American accent in her voice caught Tilly off guard.

'Sorry about that. It was busier than I expected.' She crossed the verandah to hug her sister, breathing in the perfume she suspected would have most likely cost a week's worth of wages. 'You look great, Jess,' Tilly said, stepping away as her sister sat back down and picked up her wine glass. She always did.

Her sleek hairstyle, shaped around the angles of her face, looked like she'd just stepped out of the hair salon, and her white linen pants and red blouse outlined her tall, lean figure to perfection. Unlike Tilly's clothes, which were almost always too long: the hems of her jeans had to be tucked under, and sleeves always needed to be rolled up. But despite their differences in height and personality, people always remarked on how similar she and Jess looked. Tilly could never see the resemblance.

'Well, I haven't been working all day,' Jess said, giving Tilly's T-shirt and jeans a brief glance.

As far as backhanded compliments went, this one was pretty tame for Jess, so Tilly took it with only a slight wince. 'How long are you here for?'

'I haven't decided yet. I had time to kill before I fly out on the twenty-sixth.'

'So, you're not back in Australia for good, then?'

Her sister shook her head and the silky lustre of black hair almost seemed to shimmer like a dark waterfall with the movement. How the hell did anyone manage to have hair like that? Not a strand out of place? Tilly's hand went involuntarily to the end of her ponytail and felt the brittle ends that had long been in need of the attention of a hairdresser, an appointment she just never seemed to find time to make.

'I've had back-to-back shows. It was only because of the charity event I promised my agent I'd do here that I've been back.'

*Heaven forbid.* Tilly looked again at her sister. The last time Jess was here had been for their mother's funeral almost two years ago. She hadn't stayed long then either. Things to do, shows to put on.

'Well, that's good, then,' Tilly said, mustering a smile. She looked at the bottle on the table and decided alcohol might be called for. 'I'll just go get a drink.'

'I brought you out a glass,' Jess said, picking up the extra one on the table. 'These are actually quite nice. I wasn't expecting to find real crystal.'

'They were a wedding gift.' Until that moment she hadn't taken any notice of the glass her sister was holding. They were kept at the back of her cabinet—too special to use.

'Thank God you had them. I was almost expecting Vegemite jars. Oh, come on, Tilly, lighten up,' Jess said, noticing the frown Tilly was wearing. 'I was only joking.'

'I'm not a wine drinker,' Tilly said as she headed inside. She opened the fridge and sighed. She didn't mind wine, sometimes, but she wasn't going to sit there and drink her rich sister's obnoxiously overpriced fancy wine and give her something to gloat about. She took out a can of beer and grabbed the pre-opened dip from the fridge and a packet of cracker biscuits to take back out.

She bit back a grin at her sister's dubious look as she plonked the food unceremoniously onto the small table in front of them and took maybe a touch too much delight in the disapproving glance she was shot as she cracked open the can of beer and took a long sip. As a rule, she really only enjoyed a beer after a hard day's work outside. As a thirst quencher there was nothing better, but tonight she made the exception, knowing how horrified her sister would be. It was childish, she knew, but they had spent less than ten minutes in each other's company and already Tilly was feeling the judgemental weight heavy on her shoulders.

'I thought maybe you'd gone in to shower and change out of your work clothes.'

'There's no point really. I still have to go down and feed the horses yet.'

'I was hoping we could go out for dinner.'

'Out?' Tilly said, eyeing her sister oddly. 'You do remember where you are, don't you?'

'Yes. I thought it might save you cooking.'

'Sure. We can go out. Where would you prefer, the Ex Services or the Bowling Club?'

'Whichever has the better menu,' Jess said, doing an outstanding job of keeping her voice level.

'Well, there's the meat raffle on at the Bowlo,' Tilly said, 'but that might make it a bit crowded and noisy, so maybe the Ex Services would be the go.'

'Sounds lovely.'

Tilly grinned across at her sister—her evening seemed to be looking up after all. 'I'll do the horses and get ready,' she said, downing her beer. 'Unless you want to come and help?'

'I don't think I'm dressed for it,' Jess said, sending an unamused glance Tilly's way.

'Won't be long. Make yourself at home,' Tilly added, and sent a quick look at the wine glasses as she left. *Like you haven't already.*

She didn't stay and work with the horses today, not because it would be rude to leave a guest alone at the house—quite the contrary, under normal circumstances she would be quite happy to stay down and play with horses instead of hurrying back to the house where her sister waited. Today, though, she was kind of looking forward to going to the club for dinner. It was a rare treat and she was curious to see how her sister handled it.

&

Tilly parked out the back of the club, glad the trip was over. The silence had been a little uncomfortable until Tilly asked about Jess's latest fashion show and then she hadn't needed to worry about small talk. She just let Jess bang on about people she was supposed to have heard of but hadn't, and only had to nod now and again to keep up her end of the conversation.

They walked inside and Tilly greeted a few familiar faces from the cafe, nodding and smiling as they headed for the bistro. Tilly led the way to the counter and looked up to read the evening's specials written on the chalk board above the serving window.

'Do you know what you're having?' she asked Jess. Her sister sent her a sharp glance, before turning back to the options with a look of what could only be described as desperation. 'What's wrong?'

'Haven't these people ever heard of a low-carb diet?' she hissed. 'Every single thing listed has meat or carbs ... or both.'

'Well, what are you planning to eat if you don't want meat or carbs?'

'What can I get you, love?' a woman asked, appearing from the back of the kitchen.

'Hi. I think I'll have the scotch fillet and chips, please,' Tilly said, smiling at the woman as she wrote down her order.

'And what about you, darl?' she asked, looking up at Jess.

'Would it be possible to get some mung bean with veggies? Or maybe a paneer salad?'

The woman blinked, then switched her gaze to Tilly as though hoping for a translation.

'I don't think they do either of those here,' Tilly said in a low voice.

'A paneer tikka with vegetables?' Jess continued hopefully.

'I think you lost the conversation at mung beans, Jess.'

'There has to be something without meat or carbs for goodness sake.'

'You can have a salad,' the woman offered.

'What's in the salad?'

'Lettuce. Tomato, bit of cuie, dressing,' the woman said then looked at Jess expectantly.

'That's it?'

'It's a side salad.'

Tilly rolled her eyes.

'Fine. That'll have to do. Unless you can make an egg-white omelette to go with it.'

'We don't do egg-white omelettes.'

'Of course not. Fine. Just the salad, then. No dressing.'

Tilly took the number the woman passed them and followed Jess to a table off to one side of the room.

'Well, that went well,' Tilly said, settling in her chair.

'Honestly, you'd think this place would have at least had someone who could drag it into the present day. I knew this would happen,' Jess exclaimed.

'Then why did you insist on eating out?'

'I thought it would be nice.'

*It would have been if you hadn't just made a scene out of ordering a meal.*

Tilly suppressed a sigh. It was going to be a long night. 'Do you remember coming here with Gran and Pop?' she asked, hoping to avoid another scene.

'Yes,' Jess said, glancing around the room. 'Doesn't look like it's changed at all.'

'I'm pretty sure they've just finished some renovations to the club.'

'Nothing really seems to have changed around here, though. Even the farm.'

'That's what I like about it. It's nice to feel like things are the same.'

'It's called being stuck in the past and it's not healthy, Matilda.'

If her condescending tone hadn't been bad enough, the use of her full name was like fingernails down a chalk board.

'There's nothing here for you,' Jess continued before Tilly could speak. 'You have your whole life ahead of you and you're sinking all your money into a rundown farm and a business that you don't even know will make enough to be worthwhile.'

Tilly forced herself to take a deep breath. They were out in public and there was no way she was going to make a scene in front of people she knew. The last thing she wanted to be was gossip fodder. 'I'm not doing it to become rich. I'm doing it because I believe in it.'

'If you want my advice—' Jess said, but Tilly cut her off abruptly.

'I don't. You don't get to drop back into my life when it's convenient to you and throw your opinions around like you're somehow entitled.'

For a moment, a flicker of something resembling hurt flickered across her sister's face, but it was gone too fast for Tilly to be sure.

'I'm your sister,' Jess said tightly. 'I'm the only family you have left. I think that gives me the right.'

'No, it doesn't. Maybe if you'd stuck around during at least one crisis and helped out, you might have some kind of right to an opinion. But you didn't. So, you don't,' Tilly said in a low, harsh voice and felt her cheeks redden in anger.

Jess seemed to take a mental step backwards, before a note of defensiveness crept into her tone. 'You can't blame me for any of that.'

'Really?'

'It wasn't my fault. I couldn't help that I wasn't here when Mum got sick.'

'Or after Jim died. Or when David was killed.'

'We were both kids when Jim died,' Jess said, throwing her hands up in the air.

'Keep your voice down,' Tilly said in a furious whisper.

'This is still about New York, isn't it?' Jess folded her arms and leaned back in her chair. 'You're never going to let that go, are you?'

'You made your choice.'

'Mum understood. Mum supported my decision. This hasn't got anything to do with me not being here for her. It's about *you* being jealous of *me*.'

'I am *not* jealous of you, Jess,' Tilly said adamantly. 'I'm glad you've been able to follow your dream.' Tilly slumped back in her own chair feeling defeated. What was the point? It didn't matter what she said now. She had needed her sister during some of the worst times of her life—losing their brother, their dad, their mum, and then her husband. But Jess hadn't been there for any of it.

Tilly just didn't understand her sister, but then, she and Jess were like chalk and cheese. Always had been. Always would be.

∽

They drove home in silence, and Tilly felt her heart sink lower. Why was it always like this? Why couldn't they break down this wall that always seemed to stand between them? Guilt added to the weight on her heart. She'd made a promise to her mother.

'Jess isn't like you, Tilly,' her mother had said one day when they'd been sitting outside in the warm afternoon sun. 'She's never really recovered after losing your father.'

Their father hadn't been living with them when he had the accident. Her parents' on-again–off-again relationship had been more off than on by that stage.

Jess and their dad had been close—he'd loved them all in his own way, but he had a soft spot for his first-born daughter. He had always been her greatest fan, praising her artwork and designs, and telling anyone who would listen how his daughter was going to be famous one day.

His accident had set off a chain reaction through the family. Their life had never been smooth sailing, but it was something they'd got used to. Their father's death, though, changed everything. Their mother went into a severe depression, Jim started going off the rails, Jess became increasingly withdrawn and then left home, and Tilly pined for her grandparents and wished she was anywhere but where she was.

'None of us were the same after Dad died,' Tilly had said to her mother.

'No. And I let you all down too by wallowing in my own grief. But Jess lost something. I don't know, it was like she channelled all her emotion into her art and there wasn't any left for anything else.' Tilly watched her mother turn her gaze out to the mountains before them. 'I told her not to give up the chance to do the New York show, Tilly. It was my idea. She would have given it up if I'd asked her to, but I couldn't do that.'

'You could have, Mum.'

'No,' she said sadly. 'This is what she's been dreaming of for years. I didn't want her to think about me and always be reminded of the chance she gave up.' Her mum turned back to look at her solemnly. 'I know I've asked a lot from you over the years, darling, but the truth is, you're my rock. I don't know what I would have done without you. You've always been so strong and dependable, even as a child,' she said, squeezing her hand gently. 'It's not fair, and I'm so sorry to continue to be a burden on you.'

Tilly blinked hard. 'You're not a burden, Mum,' she said, forcing the words through a tightening throat.

'Be patient with her, Tilly. You only have each other now. I know deep down the Jess I raised is still in there. You just have to find a way to reach her. Promise me you won't give up on her?'

Tilly nodded. 'I won't.'

She'd made the promise to her mother, but she wasn't so sure that Jess could change. She continued to hope, but each time they saw each other she was left disappointed.

# Eight

'You look terrible,' Josie announced as Tilly passed her while she was getting ready to start her shift.

'Thanks.'

'Nothing a bit of make-up couldn't hide. You should try it sometime.'

'And people say you have no tact? I don't understand it,' Tilly told her dryly as she deposited a tray of dirty cups on the sink.

'Ignore her,' Allie said with a frown. 'You don't look terrible, but you do look tired. Are you okay?'

'Yeah. I just didn't sleep well last night. Jess is home for a visit.'

'The prodigal sister?'

'Yep.'

'Oh dear. Visit not going well?'

'Nope.'

'How long is she here for?'

'I don't know. I don't even know why she bothered coming. She could have lectured me on everything I'm doing wrong with my life on the phone without going to all the trouble to drive up here.'

'Oh dear,' Allie repeated with a kind smile.

Tilly let out a weary sigh before turning and heading back out to the cafe. She pulled up short when she saw Jason seated at his usual table. 'You don't usually come in two days in a row,' she said and did a double-take, swearing she saw a slight blush creep up his neck.

'I had to come in and pick up some stuff.'

'I wasn't complaining,' she said, then felt her eyes widen as he glanced up sharply, eyeing her curiously. 'I mean, business-wise—it's good to have returning customers.'

'Yeah, right.' He nodded hastily and Tilly closed her eyes briefly. Just when she thought they could have a civilised conversation, there was that awkward exchange again. 'So, did your visitor turn up?'

'Yep, she turned up.'

'I gather from your tone it's not going well?' he said, watching her in a way that made Tilly feel as though he could see far more than she intended him to see. 'I told you the best way to keep them away is to pull down a few walls.'

She appreciated his attempt at lightening the conversation. It was strange that for someone she had only known a short while, she'd already shared a lot more of her private life than she had with most people. The usual customer banter didn't include any of her actual daily life problems.

'It is what it is.' She shrugged.

'Sounds like next time they plan a visit, you should tell them you're out of town for the week.'

'It's my sister and she knows me too well. Unfortunately.'

'Ah, I see.'

She considered him thoughtfully. 'Do you have siblings?'

'No,' he said, shaking his head, 'but I remember my best mate and his brother growing up. They fought like cats and dogs.'

'Well, we don't exactly fight. It's more she likes to give her opinion about everything I'm apparently doing wrong and how I'm throwing away my life up here.'

Jason gave a small grunt. 'Everyone's entitled to their opinion, I guess,' he said. 'But in the end, that's all it is, an opinion. You're the one who makes the decisions on how to live your life.'

'Yeah, I know.' She shook her head sadly. 'I just wish we could have conversations with fewer opinions,' she said dryly. 'I better keep moving. I'll get your order ready.' It was nice to vent to someone who didn't judge her, although it wasn't something she normally did. Around here it didn't pay to complain about people too often; it almost always got back to them. She wasn't worried about that being the case here, though. Jason Weaver seemed to be even more tight-lipped than she was.

Tilly leaned against the verandah post and watched the softly falling morning rain. It had come in the nick of time. The tanks had been getting low and the last of the summer grass was dying off. A good soaking now would help boost the winter feed she'd only just sown. She should be feeling a high of contentment, but she couldn't shake the melancholic cloud that seemed to hang above her.

The screen door opening drew her gaze. 'I wish this rain would go away,' said Jess. 'I wanted to go for a bushwalk today.'

'We need it,' Tilly said, looking back out across the damp paddocks. In the distance she could see her horses happily grazing, blissfully ignorant of their wet coats, all looking sleek and somewhat drenched.

'I thought you were supposed to rug them or something?' Jess said, moving to stand beside her.

'They're brumbies. They're used to the weather.'

'They look unhappy.'

Tilly kept her eyes on the horses grazing unperturbed in the paddock. 'You could still go for a drive,' she suggested dryly. 'Maybe get out of the house for a bit.'

'It's too miserable.'

Tilly watched as her sister sat down on the timber bench against the wall, wrapping a woollen shawl tightly around her shoulders. 'I'd forgotten how bone-chillingly cold it gets here. And it's not even winter.'

'It's just because it's raining. It always gets cold when it rains.'

For a moment Tilly enjoyed the silence that had fallen between them, before it was broken.

'Is this really what you want, Tilly?'

'Why is it so hard to believe? You get to do what you love—why wouldn't I want to be here, working with horses and doing what I love?'

'Because what you love to do puts you in the back of beyond, hidden away from the rest of the world. You've got the rest of your life to live.'

'I hate to break it to you, but this is hardly the back of beyond. There *are* actually people here, a whole town full of them. I'm not hidden away.'

'Seriously, Tilly. How are you going to meet someone living here?'

Jason Weaver's face flashed before her eyes briefly and she shifted uncomfortably. 'I'm not looking to meet anyone. Anyway, like you can talk. You live in the busiest city in the world and you don't have a serious relationship . . . that I know of,' Tilly added, narrowing her eyes at her older sister.

'I've had my share of relationships—but none of them were serious enough to give up my freedom. But I'm not like you. I don't need other people the way you do. You were happier when you were married. You're different now. I just want you to be happy again.'

'I *was* happy when I was married,' Tilly said quietly, 'but then David died. I can't just replace him with a new husband. It doesn't work like that. I don't want to replace him. Believe it or not I'm the happiest I've been in a long time.'

She saw Jess hesitate before deciding to push on. 'I'm saying this because I care. I know you don't believe it, but it's true.'

'I do believe it. And thank you for worrying, but I really am happy here. I've got big plans for this place. One day soon you'll see.'

'And what if they don't work out the way you hoped? You've just thrown all that money away.'

Tilly frowned across at her older sister. 'Is that what this is all about? Mum's money?'

When most people thought of artists, they thought of free-spirited, creative beings who only focused on their chosen field, with little thought given to the pesky realities of finances. Her sister was not that kind of artistic soul. Jess had equal measures of creativity and financial savvy. Maybe it was because she was brought up in a family dictated to by a tight budget, or maybe she was just blessed that both sides of her brain were able to function equally.

'As Mum's executor, it's my responsibility to make sure you're using it wisely.'

'No, it's not,' Tilly replied, staring at her sister accusingly. 'It's none of your business what I do with my share of the money.'

'I just don't want to see you wasting an opportunity to invest it in something a lot safer than some business idea that may or may not even get up and running. You need to think about your future.'

'This hasn't been some spur-of-the-moment idea. Maybe if you'd been around more often, you would have heard us talking about it and planning it,' Tilly snapped. 'David and I worked on this for a long time, and then we bought the property. Everything was leading up to us moving here and renovating. I know what I'm doing. Work's due to start in a couple of weeks on the renovations to the old shed to turn it into a bunkhouse, and I'm already in the final stages of planning for the youth-at-risk program. Everything is starting to fall into place.'

'And what if it doesn't? Are you just going to continue working as a waitress till you're old and grey? Mum wouldn't want you to throw your life away like that.'

'Mum would have wanted me to do what makes me happy, Jess . . . or was that only supposed to be what she wanted for you?'

The two women turned away from each other to look out at the view, before Jess gave a tired sigh. 'How do our conversations always end up as arguments?'

'Beats me,' Tilly said irritably, still looking at the horses in the paddock. The dripping of rain from the downpipe filled the stilted silence. 'Why did you really come up here?'

'I told you, I had some time before I had to fly out again.'

'You haven't been up here before when you've been home.'

'I'm making an effort. Is that a crime?' Jess snapped.

Tilly got the feeling there was more to the visit than simply making an effort. Still, if Jess didn't want to discuss it, then she wasn't going to keep asking.

'I've got to get ready for work. Why don't you take a drive into town and have a look around? Drop in for a cuppa later.'

'I was hoping you could take some time off so we could spend it together.'

Tilly bit back her frustration. 'If I'd had more warning, maybe I could have tried to get a day off, but I can't just call in and tell them I'm not coming in on short notice like this. Not to mention, at the moment each pay cheque is important. I'm only planning to work for another few months.'

'I understand,' Jess said a little stiffly.

Tilly forced away the twinge of guilt that followed her sister's disappointed reply. *This isn't my fault,* she told herself firmly. *Being responsible doesn't make me a bad person.* 'I'd really love to see you later in at the cafe.'

'I'll see how I feel. This rain doesn't particularly make me feel like doing very much at all,' Jess said.

Tilly pushed away from the railing and headed inside to get dressed. She didn't want to start another argument, but sometimes her sister's attitude made it incredibly difficult to keep the peace.

It wasn't like this when they were younger. Tilly had always looked up to her big sister—her fun, happy big sister. Well, most of the time. Jess did tend to feel it the worst when their parents fought and their dad took off, but she always seemed to adjust. They all did. It was after their father's accident that Jessica changed. They were all mourning in their own ways. Jess had been eighteen and doing her final year of high school; Tilly had been sixteen, and Jim had just turned fourteen. While Jess had become withdrawn and bitter, Jim had gone the other way and started getting into trouble. He hung around with much older kids and sometimes wouldn't come home at night.

'You'd never pull this crap if Dad were here,' Tilly remembered snapping at him after she and her mother had been up all night worrying about him.

'Well, he isn't here, is he? He's dead!' Jim had shouted, storming off to his room and slamming the door.

Their father's death had a lasting effect on them all, and it was the tipping point for all the grief that followed.

⁂

The mothers' group was back, and Tilly had to suppress an eye roll at their noisy arrival, plastering a welcoming smile on her face as she handed out menus.

The orders kept her busy for the next part of the morning and she didn't notice when Jess came in and seated herself at one of the small tables at the back of the cafe.

'Looks like you're having a busy morning,' her sister said, raising an eyebrow at the large table nearby.

'Yeah. They keep us hopping. What can I get you?'

'Just a short black, thanks,' she said, handing the menu back.

'Nothing to eat? We've got some amazing cakes and muffins in at the moment, or our lunch specials are very popular.'

'No thanks. I'm not hungry. Just the coffee.'

'Okay,' Tilly said, biting back a sigh and smiling. 'Won't be long.'

She turned away and almost collided with a human wall. 'I'm so sorry,' she started, then caught her breath slightly as she realised who it was. 'Jason.'

'My fault,' he said, dropping his hands from her arms where they'd instinctively gone to steady her.

'Sorry, your table's taken this morning,' she said, then turned and saw her sister watching them curiously. 'This is my sister, Jessica. Jess, this is my neighbour, Jason. He's new to town.'

'Nice to meet you, Jason,' Jess said politely, smiling. 'I'm sorry, I didn't realise I was taking your table.'

'No, you're fine. It's not really my table. Guess I'm just a creature of habit,' he said, sending her a rare smile that distracted Tilly momentarily. He didn't give those out often.

'Well, please, join me. I hate dining alone.'

Tilly saw Jason start a little at the invitation and waited for him to decline, but much to her surprise he pulled out the chair across from her sister and sat down. *Well, there's one for the record books. Mr Antisocial suddenly willing to partake in some conversation.*

'Your usual?' she asked, trying not to look as though she hadn't just suddenly been sideswiped.

'Oh? What's the usual?' Jess asked sweetly, eyeing the man across from her with interest.

'Bacon-and-egg roll and a strong coffee,' he told her with a shrug.

'Oh my God, I haven't had a bacon-and-egg roll in years,' Jess said, lowering her voice. 'Make that two,' she said, swinging her gaze across to Tilly.

'You want to eat a bacon-and-egg roll?' Tilly asked doubtfully. 'It's real bacon, not fake vegan meat.'

'I know, *Matilda*. You're the one always telling me I should try things. Well, I am.'

'Okay, then,' Tilly murmured as she jotted the order down and turned away. Jason Weaver was suddenly being social and her sister was eating normal-people food. What next? Paul might suddenly smile and be friendly?

'Oh good, you've brought an order over. I hope we didn't interrupt your social life or anything,' Paul muttered as she handed over the order slip.

*Well, thank goodness there are some things I can still rely on.*

❦

Jason swore silently as Tilly walked away. He hadn't meant to accept her sister's invitation, but he couldn't think of a way of declining that wouldn't either offend her or make him look like a dick in front of Tilly. Now he was stuck making small talk—the thing he hated the most. Still, it was a good way to maybe get some intel on Tilly.

'Tilly mentioned you were here visiting. Where are you up from?'

'Sydney, at the moment, but I'm only there briefly before I head back to New York. I spend my time between both cities for work.'

'Wow. That's a fair commute.'

She smiled politely, before tilting her head slightly while she looked at him, as if trying to work something out. 'So, you know Tilly because you're neighbours?'

'Well, we only recently figured out we live on the same road.'

'I see,' she said slowly. 'And what do you do?'

Hang on, wasn't he supposed to be the one asking questions? 'I'm a builder by trade. But right now I'm renovating the place I just bought.'

'So, you're out of work at the moment?' she asked.

'No, I'm working on my own place,' he said, striving to keep his voice neutral. 'Once I've finished renovating, I plan to buy another one to fix up.'

'Oh, I see, like that TV show *House Flip*?'

TV show? He didn't watch TV; if this was the kind of stuff they were showing, then he clearly wasn't missing much. He gave a noncommittal reply and was relieved when Tilly delivered their coffee, and managed to sneak a look at her T-shirt. *May your coffee kick in before reality does.*

'The food won't be long,' she said, making him lift his gaze and notice her guarded glance before she walked away once more.

'So, what is it you do in New York?' he asked Jess, aiming for deflection.

'I'm a fashion designer,' she said, taking a delicate sip from her cup.

'Excuse me,' a woman from the table across from them interrupted tentatively, 'I couldn't help but overhear just now, but you wouldn't be Jessica Lewis by any chance, would you?'

Jason saw Jess shoot a startled look at the other woman. 'Yes. I am.'

'The fashion label?' the woman pressed insistently.

'Yes, that's me,' Jessica said, and he saw her wariness slip a little more.

'Oh my God!' the woman shouted, causing everyone in the cafe to turn towards them in alarm. 'This is Jessica Lewis. She's famous, and she's right here in Ben Tirran.'

Jessica's surprised expression matched the other woman's, briefly, before she started to play down the unexpected attention.

Undeterred, the other woman got out of her chair and dragged out one at their table. 'What are you doing out here? I'm a total fashion-blog tragic! Actually, I've recently started my own blog. I feature new and fun brands and I plug clothing lines I like . . . I could do a post about you! Oh my God, could I interview you? We could do a live blog piece right now,' she said, pulling out her phone and scrolling through the screen pages.

'Ah, well, I'm . . .'

'Oh sorry,' she laughed, covering her mouth with a hand. 'You were about to eat. Can I just get a selfie with you first?' Without waiting, the woman leaned across and snapped a few dozen photos on her phone, before Tilly saved the day by plonking down the plate of food in between her sister and the uninvited guest, glaring at her without apology.

The woman seemed to take the hint, sliding her chair from under the table and heading back to her own.

'Sorry about that,' Tilly said to Jessica, frowning at the table across from them.

'That's all right. I'm actually more surprised than offended. I had no idea anyone would have even heard about fashion this far out in the back of beyond.'

Tilly swapped a dry glance with Jason as she placed his plate on the table. 'Enjoy.'

'Actually, Jason, if you'd excuse me, I hate to be rude, but I think I might go and sit with these ladies for a bit. It seems a shame not to say hello.'

'What about your food?' Tilly asked.

'Oh, I'm not hungry after all. Jason, you're a virile-looking man, I'm sure you can manage to take care of it,' Jess said, waving it off as she rose from her seat elegantly and crossed to the other table.

Jason sent a bewildered look up at Tilly, who gave a small chuckle. 'And that was my sister.'

'Wow,' he said, shaking his head slowly. 'Are you sure you two are even related?'

'I know,' she agreed meaningfully. 'Oh well, you won't be needing lunch or dinner tonight after this.'

He stared down at the two plates before him and let out a resigned sigh. A man had to do what a man had to do, he supposed, picking up his roll and biting into it with relish.

∽

Tilly followed Jess down the front path and watched her put her bag in the boot of her car.

'Are you sure you have to go back so soon?' Tilly asked. 'Seems a shame since you just discovered you had a fan club in town.' She grinned, still shaking her head over yesterday's events in the cafe.

'I have a few appointments that can't be put off,' Jess replied, turning to face her. 'I'm glad I came up . . . to see you,' she added, digging through her handbag to find her sunglasses. She put them on and straightened, her posture now a little stiff. 'I'd better go so I get back before rush hour.'

'Okay. Call me when you get home.' Tilly hugged her and stepped back so she could close the door.

As she watched the car disappear, Tilly wrapped her cardigan closer around her until she could no longer hear the sound of the engine, then turned and walked back inside to get ready for work. All in all, it hadn't been a horrible visit, she supposed, as she dug through her washing to find some clothes. Jess had been in, dare she say, almost high spirits after an afternoon of talking fashion with the mean girls for the better part of two hours.

She grabbed the shirt with *Coffee spelled backwards is eeffoc. Don't eeffoc with my coffee* and pulled it on. Sometimes she wondered about Paul's sense of humour, but it kept the customers coming back to see what the latest T-shirt quote would be.

Maybe it was all that talk yesterday about fashion and blogs that had made Jess suddenly homesick, or maybe she really did have appointments—who knew? Whatever the reason behind the visit, it hadn't been as much of a disaster as it could have been, and Tilly told herself she should be happy that the unexpected visit was over. Only, she wasn't. It *had* been nice having Jess here again. Maybe if she could get her up here again for a few days, away from work, she would finally manage to unwind. Then again, her sister seemed to thrive on keeping busy and Tilly wasn't sure she even knew *how* to relax.

As she drove into work later, her thoughts returned to her sister. She just wished she could shake the feeling that there was something more behind the visit.

# Nine

'Hey, Tilly, I was just out in your neck of the woods,' Tommy said when she went out the back to grab her handbag on her way home. 'I had a delivery for the new bloke who's in Browning's old place.'

'Oh yeah? Jason?'

'Yeah, Jason. Nice enough fella,' he added conversationally. 'Are you heading home now?'

'I was, yes,' she said.

'I don't suppose I can ask a favour?'

'Sure, what is it?'

'Old Bill at the hardware store said that Jason ordered a box of special screws he's apparently been keen to get and he wanted me to take them out when I was going that way, but I forgot they were in the front of the van. Any chance you could drop them off to save me another trip out there today? I'd do it tomorrow, but I promised Bill I'd get them to him today and I feel kinda bad that I forgot.'

'Sure, I guess. I'm driving right past anyway.'

'You're a legend,' he said with a sigh of relief. 'I've got training in a few minutes and I don't want to be late. Some of the kids get dropped off and I don't like them waiting at the park alone.'

'No worries.' She smiled, taking the surprisingly heavy box from him, and juggling it in her arms as she swapped her handbag to the other shoulder, heading out to her car.

Arriving at Jason's a few minutes later, Tilly knocked on the door and waited. The sound of a power tool came from the back of the house, so after another a couple of minutes she followed the noise.

As she rounded the corner she stopped. She'd seen men working before, sure, but this one caught her off guard. Jason was bent over, carefully guiding a saw through a piece of timber. The noise masked her approach, so he was oblivious to the fact he had an audience and was totally absorbed in the task at hand. It was a rare chance to observe the man unobtrusively. In the cafe he always seemed so on edge, alert, as though he were unable to completely relax. She recognised it, now that she knew a little of his past. She had seen the same in her husband, though in a slightly less noticeable way. As a police officer David could never truly switch off that instinct to be aware of his surroundings either.

She ran her eyes over Jason, moving from the denim-clad thighs, up along the length of his back and shoulders she could trace beneath the snug fit of his work shirt, and across his strong, tanned arms, her gaze lingering on his hands. They were large and hard looking, from hours of outdoor work. She often noticed them in passing—the way they held a mug or handed over a card. There was something comforting about a pair of calloused hands. Maybe because they reminded her of Pop. Years of working horses and the farm had toughened his hands and yet they were still gentle enough to hold hers as a child. Strong, safe hands.

The noise died down as Jason finished cutting the timber and it jolted Tilly from her thoughts. As he turned to throw the cut piece of wood on to a pile beside him, he noticed her and straightened quickly.

'Hi, I didn't mean to sneak up on you. I followed the noise,' Tilly said.

'Sorry. Can't hear a thing with these on.'

She waited as he took off his earmuffs and tossed them on the bench behind him. 'I didn't mean to interrupt. I believe you've been waiting on these? Bill wanted you to get them today.'

'It's all good. I'm done,' he said, heading towards her. 'Great, I haven't been able to finish off a job without these. Thanks for bringing them out. Dare I ask how you got stuck with the delivery? Seems a bit out of the cafe jurisdiction,' he said with a hint of a smile in his eyes.

'Bill gave them to Tommy,' she explained, 'but . . . long story, Tommy forgot they were in his van and asked if I could stop in on my way home.'

'That's customer service,' he said, taking the box from her.

Tilly shrugged. 'We don't tend to stand on ceremony out here.'

'Apparently.' He grinned. 'Well, thanks for doing this.' Then he looked at her, his smile still in place. 'I didn't know your real name was Matilda. Are you named after a relative or something?'

Tilly couldn't suppress a sigh. 'No. It's from *The Man from Snowy River*. You know, after Jessica Harrison's mother?'

Jason looked at her oddly.

'I'd have preferred Jessica, but my sister already got that, so it was either Rosemary or Matilda.' Tilly shrugged. 'My brother got Jim . . . after Jim Craig,' she explained, before realising he really had no idea who she was talking about.

'Your mother named all her kids after characters in a movie?'

'Yeah, I know. After a while it's not as weird as it first sounds.'

'I don't know, that's pretty . . .'

'Weird,' she supplied dryly.

'Dedicated,' he corrected. 'She obviously thought it out.'

'At least it wasn't from some horrendous movie, I guess.'

'I can't say I've ever seen it.'

'What?' Tilly gaped at him. 'How can you have never seen it? It's only the *greatest Australian movie ever made*.'

'I don't know,' he said with a shrug, 'I guess I've just never beeen that into horses.'

Tilly was pretty sure she'd never met anyone who'd never seen *The Man from Snowy River*. It was unheard of. 'You have to watch it,' she said simply.

'I'm more an action movie kind of guy,' he said, hedging.

'This has action. He rides a brumby down the side of a mountain, for goodness sake. You don't get more action than that.' Tilly could see he wasn't overly convinced, but this was her civic duty. The poor bloke didn't even know how un-Australian he was. It would almost be funny if it wasn't so damn tragic. 'Tomorrow night. My place. I'll even throw in a hot meal.'

'You're cooking?' he asked, lifting an eyebrow.

'Well, kind of. I'll probably be bringing home whatever's leftover from Allie's specials board, but it'll be hot.'

Jason gave a small grunt. 'Good thing I like Allie's cooking, then.'

'If you're really good, I might even throw in dessert. Six o'clock. Don't be late.'

'Yes ma'am,' he said, giving a small salute as she turned and headed back around to the front of the house.

As she walked towards her car, Tilly suddenly realised what she'd just done. She hadn't even thought it through before the words came out. Now, though, as she sat in her car, the magnitude of her actions began to sink in. She had invited Jason Weaver to her place for dinner. Was this a date? She hadn't been on a date since before meeting her husband.

A sickening sensation washed over her and she immediately decided to cancel. *What are you doing? You can't do it. It's too soon. What were you thinking?*

She *hadn't* been thinking, and that was probably why the invitation had come so easily. She'd found herself caught up in the moment; she was happy and Jason was good company. It was a natural, perfectly normal thing to do, a little voice inside her head soothed, and Tilly took a deep breath and let it out slowly.

It was just a movie, she told herself firmly. He was just a neighbour. She could do this; it was only a big deal if she turned it into one.

∞

'You invited him over for dinner and a movie?' Josie gaped at her the next day as they gathered in the kitchen before closing.

'He's never seen *The Man from Snowy River*,' Tilly said, and realised that saying it out loud did seem to lack a certain logic, compared to saying it in her head.

'You *have* heard the term "Netflix and chill", haven't you?' Josie asked, hitching an eyebrow suggestively.

'Yes,' Tilly said, swapping her confused gaze to Allie for some kind of support. 'And that's what we're doing: watching a movie and . . . chilling.'

She frowned as Josie gave a hoot of laughter. 'What? We are.'

'*Sure* you are.'

'Leave her alone, Josie,' Allie said, but she was smiling as she turned back to packaging up the leftover food from the lunch service.

'All I'm saying is, if you have that man on your lounge tonight and all you do is watch some dumb old movie, you need your head read.'

'It's not a dumb old movie. It's a classic,' Tilly said, picking up her bag.

'Well, you enjoy your ... *movie* tonight,' the younger woman called after her.

On the drive home, Tilly felt her hands begin to sweat on the steering wheel, and she swore under her breath at the ridiculousness of it all. After her initial bout of nerves yesterday she had calmed down, but now, if anything, it had got worse. Josie's words haunted her the whole way home. Did Jason think her invitation was more than a movie and dinner? What if he thought it was a code for something else? *Oh God*. She felt her cheeks begin to burn. Then she had a sudden thought, *He hadn't come in today ... Was he trying to avoid her?*

She had to cancel. She would call him and say she didn't feel well and was probably coming down with something infectious. She wouldn't really be lying—she did feel sick ... with humiliation. She'd call him as soon as she got home. This was just all too embarrassing.

She pulled into the driveway, then swore as she spotted the four-wheel drive already parked in front of the house.

*Crap.*

## Something Like This

Jason heard her car coming long before he saw it. He felt like a dill getting there so early. *Way to seem eager,* he thought when he arrived and realised she wasn't home yet.

He took his sunglasses from his head and threw them onto his passenger seat before climbing out of his car. That weird tingling sensation began in his gut again and he swallowed hard as she came towards him, looking somewhat anxious, wearing a T-shirt that read, *How do I take my coffee? Seriously. Very seriously.*

It wasn't enough to distract him from the thought that coming here tonight was probably the worst idea in the history of bad ideas. He couldn't make himself stay away from the damn cafe, but at least there he was saved from doing anything too stupid in the brief few minutes of conversation they had. But here, tonight, without the safety net of other people around, who knew what stupid thing he might say or do?

He shouldn't care so much about doing something to jeopardise whatever this thing was between them, but he did. He really liked Tilly. He hadn't wanted to. God knew he didn't need the whole rigmarole that went along with meeting someone. All he'd wanted was some time to clear his head and renovate his house. And yet, here he was all tongue-tied with sweaty palms like he was a fifteen-year-old kid again.

'Come on in. There's a beer in the fridge if you want to help yourself. I'm just going to clean up. Won't be long,' she said, waving her hand in what he assumed was the direction of the kitchen before disappearing down a hallway.

Jason looked around the room, noting that there wasn't a great deal in the way of decoration. Not that he knew a lot about such things—his place was more politely described as minimalist and not entirely on purpose. He just didn't have much stuff. He'd lived on base for most of his army career, and on the few occasions he had lived in a house, it was pre-furnished shared accommodation with other army blokes.

After his mother died, he'd cleared out the house before putting it on the market, keeping only a few things that held sentimental value—photo albums and pictures that had hung on his mum's walls. He didn't believe in holding on to stuff. Maybe it was due to his nomadic life in the army, always being moved around the place, or maybe it was just the way he was, but material things had never been important to him. He knew blokes who bought all the latest gadgets, had to have the biggest TV, the latest model car, the newest phone on the market, but that had never been him. Hell, he'd only bought a phone when he got out of the army and started his business; up until then he hadn't felt a need to be contactable twenty-four seven. For Jason, there was more to life than just accumulating stuff.

He wasn't surprised by Tilly's taste in furniture. Her dining table was a solid, sturdy timber, as was the coffee table and wall unit and cabinet. They looked like they'd been purchased as a package, rather than individually sourced to complement each other or be artfully coordinated.

The fridge wasn't new or a fancy state-of-the-art model, and no photos or magnets covered the front. He took out a beer and opened it, moving back out to the lounge room.

There were a few photos sitting on a fireplace mantel and he wandered over to take a closer look. A young girl sat on a brown horse, grinning at the camera; there was no mistaking that it was a young Tilly. Nearby, an older girl leaned over a fence beside a younger boy in a helmet, perched on a motorbike.

A movement caught his eye and he straightened as Tilly came back into the room dressed in a pair of soft denim jeans and a loose-fitting top. 'You haven't changed much.'

He caught her half-amused snort as she flicked a brief glance at the photo.

'Is that your brother and sister?'

'Yep.'

'Was that taken here? Near the stock yards?'

'Sure was. During one of our extended visits,' she said, looking back at the photo almost wistfully.

'Extended visits?'

For a moment he didn't think she was going to answer, but then she dragged her gaze from the photo and looked up at him. 'We lived in Sydney. My dad was a truck driver,' she said. 'He was away a lot, and he and Mum used to fight when he was between driving jobs, so Mum would often bring us back here to visit her parents. We'd stay anywhere from a week to a couple of months, depending on how bad the argument had been,' she said dryly.

'That must have been tough on you with school and stuff,' he said, glancing back to the photo and trying to imagine Tilly being that age.

'Yeah, it was a bit. It was harder on my brother. He was struggling at school to start with. It was always difficult for him to catch up.'

'Are you and your brother close?' As an only child, it always amazed him to see the difference in sibling relationships. He knew plenty who were close, and it always made him feel as though he'd missed out on something, but then there were a few who gave a whole new definition to the term dysfunctional families.

'We were. Jim died when he was sixteen.'

Jason had never known the kid, but he felt almost winded by the news. 'Jesus, I'm sorry, Tilly. I didn't . . .'

She gave him a small smile and shook her head. 'It's okay, there's never any easy way to bring it up.' Her smile turned a little crooked. 'It's okay to ask about it.'

'I don't want to dredge up anything,' he said, but was relieved she'd clearly been able to read him. The question of what happened was burning on the tip of his tongue.

'He got in with the wrong crowd. They started off doing stupid teenager stuff, sneaking out to parties and roaming the streets at all hours, but then they got mixed up in the drug scene and he ran away from home. We hadn't been able to find him for three months when the police came to the house to tell us he'd been killed in a car accident—running from the police.'

## Something Like This

He wanted to reach out to her or make some kind of gesture of comfort, but he didn't know how to start. He'd seen his share of death and the aftermath of violence, but how to deal with it, and what to say, had never been in his job description. The army had taught him a lot of things—but not how to comfort someone suffering, or give words of condolence, so he shoved his hands into his pockets instead. 'That really sucks.'

'Yeah. It does.'

'Is that why you're doing this program? Because of what happened to your brother?'

She nodded and turned away from the photo, and he assumed that was the end of the discussion as she moved towards the kitchen.

'There was this place that offered therapy with horses for people with emotional issues,' she said as she took two containers of creamy chicken carbonara out of the fridge and placed them in the microwave. 'It came in a pile of pamphlets Mum had been given from social workers when she was trying to get help for Jim. The flyer was in the bin, after Mum had gone on a massive cleaning frenzy following the funeral. It caught my eye, so I picked it out and read it.' A small smile touched her lips. 'If I'm honest, it was the fact they had horses that drew me to it in the first place. I'd always loved horses and I hated the city because I couldn't ride there.'

Jason watched as she took the food out of the microwave and plated it up.

'I caught the bus there on a whim one day. The owner saw me hovering outside and took me on a tour of the place. I told her about my Pop and how we rode horses at his place, and she offered me a part-time job helping out with the horses.'

'How old were you?'

'I was seventeen. I ended up working there for four years.'

'So, what happened between then and now?'

'Life,' she said with a weary smile.

He sensed there was a lot more to her story but didn't want to push. He had always trusted his instincts, and right now they were telling him to back off. 'Can I help with anything?' he asked instead.

'Nope. All ready. Do you want to eat this outside?'

'Lead the way,' he said, stepping back to let her pass and catching the faint smell of perfume.

The small table they sat at overlooked a yard planted with colourful shrubs and trees, and separated by a gate was another yard further back where contented-sounding chooks scratched around the base of fruit trees. 'Someone took a lot of time planting all those trees.'

Tilly glanced over towards the orchard, and her smile this time was happier. 'My grandparents planted them. They've been there for as long as I can remember. I had to do a lot of clearing up when I first moved back. The previous owners didn't get here very often and the orchard was pretty overgrown. I was worried I'd lost most of the trees, but they were fine.'

Jason suspected most of the garden was also her grandparents' work. It reminded him of his mother's garden, full of the old-fashioned plants that had started disappearing from yards. Landscaping was now full of trendy plants—structured, with colour-coordinated grasses, full of clean lines and stone pathways. There was none of that in this garden, and yet he found a peace here he rarely felt in other places.

Something about the way she held herself, a little stiffer than usual, caught his attention through the meal. Clearly something was bothering her. She seemed nervous, and the realisation made him feel a little better about his own feelings. Was she anticipating how things would go from here between them too? Or was she regretting inviting him over? He tried to gauge her mood, but he didn't have all that much experience with women and moods, so this was one area he couldn't rely on his instincts. When she dropped her fork, and jumped, he knew he wasn't going to be able to sit there wondering and second-guessing any longer.

'Is everything okay?' Jason asked, watching her steadily even though she didn't make eye contact for very long.

'Yep. Sorry. Just a bit clumsy.'

He found that pretty unbelievable. He'd seen the woman balance plates and a pile of coffee mugs and carry them with the steady hand of a seasoned circus juggler. 'Are you having second thoughts about inviting me over?' He held his breath waiting for her answer, wondering what the hell he would do if she said yes.

'No,' she said quickly. The answer should have been a relief, but the fact that she said it so fast wasn't exactly confidence boosting.

Tilly glanced up and must have seen the doubt on his face, because she sighed and put down her fork carefully. 'When I invited you to have dinner and to watch a movie, what did you think I meant?' she asked, the words coming out in a rush, catching him a little off guard.

'To have dinner and watch a movie,' he said slowly, trying to figure out if this was some kind of test and if he had just failed miserably.

'Really?' Her hopeful tone only confused him more.

'Yes. Why? What *did* you mean?'

'To have dinner and watch a movie,' Tilly replied, almost defensively.

'Okay,' he said, holding up his hands and sitting back in his chair. 'Did I miss something?'

'No.' She sighed again. 'It's just that apparently I'm really out of touch with how things are done and that inviting someone over to watch a movie is code for . . . something else,' she finished in a murmur, lowering her eyes uncomfortably.

'Ah,' he said, as understanding finally dawned.

'I wasn't inviting you over for anything . . . well, you know . . .'

'It's okay. I didn't think you were. Truth is, I was just glad I didn't have to cook dinner for myself tonight.'

'Really?'

'Yeah. Cooking for one gets a bit monotonous.'

'I mean, you really weren't expecting this to be some kind of . . .'

'Trick to lure me into your bed?' He chuckled at the incredulous look on her face and shook his head. 'It's okay, I'm kidding. But since you pointed out that I've apparently missed out on some vital part of my education by not having watched this movie, I was too scared to turn down the invitation.'

Jason caught her droll smile and saw her relax slightly across from him.

'It *is* pretty embarrassing that you've never seen it,' she agreed.

'Well, I'm ready to be enlightened.'

As they finished the meal he was relieved that the conversation felt a lot less forced between them, although hearing her rule out any kind of extra-curricular activities so emphatically had been a tad disappointing. Not that he'd really expected anything, but he was hopeful that an invitation for dinner was at least an indication that maybe she didn't mind his company and from there something could possibly grow. Maybe not, it now seemed.

He got up and followed Tilly into the kitchen, helping her to clean up despite her protests, then they headed into the lounge room. There was a three-seater lounge and a single chair to choose from and he momentarily wondered if he should take the single seat, before she indicated towards the lounge and sat down beside him, picking up the remote.

'Do you remember when there was only one remote to operate a TV?' she said as she swapped to a second remote on the coffee table and then picked up a third to complete the task of searching for the movie.

'I feel old,' he agreed with a smile. 'But tell me again, what's so special about this movie?'

'Well, aside from the fact it's about horses,' she said in a tone that virtually said, *dumb arse*, 'it's an underdog story, and who doesn't love one of those?'

'Won't hear me complaining.'

'Shh,' she said, as the screen lit up. 'It's starting. You have to watch this.' She reached for the other remote and turned it up.

'Nothing's happening,' he said, then jumped at the roar of a hundred horses galloping across the screen. 'You did that on purpose,' he muttered, watching her laugh beside him.

'It gets 'em every time,' she said, still chuckling and turning the volume back to an acceptable level.

'Who's that guy?' he asked as the scene opened.

'Are you *seriously* going to do this through the entire movie?'

'Okay, fair enough . . . I'll figure it out on my own.' Jason hid a grin as he saw her shake her head, and settled in to watch the movie that was important enough for Tilly's mother to name her children after. A few minutes in, he began to notice he and Tilly were sitting a lot closer. Maybe it was because with the lights turned low, it was easier to relax and get comfortable. He could feel the heat of her leg as it rested beside his.

On the screen, Jim was having a moment with Jessica in the stables, and Jason covertly glanced over to watch Tilly staring at the screen, mesmerised by the unfolding story. He grinned when he saw that she was mouthing the words as the actors spoke them.

'You know every line word for word?' he finally asked, after giving up trying to be inconspicuous about watching her.

Tilly jumped guiltily, sending him a startled glance. 'Are you watching the movie?'

He turned back to face the screen but continued to smile. Jason couldn't remember the last time he'd watched a movie with someone. He frowned a little at the thought. It had to be years. He hadn't dated for a long time, and even before he lost his leg he hadn't taken women to the movies. He was more of a pub-and-meal kind of bloke back then. This was nice, though. He could get used to doing this. As the movie continued, he found himself distracted by every little movement Tilly made. Jason could feel each time she tensed, when she relaxed, when she shifted her position the slightest bit; he was completely in tune with her and he prayed that *The Man from Snowy River* was one of those movies that dragged on forever.

# Ten

Tilly couldn't concentrate on the movie. She tried, but for the first time in her life she just couldn't make herself focus, and she knew the reason was the man sitting beside her. He smelled good. She had a crazy urge to turn her head and bury it into his neck and sniff . . . She almost snorted when she imagined the reaction that would get from him. *Do not attempt to sniff the man,* Tilly repeated firmly in her head, not altogether sure she could trust herself. Sitting together like this in the darkened room, it was all too easy to fall into the trap of feeling at ease. Despite the fact she instinctively knew she could trust Jason, there was the underlying factor of something she dared not try to label that flowed between them, just under the surface.

At least she thought there was something there. Then again, it had been so long since she'd had any experience with men that she was a little concerned maybe it was just wishful thinking. The thought made her frown. *Was* she thinking of Jason like that? There was no denying he was attractive, in a surly, rough kind of way. But he had a softer side. She had seen him watching the horses and she knew he would be gentle with them. She didn't know how she knew; she just did.

There was something about Jason that she found herself drawn to. Maybe it was his vulnerability, which she occasionally caught a glimpse of. He seemed lost, lonely even, although she was fairly sure he kept people at a distance and created his own isolation. Tilly could relate to that. She didn't like crowds—she was totally fine with her own company. If it wasn't for the need of an outside income, she could quite happily never leave her property again. But there were times when even the most content of hermits longed for company.

Jason shifted slightly, and the movement brought his arm in contact with hers. She felt the heat of his body burn her own. It would be so easy to rest her head on his shoulder. He would put his arm around her and they would fit perfectly ... *Stop it*. Jason was her neighbour, of sorts, and a customer at the cafe. They were friends, and that was all.

She should have left the lights on. She wouldn't be having all these crazy fantasies if the lights were on and she was forced to remember who and where she was. A man in her life right now was not a complication she particularly needed. No matter how tempting the thought of snuggling together on a lounge might be.

The big ride was about to come up on the screen, and thankfully her attention was once more caught by Jim Craig and his mighty brumby, Denny. She would never tire of watching that scene, as he finally brought the mob in singlehandedly.

'That hat tip at the end gets me every time,' she said wistfully, as she watched Jim give a little tug to the brim of his hat before riding off to claim his inheritance, then she remembered she was sitting next to Jason and cleared her throat.

'Really?' Jason asked with a raised eyebrow.

'So, what did you think?' Tilly asked, sitting up and attempting to get things back on track.

'It was okay,' he said, shrugging.

She stared at him, waiting. There had to be more, surely? 'That's it? It was *okay*?'

'The mountain ride was pretty cool,' he acknowledged.

'I'm not sure we can be friends anymore,' she said with a defeated sigh, standing up.

'Aw, come on. It's not exactly high-quality acting.'

'It's more than the acting, it's . . . You know what, I tried,' she said with mock regret.

'Okay, I did like it, but don't tell anyone. I have a tough-guy image to maintain and if anyone found out I liked a movie about horses, I'd never hear the end of it.'

'Exactly who would I tell? Do you even know anyone else in this town?'

'I know people,' he protested.

'Who?'

'I know the guy at the hardware store.'

'Oh really? What's his name?'

'Bob . . . or Brett . . . or . . .'

'Bill?' she supplied helpfully.

'Yeah, that's him. Bill.'

Tilly rolled her eyes. 'You really should get out more, you know.'

'Why?'

'Because you've moved to town and you hardly know anyone.'

'So?'

'*So?* How are you going to make friends if you don't go anywhere?'

'What gave you the impression I wanted to make friends?'

Tilly looked at him, wondering if he was joking, then realised he was serious. 'Really? You don't want to meet anyone?'

'I met you.' He shrugged.

'Only because you had to order food,' she pointed out.

'Yeah, well, that's pretty much all I need.'

'Everyone needs friends.'

'I've got friends.'

'That live here, I mean.'

'Why? I'm happy with my own company. I don't need to meet a bunch of new people I'm never going to hang out with. So, why bother?'

'Well, because . . .' This was crazy. 'Because no man's an island and all that.' She gave up even attempting to cover her exasperation.

'Consider me Great Keppel,' he said with a grin, resting his arms out either side of him along the back of the lounge.

'Well, I think you're wrong. I like my own company, but I still need friends. Everyone needs a friend.'

'The fact that you trusted me to watch a movie with, I'm taking a punt and guessing that makes us friends. I'm okay with that.'

'Oh, you're okay with that? What a relief. I feel honoured.'

'You should.'

'Whatever.' She dismissed him with a shake of her head, trying to ignore the little flutter that his slow, cocky grin sparked inside her. 'You want a coffee and some dessert?'

'Sure. I've worked up a bit of an appetite.'

Tilly wasn't sure if Jason was being deliberately flirty, but she needed no help in coming up with ideas to satisfy an appetite. She quickly made for the kitchen and dished up apple pie with custard.

As they ate at the kitchen bench, Tilly took the time to study Jason as he answered her questions about where he'd come from. She sensed there was a story behind his move here that he hadn't told her about.

'I'm sorry about your mum,' she said after he shared the details.

'Thanks. It was pretty hard to watch her in so much pain. I wouldn't wish it on anyone.'

'I nursed my mum through the same thing. It's awful.'

'I'm sorry,' he said, holding her gaze steadily. She saw in his eyes the look of true sorrow that only someone who had seen the same heartache could share.

'Was it because of the memories of your mum that you wanted to move?' She scooped up a small spoonful of pie while she waited for him to answer.

'Kind of.'

'Kind of?'

For a moment she wasn't sure he was going to continue, but eventually he spoke, though clearly with some reluctance. 'It was a lot of things. I'd been through a bit of a rough patch after I was released from the hospital. I was drinking a bit and pretty much became the grumpiest bastard on earth. I hated everyone and everything . . . I wasn't particularly fun to be around.'

Tilly remained silent as she waited for him to continue.

'When Mum got sick, I guess it shook me up a bit. I started to get my act together because she needed me. I got back into work, started my own business and pulled my sorry arse out of pity land and back into life.

'For a while I thought I'd found someone, a chance to have something I hadn't really thought about once I lost my leg,' he said, stirring his spoon idly through his custard. 'But it fell through, so I decided to move—have a change of scenery, that kind of thing.' He went quiet for a moment then seemed to shake off the memories before glancing up at her. 'What about you? Why did you move back?'

For a moment Tilly didn't answer. Talking about David wasn't something she did very often. 'My husband and I had bought this place, and were planning on moving here, but then he died. I put off the move for a bit, but then Mum got sick, so she moved in here with me and I took care of her once she couldn't look after herself anymore.'

She felt Jason staring at her but didn't glance up. She hated seeing that horrible look of pity on people's faces.

'That must have been tough,' he said quietly.

'Yeah. It was pretty horrendous actually, but that's life, isn't it?' She looked up quickly. 'It has a particularly sick sense of humour.'

He nodded slowly, giving her a wry, sad kind of smile. 'It does at that.'

It had been a surprise to learn that Tilly had been married. Of course, maybe if he had gotten out to meet more people someone would have mentioned it to him. Small towns always saw it as a civic duty to share information about everyone to make sure you were up to speed as a newcomer.

He was glad he was a pro at hiding his reactions. Automatically his gaze swept the room, looking for any clues he must have missed, and he spotted a timber photo frame on the hallway wall he hadn't noticed before. He couldn't get a clear view of the image but he could make out a woman in a long, white, sequined gown, and a tall, dark-haired man beside her. *That must be him,* he thought. He felt sorry for the guy, of course—dying young was always a tragedy—but he'd seen enough dying and had lost too many good mates over the years to waste any kind of polite grief on someone he'd never even met.

His mother had commented once that she had lost the boy he'd once been before he joined the army. Most people probably thought that was a natural progression, but he knew his mum was right. In order to do his job, he'd had to sacrifice part of himself, and that part had never come back. But he was also a realist. He wouldn't be here with Tilly now if her husband hadn't died. He knew he could be a cold-hearted bastard, but he was working on it.

Meeting Hayley had woken him up to the fact that he needed to change. His old life was gone, along with his leg, and if he didn't adapt and change, then the road ahead would look pretty lonely.

He saw her smother a yawn, and he glanced at his watch. 'I guess I should get out of here and let you go to bed,' he said, standing and carrying his bowl to the sink.

'Leave it, I'll do it in the morning,' she protested when he reached for the tap to run water in the sink.

'I'm here now, may as well get it done.'

'You know, for someone who was in the army, you don't take orders very well,' she grumbled, bringing her own bowl across to place in the sink.

He grinned down at her and caught the smell of warm coconut and vanilla—from where he had no idea, but she always smelled so damn good. She glanced up and he held her gaze; it was only for a moment, but it felt much longer. There was something there, he felt it. She had the ability to make him feel things he hadn't experienced in a long time.

It was different to the way Hayley had made him feel—he saw that now. There'd been a spark of something there too, but it hadn't been this intense. With Hayley it had been the awakening of hope he'd felt. With Tilly, it was something far deeper. His chest filled with a warmth he couldn't truly recall ever feeling before. It was more than attraction—he wanted to know everything there was to know about her. He wanted to be part of whatever was important to her. He cared about her.

She lowered her eyes, breaking the spell, and he washed the bowls and cutlery, handing them across for her to dry, working in a companionable silence, lost in the comfort of sharing a mundane domestic duty.

A few minutes later, when they reached the front door, Jason turned to say goodnight.

'What are you doing Friday night?' she asked unexpectedly.

'I don't know, I'd have to check my diary. I'm pretty booked out with social engagements usually.'

'Well, if you find that you're free, I'd like to continue your education.'

'Oh? There's another classic I haven't watched?'

'Yep. *The Man from Snowy River . . . Two.*' She smiled sweetly, closing the front door on him before he could reply.

Jason lowered his head in defeat. Jesus, how many movies could they make about a bloke riding a horse down a mountain? But he found himself smiling as he walked to his car. It would mean he could be alone with Tilly again—he could think of worse ways to spend a night.

∽

Life suddenly got even more hectic for Tilly as the renovations for her business started. Her every waking minute was once again consumed by plans and quotes and making decisions about a whole range of things she knew pretty much nothing about. It was harder than she'd expected. David was supposed to be here and handling this side of the business venture. Her job was the horses. But not anymore. Now she was doing it all on her own and for the first time since starting on this journey, she was beginning to have doubts. Jess's words echoed in her mind. What if she *did* fail? What if she couldn't manage all this on her own?

*You got this, babe.* The words floated to her from somewhere deep inside and Tilly blinked back tears. She missed David so much, but especially when she found herself out of her depth, like now. He had always been the one who helped shoulder the burden. He had been her rock. He was supposed to be here now so they could make all these decisions together. But he wasn't.

It was all becoming very real. Bob Peterson, the local builder she had hired to undertake the renovations, was a nice guy but he worked on Ben Tirran time, which meant often he would stop work and leave because he didn't have a part, or another job came up that he decided he could squeeze in, and work would suddenly be at a standstill for days at a time. With the paperwork completed and the majority of her approvals rubber-stamped, she had been confident enough to set an opening date for Healing Hooves, but at the rate the renovations appeared to be moving, or rather *not* moving, now she was wondering if everything would be completed in time.

She was leading two of her riding horses out from the undercover area outside the tack shed when her first two riding students arrived.

She loved working with the little kids—they were so full of energy and had no fear when it came to learning new things. Denny and the other bay mare, also a Guy Fawkes, stood patiently while the six-year-olds clambered up into the saddles.

Today they were practising some tricks to perform at the local show in a couple of months' time as part of the horse events program.

'Okay, Serina, now you're going to stand up on Denny. Slowly now, wait until you have your balance,' Tilly said, holding on to the child's hand. 'You right?' she asked, looking up into the girl's widening smile.

'Yep, you can let go now, Tilly,' she said confidently.

'Okay,' Tilly said, carefully taking a small step back. 'Look at you. You did it.' She grinned. 'Do you think you can catch a ball?'

'I'm not a real good catcher,' Serina said, sounding a little doubtful.

'Well, it's a big ball. Do you want to give it a go and see?' Tilly asked, sitting the little girl back down in the saddle while she walked over and picked up a large beach ball. 'Okay, now stand back up.' She waited for Serina to regain her balance and then gently tossed the ball up to her. 'Well done,' Tilly said as she helped the beaming child hop down from Denny, who had barely moved during the entire lesson.

'You wild, ferocious brumby, you,' she crooned to the docile Denny, rubbing his furry face.

They had worked on the routine for the past few weeks, and the girls were gaining more confidence with every lesson. They were preparing for a riding event and a freestyle demonstration, and Tilly couldn't wait to see them perform in the show. There was nothing cuter than horses and kids enjoying what they were doing, and the publicity for the brumbies as a breed and her business was an added benefit. But she was really doing it for the kids. They got so much enjoyment out of riding, and for them to do it in front of the town at the show was a highlight of the year.

Later, as she packed away the equipment, Tilly smiled when she turned and saw Denny kick the beach ball ahead of him as he walked around the arena.

They never ceased to amaze her, these gorgeous animals. She let out a long, contented sigh and tipped her head back, allowing the last few warm rays of afternoon sun to touch her face. She counted her blessings every day. It had been a hard road getting this far, with a lot of pain along the way, but she was truly grateful for everything she had.

Tilly opened her eyes when she felt a warm puff of breath on her shoulder, and smiled as Denny came to stand beside her. 'We're pretty lucky, aren't we, old fella?' she whispered, resting her head against his, happy to just be in the moment with her best friend.

# Eleven

Two days later, Jason walked into the cafe and took his usual seat, waiting for Tilly to finish serving a customer before she came over to take his order. When she did make her way across to his side, she seemed distracted.

'Everything okay?'

'Bob Peterson had an accident yesterday.'

'Who's Bob Peterson?' Jason asked.

'He's a builder around town. He fell from a ladder on a building site.'

'Bugger,' Jason said with a wince. 'Is he okay?'

'They're not sure how extensive his injuries are yet, but apparently he's lucky he survived the fall.'

'I take it he was a regular in here?'

'Yeah. Nice fella. I actually had him booked in to finish the bunkhouse. He was supposed to be starting next week. I'm going to have to move the opening date back.'

'Can't you just get someone else?'

'Not on short notice.'

'Gee, if only you knew a builder,' he said dryly.

'You?' Tilly lifted an eyebrow. 'But you're working on your place.'

'I'm working for myself. I can shuffle things around. If you want?'

'Yes,' she said quickly. 'That would be great. If you're sure you can fit it in.'

'I can come out and take a look this afternoon after you finish here?'

'That'd be perfect. Thank you,' she said, and he saw gratitude fill her big brown eyes.

Warmth spread through his chest and he felt the ridiculous urge to puff it out like some overly proud peacock. *Jesus, mate. Get a grip.*

'I'll put your order in and be right back,' she said, cutting into his inner strutting and hurrying away. He followed her departure with a distracted frown. He didn't regret offering to take a look at the job, but it was getting harder to pretend to himself that he wasn't jumping at any opportunity to be with her or impress her in some way. What had happened to his new philosophy about taking himself away from people and complications?

He tried to ignore the little part of him that scoffed in the background as he continued to admire the way her jeans fitted around her backside and thighs. It was more than that, he told himself with a touch of annoyance. Sure, he was attracted to her, but this was more than just attraction. He liked her. Hell, he admired her. Tilly was tough yet gentle, thoughtful and funny . . . He liked her. *Really* liked her.

Jason knew he couldn't deny what was going on—not after their last movie night that was definitely-not-code-for-sex. Two nights ago he'd arrived at Tilly's place bracing himself for his ongoing education of Australian cinematic masterpieces. He'd gone in with an open mind, he really had, but found the second *Man from Snowy River* even worse than the first.

'There is really something wrong with you,' Tilly had told him, shaking her head in disgust as she got up from the lounge after the movie and collected their dessert bowls from the coffee table.

'Hey, I tried,' he said, following her into the kitchen.

'So what's your favourite movie then? Oh wait . . . Let me guess . . . *Rambo* . . . or *Rocky*,' she said, rolling her eyes.

'That's a fair guess, and both *are* classics,' Jason told her, ignoring her scoff. 'But I think it'd have to be a toss-up between *Die Hard* and the *Fast and Furious* franchises.'

'What a surprise.'

'Have you seen any of them?'

'Can't say I have,' she said before glancing across at him.

'Well, I think I may need to further *your* education.'

'But they're such . . . *man* movies,' she finished, scrunching up her nose a little.

'I sat through two movies watching Jim Craig ride horses down a mountain. I think it's only fair you sit through a couple of mine.'

She rolled her eyes dramatically and gave a hard-done-by sigh, before reluctantly agreeing. Jason had bitten back a triumphant grin that had threatened to escape.

Seeing her attempt to cover a third yawn, he'd said goodnight shortly afterwards, but he had to admit that he was enjoying their movie nights more than he'd thought possible.

∽

The cafe was busy when she dropped his order off and the place was getting too noisy for his liking, so he made short work of his roll and tossed his coffee down, then got up to pay.

'Thanks again, Jason. I'll see you this afternoon?' she asked, and he had to drop his eyes when he felt himself almost fall into her gaze—he couldn't even defend himself against the old Jason in his head who was gagging over his out of character, love-sick cliché.

'No worries,' he said, clearing his throat and putting his wallet into his back pocket. 'I better get home. I'll see you this arvo.' He made his escape before he started dreaming up reasons to hang around.

There wasn't much left to do to the back of the house. He just needed to finish installing the set of bi-folding glass doors that now opened up onto the large verandah and deck he'd been extending. The extra light that removing the back wall now revealed was remarkable. Instead of the dark, walled-in kitchen and dining area he'd once had, there was now a wide, unobstructed view of the back yard and rolling hills.

As Jason worked, his mind drifted to the troubled thoughts that had been darting around in his mind. He was doing it again, playing the knight in shining armour. His heroic deeds were in the form of paid work, but he sure as hell wouldn't be dropping everything to help out some bloke who'd suddenly found himself in a bit of a jam without a builder, not when he'd decided he wasn't going to do any contract work until he'd finished his own house. Buying this place and taking his time to do the renovations was supposed to be therapeutic. But ever since meeting Tilly, therapy had been the last thing on his mind—instead, all he'd really thought about was her.

It was weird that he seemed to be following some sort of pattern. He'd fought the attraction to Hayley when he'd agreed to take on her renovation, and lost. Why couldn't he be attracted to a woman he didn't have to work for? It would be nice for once to not have a work connection to the woman he had a thing for.

*You didn't have to take the job, dumb arse.* Up until today, Tilly hadn't been a client. So, he supposed that theory was out the window. Maybe he'd had enough of a break?

*Or maybe, you could stop being such a drama queen and do something about it.* He was sick of behaving like a stalker, going into the cafe a few times a week just so he could see her. Not to mention it was costing him a small fortune. He needed to man up and do something about it, or move on.

Standing back to survey his handiwork after adjusting the last screw on the sliding door, Jason gave a satisfied nod. That was one job down. Now it was time to do something about this other situation.

∽

'So, what do you think? Is it doable?' Tilly asked after showing Jason the shed. 'Can you squeeze it in?'

'Yeah, I reckon I can get it done.'

Tilly breathed a sigh of relief; it had been weighing on her heavily all day. It wouldn't be the end of the world if she had to put back the opening day, but she really didn't want to have to re-book her first clients and start off on such an unprofessional foot. Credibility was going to be everything if she hoped to run a successful equine therapy business.

'Thanks, Jason. I really appreciate this.' She held his gaze for a moment and felt a flicker of awareness rush through her. Surely it was just gratitude, she told herself as he shifted slightly before turning away to inspect a nearby beam.

'No worries. It's pretty straightforward, so it shouldn't take long, and you've got most of the building materials here.'

'Great.'

'I'll grab some measurements now so I can get started.'

'Okay. I'll get out of your way. Yell if you need anything.' He gave her a brief nod and she headed back to the round yard where she'd left Red.

## Something Like This

He was going to be a beauty when he stopped growing. Already he was at just a bit above sixteen hands, which was quite tall for a Guy Fawkes horse, and he still had some growing left to do.

She stood in the centre of the round yard and started moving him around her. His gait was a dream to watch, so smooth and agile. She extended her arm and the horse stopped and changed direction as she turned slowly in the centre of the circle. When he stopped, she walked steadily closer. Each session over the past few weeks she had managed to get closer, which was encouraging, but the progress was frustratingly slow.

'What is it, mate?' she asked softly, holding her ground in front of the big horse. 'What am I missing with you?'

Red nodded a couple of times and gave a few low snorts. The good old brumby snort. It wasn't unheard of in other domestic horses, but it was pretty standard communication for these ones. It was often used as a warning, and in younger horses as a way to make them sound tough. It didn't impress Tilly one bit.

'You know, you're going to wonder why you put up such a fight once you realise how good a scratch behind the ear can feel.' She stayed for a few more minutes before deciding to end on a good note. But maybe it was time to look for a different approach.

∽

A few days later, Tilly poked her head inside the shed and smiled. Her gaze was drawn to the man in the centre of the room leaning over a sawhorse banging something with a hammer. It wasn't so much what he was doing that held her so transfixed, it was the fact he was shirtless while he did it. Sweat glistened on his skin and she followed a little rivulet that beaded from between his shoulder blades and ran the length of his back, disappearing into the waistband of his jeans.

With each movement of the hammer, the muscles in his arms and along his sides bunched and bulged in a mesmerising display. She took a step backwards and bumped a piece of timber on the floor, which made a noise that caused Jason to turn his head in her direction. He paused mid movement, slowly lowering his arm and straightening to face her.

Was she still gaping at him like some sex-starved animal? She wasn't sure. God, she hoped not. Tilly swallowed hard and cleared her throat. 'Hi, sorry, I didn't mean to sneak up on you. I just got home and thought I'd have a look.'

'All good. What do you think?'

*Of the shed,* she reminded herself firmly. 'It's really coming along. You've done a great job.'

'Yeah, it's shaping up.'

*It most certainly is.* 'It looks amazing . . . the shed. Looks amazing,' she quickly added.

'I'm glad you're here actually. I wanted to find out what you wanted to do with the bathroom.' He walked across to the other side of the room, beckoning her to follow.

*Concentrate, Matilda.* She forced herself to listen to what he was asking. This was, after all, her livelihood they were discussing.

'I reckon instead of putting the bathroom on that side, you could move it to here and then we could just use the existing plumbing and tap into the electricity, which would work out cheaper for you and would also save time.'

Tilly followed his movements across the room and tilted her head slightly as she considered his suggestion. It did make sense. 'Sure. I didn't have my heart set on having it over there.'

'It won't be too involved to rearrange the layout. I was just thinking if we can save some dollars here and there, you could use them somewhere else.'

'Absolutely,' she agreed. There was always somewhere she could use extra cash. It seemed like no matter how well she'd budgeted, every time she turned around there was another thing that she needed to find money for.

Tilly suddenly realised how close they were standing and her breath did that strange little catch it had been doing whenever he was nearby lately.

Her gaze followed the trail of dark hair that feathered its way downward, across a nicely tanned chest to narrow at his belt buckle and disappear from sight. Her eyes flew to his face, and she realised, to her horror, that he was watching her.

She froze, like a startled rabbit. What could she do? There was no way of disguising the fact she was ogling him as he stood right there. It took a moment for the expression on his face to register. He didn't look insulted by her blatant gawking, far from it. If she wasn't mistaken, there was a kind of satisfied smugness exuding from his normally reserved exterior.

'Well, you seem to have everything under control here,' she said briskly. 'I'd better let you finish up so you can get home. I'll see you later.' She walked backwards and gave him a brief wave before stepping outside and groaning with humiliation. *Idiot.* She really needed to deal with this—whatever it was. It was turning her into a complete moron. But *how* did she deal with it? That was the question.

⁂

Tilly rubbed at her face as she sat at her dining table that evening, going over the last of the paperwork for her upcoming clinic. She gave an annoyed groan as her phone rang and frowned at the international number on the screen.

'Hello?'

'Is this Matilda Hollis?' an American-accented voice asked.

'Yes . . .' she said slowly.

'I'm a friend of Jessica's, I'd rather not say who.' The woman on the other end of the line sounded nervous. 'I've debated for a few days now about calling you. It's probably not my place, but I felt you should know.'

'Know what?' Tilly asked.

'Jessica's had some . . . health issues lately. I had hoped that she'd call you herself and let you know but, well, you know Jessica. She can be stubborn.'

'I'm sorry, but who is this?' Tilly didn't understand why some stranger would be calling her, out of the blue, about her sister.

'I'm a friend. A close friend. Look, I normally wouldn't interfere, but she won't let me fly over to be with her and I know she won't ask anyone else to help—she'll try to do it alone, but I'm really worried that she won't manage. I care about her,' the woman said softly, and Tilly heard the lilt of emotion in her voice that was being held tightly in check.

'I'll call her now,' Tilly said, breaking the moment of silence that followed.

'No, she'll only tell you she's fine. Please, I know it's a lot to ask and I know your relationship with your sister is no business of mine, but you need to go to her. Otherwise she'll just push you away. Like she has with me,' the woman added sadly. 'I wouldn't ask if it wasn't serious.'

'How serious is serious?' Tilly asked cautiously.

'Your sister is having a mastectomy. She goes into hospital tomorrow.'

The caller hung up before Tilly could ask any more questions, leaving her to stare blankly at the phone in her hand. Who called someone out of the blue to tell them something like that without giving any details? Panic began to gnaw at her insides. Her sister had only just been here. But there was something off, she reminded herself—she had known it at the time. There was more to it than Jess just being her annoying self. Tilly had wondered what she was really doing up here . . . now she knew. Jess had been carrying this secret, had come to share it with Tilly, but then changed her mind.

*A mastectomy?* This was so far beyond serious. This was monumental. And she hadn't said a word when she was here. Indignation momentarily overrode Tilly's shock. Why wouldn't Jess tell her? Clearly she didn't want Tilly to know. And who the hell was this anonymous woman to phone her and tell her she needed to go to her sister? It hurt that Jess hadn't told her, but it didn't surprise her. Jess had never had a great track record when it came to sharing burdens.

What if Tilly went all the way to Jess's place just to be told to mind her own business?

With a frustrated groan she tilted her head back to glare at the ceiling. She couldn't ignore it, and her mysterious caller did have a point. If Tilly called to ask what was going on, Jess would tell her she was fine. That much was certain. Pride would stop her asking for help.

Why was this happening again? Hadn't she already lost enough? The thought of losing her sister as well was too painful to think about. A tear rolled down Tilly's face as she fought not to give in to the threatening panic. It was too soon to think the worst. She needed to stay calm and wait until she'd spoken to Jess, but already she could feel the claws of grief beginning to take a firm hold.

The next morning, Tilly woke exhausted and no less worried. She packed her car in a confused rush, and then as she got off the phone to Paul, who thankfully was gracious about letting her have a few days off, Jason pulled up in his ute.

Despite the fact her mind was racing as she made a mental list of things to do before she headed down to Jess, she could still appreciate the wide-shouldered figure dressed in a white T-shirt and caramel cargo work pants as Jason gathered the equipment from the back of his vehicle.

'Morning,' he called as she walked out to greet him.

'Morning,' she said, remembering to concentrate on what she had to do.

'Everything okay?'

'I'm not sure, actually. I have to go to Sydney. I had a phone call about my sister.' She waved a hand quickly, realising he probably wasn't interested in all the details. 'Anyway, I have to head down there, so I just wanted to check that you didn't need me for anything before I go?'

'You're going now?'

She nodded. 'As soon as I get back from next door to ask about feeding the horses.' Feeding was a bit of an issue. They didn't require a strict routine as such—her brumbies were hardy, but it had been a particularly dry start to autumn, and winter wasn't looking all that promising either, so she still needed to supplement their grazing with hay.

'I can do that,' he said.

'Oh no, you don't have to.' She shook her head, caught off guard by his offer. 'You're busy with all this,' she added, waving a hand vaguely at the building site.

'I'm already here every day. It's not like I'm making a special trip. Show me what needs doing,' he said before she could object further. He put down his toolbox. 'That is, if you trust me with the horses,' he added when she hesitated.

'Of course I trust you,' she said, and felt something warm unfold inside her chest.

'Well, then? Show me what you want done,' Jason said, stepping aside to let her lead him to the tack shed.

She led him inside, fighting a strange feeling. It was hard for her to hand over responsibility for her precious animals. Tilly pointed out the hay stacked neatly in the corner. 'It's easier to wheel them down in the wheelbarrow,' she told him, heading back out of the shed. 'Just break it up and toss it over the fence in each paddock, here and over there,' she said, pointing to the far pasture where Red was grazing.

'I can handle that.' Jason nodded confidently.

'That would be great if you could. One less worry,' she said with a small smile as she turned to walk out of the shed.

'Hey,' he said softly, his hand grasping her arm lightly, stopping her. 'Are *you* okay?'

His question caught her by surprise.

'I'm fine,' she managed to get out, but she was overcome by a flood of weariness. She hadn't been able to sleep the night before and her mind had been racing ever since the phone call, but she hadn't had time to stop and actually think about it. There would be time for that later.

'It'll be all right. Your sister,' he added when she glanced up at him, holding her gaze firmly. 'She's got you on her side, so she'll be okay. You just take care of you.'

She wanted to brush off his concern, but his gentle words touched her and an overwhelming surge of fear flowed through her instead. 'But what if she isn't?' Tilly heard herself ask, searching Jason's gaze fearfully. 'What if I lose her too?'

Tilly saw his eyes soften into a look she hadn't witnessed from him before. 'You won't,' he said with an unwavering certainty, and she felt his hand tighten slightly on her arm. She knew he was only saying it to calm her, but right here, in this moment, she believed him and instantly the panic subsided.

Suddenly, she was aware of a very different emotion filling the void between them. She could feel the heat from their bodies, smell the earthy scent of sawdust and hay floating around them and hear the soft nicker of horses nearby. Then she felt the soft warmth of Jason's lips on hers and the world tipped crazily. His arms went around her as he pulled her closer. Beneath her hands on his chest, she felt the cool cotton of his shirt, and his chest felt hard beneath the fabric as she slowly moved her hands upward and around his neck. Tilly found it impossible to think, all she could do was feel. His lips coaxed her own in a slow, almost curious dance and she had no idea how long they stood there in the doorway of the tack shed, but it felt like an eternity. When they did pull apart, there were no words. They continued to hold each other's gaze, reluctant to break the spell they seemed to have fallen under. Eventually, though, she eased back, becoming aware of their surroundings once more.

'I probably should get going,' she said quietly, missing the warmth and strength of his body immediately as she stepped away.

'Yeah, you probably should.'

'Are you sure you're okay to do this?' she asked with a look back at the hay, before she stuck her hands in her back pockets, looking at him nervously.

He gave a small grin before nodding. 'I'll treat them as though they were my own,' he promised.

'Okay, well . . .' Her words faltered as she looked at him and could only think about the kiss they'd just shared.

'Don't worry about anything back here. Just concentrate on your sister.'

*Jessica. Yes. Right.* She took a deep breath and focused on the job at hand. The rest could wait until she got back.

Jason followed her to her car and stood back as she climbed in. 'Drive safe,' he said, leaning on the door.

'I will,' she replied, managing a smile that felt ridiculously shy all of a sudden.

He leaned in and kissed her softly once more, before stepping away and closing the door.

Tilly pulled out onto the driveway and glanced back in her rear-view mirror to see Jason standing there watching her leave. What had just happened? She felt as though she were in some kind of daze. She supposed it was destined to happen sooner or later, she just hadn't been expecting it five minutes before she left town. She knew everything had been building to that moment, and it was kind of a relief to get it out of the way. But it didn't do them any good when they wouldn't be able to talk about it until she got back, and she had no real idea how long that was going to be.

# Twelve

'Tilly?' Jessica stared at her as Tilly stood on the doorstep of her sister's Sydney home.

'Are you okay?'

'What?' Jess said, frowning in confusion as she continued to gape at her sister. 'Of course I am. What's going on? What are you doing here?'

Tilly had half expected to get here and find her looking sick, but Jess looked the same, which was a relief. Maybe the woman who'd called had got it all wrong. 'I know about the mastectomy.'

Tilly saw her sister's face pale slightly before she managed to get her shocked expression back under control.

'Who told you about that?'

'It doesn't matter who told me. Why on earth didn't *you* tell me you were about to go into surgery when you were up last week? What's going on?'

'There was nothing you could do.' Jess shrugged, stepping back and silently motioning Tilly inside off the street.

Tilly followed her sister down a long narrow hallway and into the open-plan kitchen–lounge area of the inner-city townhouse.

'Would you like a coffee?' Jess asked, holding up the glass coffee pot from the kitchen bench.

'I'd prefer some answers,' Tilly countered. 'Are you all right? I mean, Jesus, Jess, I'm worried about you!'

Jess gave an impatient sigh, bracing her hands on the kitchen bench. 'Please don't make a big deal about this.'

'Jess, you're about to have a breast removed. I'd say that is a pretty big deal.'

'Two actually. I'm having a double mastectomy.'

Tilly stared at her.

'And this is why I didn't tell you,' Jess said dryly.

'Why? Because I might be concerned about you?'

'Because I knew you'd go into Florence Nightingale mode again. And here you are.'

'What's that supposed to mean?'

'Look, my first reaction was to come and tell you, but then, I don't know ... I changed my mind. I don't want to be a burden, or a charity case.'

Tilly stared at her sister. 'Why would you think that?'

'Because you always get stuck with taking care of everyone. I don't want to be another family member you've been forced to be responsible for.'

*Forced to be responsible* . . . Tilly frowned at her sister's choice of words as she processed them. 'Is this about Mum?'

'Of course it's about Mum,' Jess said, pushing away from the bench. 'You got stuck with all that because I couldn't step up and do it. Are you happy? Is that what you've been waiting to hear all this time?' Jess raised her voice even though Tilly could hear it shaking with emotion.

'I didn't get stuck with it. I chose to do it,' Tilly said quietly. She couldn't recall a time she had ever seen Jess this emotionally vulnerable before. She was always so in control.

'Luckily for Mum she had one daughter who didn't fail her.'

'You didn't fail her, Jess,' Tilly said wearily. 'I told you, Mum wanted it that way. She would have hated to have been the reason your big break in New York didn't happen. She was proud of everything she saw you achieve.'

Jess crossed to the fridge and pulled out a bottle of wine, uncorking it angrily and poured herself a glass, before holding the bottle up in question to Tilly, who shook her head irritably. 'Come on admit it, Tilly, you hated me for it. All these years you've been angry at me,' Jess challenged, although underneath the accusation was a glimmer of something that looked a lot like regret.

'I don't hate you,' Tilly said, shaking her head. 'I admit there were times I was angry at you for not being there, but that wasn't anything to do with Mum, it was me. Mum was always okay with you doing what you had to do.'

'But you resented me,' Jess said, taking a sip of her wine.

'I didn't understand you putting work before Mum, no,' Tilly admitted. 'But then I saw how proud Mum was and excited for everything that came from the New York show. I'm glad she got to see that before she died.' She and her mother had sat in front of the computer screen watching the live feed of the New York fashion show that featured Jess's clothing line; she had held her mother's hand and seen her beaming smile full of pride. Even now, it made her blink back tears. Their mum had been so happy watching the show, and then later as Jess told them about all the offers she'd received as a result, and the plans she had to expand her fashion label. It was only a few days later that their mother passed away, but seeing Jess's success had managed to distract her from the pain she was in, and brought a smile to her face.

'You did the right thing, Jess,' Tilly said, holding her sister's gaze steadily.

'I hate myself for it,' Jess said, lowering her eyes. 'At first I managed to justify it and then I buried myself in work, but lately, I find myself thinking about it a lot.'

'Mum wouldn't want you to feel like that.'

'Well, I'm pretty sure karma has come to collect,' Jess said dryly.

Tilly eyed her sister quietly as she drank the remainder of her wine in one long gulp and reached for the bottle.

'Was this what the visit was really all about? To tell me about the mastectomy?'

'I don't know. Maybe. At first,' Jess said as she poured another drink. 'I'd gone in for a routine mammogram and the doctor found a lump. He did a biopsy and a few days later I got asked to come back and see him,' she said, looking up. Tilly felt her throat tighten at the look of utter despair in her sister's eyes. 'It was a rough few days and I realised I was suddenly alone. I wasn't sure if I should tell you or not when I got to your place, but then once I got there, I decided not to.'

'I'm sorry you didn't feel like you could tell me,' Tilly said quietly.

'I felt ashamed.'

'Why?'

'Because I've always been able to handle everything on my own.'

'You don't have to, though.' They exchanged a look that was tempered on both sides, but held a note of optimism. 'What did the doctor say?'

'The biopsy came back as a lobular carcinoma.' Jess shrugged.

Tilly felt her stomach drop. She had no idea what that was, but it didn't sound good. 'Is that a type of cancer?'

'No. It's abnormal cells in the breast ducts, but if you have it you're more likely to develop breast cancer. With Mum's history . . .'

More likely? Tilly frowned as she considered her sister's reply. 'But if it's not cancer yet, is taking both breasts necessary?'

'I requested the double mastectomy.'

'Why?' Tilly asked, somewhat shocked.

'To prevent it *becoming* breast cancer. The doctor agreed with me that because Mum had cancer, there was significant reason to be cautious.'

It sounded logical, but somehow it just seemed so... excessive. 'Does it work? Do they guarantee you won't still get cancer?' Tilly knew the basics about breast cancer and removing breasts—her mother had gone through it—but in her mother's case the diagnosis had come too late.

'They give it about a ninety per cent success rate. I'm okay with those odds.'

'Are you sure? I mean, that's pretty drastic.'

'So is dying of breast cancer,' Jess said. Which was a fair point. It seemed that she'd made her mind up.

'Okay,' said Tilly. 'What happens now?'

'All that's left to do is wait. I'm booked in to have the operation tomorrow.'

They certainly weren't mucking around. Tilly was glad she'd decided to come down straight away after all. 'And how long do they think it'll take you to recover?'

'A month. I've taken time away from the office, but I can work from home, so I'll see how I go.'

'Well, you'll need help initially, and I can stay until you're back on your feet.'

'You can't do that.'

'Yes, I can.'

'What about your horses?' Jess asked, taking Tilly by surprise. Her sister rarely mentioned her horses—they had never been something terribly high on her list of topics to ask about. 'And your business? You were getting ready to start renovating. I can't ask you to take time away now.'

'You don't have to go through all this alone, Jess.' The thought of her sister waiting all by herself the morning of her operation hit her like a kick to the chest. 'I'm staying. So, deal with it.'

She watched Jess blink quickly before ducking her head. 'I didn't want this to happen—for you to have to reorganise your life again.' It was strange hearing her usually self-sufficient sister sound so uncertain, so humble, and it tugged at Tilly's heartstrings.

'It'll be okay,' she said gently, echoing Jason's words earlier that morning. Now more than ever she hoped he was right.

∞

It was another night of restless, broken sleep for Tilly. All she could think about was Jess. As her mind wandered back and forth, she tried to imagine what she would do in the same position. Removing both breasts was a huge decision to make, especially when it was as a precautionary measure. Yes, their mother's breast cancer did put them in a higher risk bracket, but it wasn't a certainty that they would get it in the future. Having that biopsy come back with a warning like that would have shaken Tilly up too, a lot. She knew her sister wouldn't have made the decision lightly, yet it was still a tough one to make.

They had an early start to check Jess in at the hospital, and Tilly found herself feeling just as nervous as Jess as they settled her into her private room and waited.

'I don't know why we had to be here this early if all we have to do is sit around and wait,' Jess complained after a while.

'Do you want me to go and find you some magazines?' Tilly offered.

'No, I don't want to read about diets and whose celebrity marriage is about to break up,' Jess snapped.

'Okay. Well, do you want to watch some telly?' Tilly suggested, reaching for the remote to the small TV mounted on the wall across from them.

'It's only those stupid infomercials,' Jess muttered irritably.

Tilly let out a silent breath and reminded herself that her sister was just nervous. 'Tell me what's going on at work. Are you designing a new line?' she asked, trying to distract her, and what better topic than her business—something Jess had always been able to rave on about without any trouble.

'No.'

*All righty, then.*

'I'm sorry. I know you're only trying to help.'

'It's okay. It's a big day. I get it.'

'You don't have to be here,' Jess said quietly. 'You have every right to turn your back on me.' Tilly saw the uncertainty in Jess's eye, heard the words catch in her throat. Her big sister wasn't as tough as she liked people to think. 'Seriously, you don't have to stay. I'm fine.'

'Too bad. I'm not going anywhere.' Tilly dragged a chair over to the bed and made herself comfortable.

Around them the sounds of daily hospital life echoed but there was an awkward silence in the room. Tilly watched Jess pick at the white bed sheet under her fingers.

'It's going to be all right,' she said, reaching across to still her sister's fidgeting. Jess looked up and Tilly swallowed slowly. Jess had always been so in control of her life, so focused on her own path, and to now see this flicker of vulnerability sent a wave of protectiveness rushing through Tilly.

'What if it isn't?' Jess asked, searching Tilly's eyes earnestly. 'What if even after all this, I still get cancer like Mum?'

'Then we'll fight it, together,' Tilly said solemnly.

An orderly wheeled in a bed, and she felt Jess's hand tighten on her own.

'I'm scared, Tilly,' Jess said softly, so softly that Tilly wasn't sure she'd actually heard it.

'It's all going to be okay. I'll be here when you get back.'

'Promise?'

Tilly's eyes burned with the sting of unexpected tears. 'I promise.'

She waited as the orderly helped transfer Jess to the other bed, turning away to wipe at the tear that made a warm trail down her cheek. Once Jess was settled, Tilly forced a bright smile onto her face. 'I'll be right here,' she promised again.

She watched as the bed was wheeled through the doorway and out of sight before she sank back down on the chair and wished she had something she believed in that could offer some comfort. She had never really got the hang of praying. There'd been no point when Jim died—he was already dead, he couldn't be saved; nor could David. She had asked *Why?* though. Both times. Why would two lives be taken so brutally and so young? Why couldn't anything have been done to save them? There hadn't been any answers.

When her mum got sick she had tried again, asking for a cure, then for each trial of a new medication to at least stave off the worst, but those calls for help went unanswered too.

She didn't understand faith. Tilly had always thought she was a good person—she'd always tried to be—and yet she'd lost so many people in her life over the years. Surely good people shouldn't be punished this much?

She had eventually come to the conclusion that there was only this life—right here, right now—and she had better start living it to its fullest while she had the chance. There was no one watching over her who could step in and do anything. No higher power—at least not that she'd ever experienced.

The way she saw it, life handed out the cards and you played whatever hand you were dealt. Still, she could understand people needing some kind of comfort—any kind, really, in times like this.

Her phone beeped and she looked down as she took it from her pocket. She couldn't stop her smile as she saw it was a text from Jason.

*Just checking in. Everything's good here. Horses fed. All still upright. How's things there?*

It might not have been the comfort she was thinking of, but it was a very welcome distraction.

*She's just gone into surgery. Got a couple of hours of waiting ahead. Thanks for feeding the horses.*

As she waited to see if there would be a reply, her eyes widened when the screen on her phone lit up with an incoming call.

'Hi,' she tentatively answered.

'I figured if you had some hours to kill, I'd call. I don't like texting.'

'I know what you mean.' Of course Jason wouldn't like texting. She was surprised he even used the phone.

'Are you doing okay?' he asked after a brief moment of silence passed between them.

'Yeah, I'm fine. Well, a bit nervous for her, but now that she's in surgery I feel better. I think it was worse waiting for it, you know?'

'The lead-up to anything like that always is. Is it very involved? The operation?' he asked.

'She's having a double mastectomy,' Tilly said quietly.

'Geez,' he breathed. 'That's pretty full on.'

'Yeah,' Tilly agreed, 'it is.'

'So, will she need follow-up radiation and treatment?'

'No, I don't think so. This was a precaution against getting breast cancer. She was flagged as being high risk, so she decided to take matters into her own hands before it came to that.'

'Wow. That must have taken a bit of consideration.'

'I guess so. I didn't know about it until the day before yesterday.'

'Wow,' he repeated.

'Yeah. It's been a rollercoaster.'

'Speaking of rollercoasters, I guess I didn't help things yesterday.'

If she hadn't been thinking about the same thing, she might have been distracted enough to not understand what he was talking about—only, she had been thinking about it. A lot. The kiss.

'Look, I don't do this kind of thing real well,' Jason started. 'My track record isn't that great lately. I just didn't want you to worry about it while you've got all this other stuff on your mind. It didn't have to mean anything, if it's going to be a problem.'

'But it did,' Tilly said. 'Mean something. Didn't it?'

'Truthfully? I've pretty much wanted to do that ever since walking into that cafe for the first time.'

'Really?' She winced shyly, suddenly grateful that he couldn't see her.

He gave a small chuckle that made her own lips twitch a little. 'I don't think I've eaten so many bacon-and-egg rolls in my entire life. My cholesterol's probably through the roof.'

'So why didn't you say something?'

She heard Jason sigh. 'Because I suck at reading women. I wasn't sure if I'd get a slap in the face if I said anything.'

'I think we established the answer to that,' Tilly said dryly, recalling the warmth of his lips against hers and feeling a funny little flutter in her stomach at the memory.

'The timing wasn't great. We didn't get a chance to talk about it or anything, I just didn't want you to be down there stressing, that's all.'

'I'm not stressing.'

'Okay, then,' he said quickly. 'That's good. I didn't want to add to your dramas. I better get going. I need to catch the hardware store before it closes. I hope it all goes okay.'

'Thanks, Jason. I'll talk to you later.'

Tilly heard the phone disconnect and cringed a little at his abrupt end to the conversation. Why did it suddenly feel like she was a kid back in high school talking to a boy for the first time? She was a grown woman, for goodness sake. Still, that kiss had thrown her. It'd been a long time since she'd kissed anyone like that. Too long. A fleeting ache of sorrow passed through her at the memory of her husband. It happened a lot less often nowadays, but it could pounce at the most unexpected times. Tilly knew that David would want her to move on eventually, but until now she really hadn't given it much thought. She'd been too busy getting used to life on her own. She would always miss him. They'd only had a handful of years together and she would always feel robbed of the time they could never have. They'd had so many dreams, but not enough time to achieve them. Well, except one: Brumby Creek. It was the gift David had left her without knowing it. His life insurance had paid out their loan on the property, leaving her mortgage-free. Tilly's share of her mother's estate was covering the majority of the renovations, but things were still tight. Jess had been right on one count—it was a lot of money to invest in a business if it didn't take off. She was using almost all of her nest egg. If this didn't work out, she was going to have a farm with spectacular accommodation and a horse arena, but no cash.

The reminder of how much more needed to be done before she could open dragged her thoughts back to the present, and she went over the daunting list in her head and calculated the costs. David might not be here to see their dream fulfilled, but that didn't mean she couldn't make it happen for them both.

# Thirteen

Jason threw a bale of hay on the wheelbarrow and lifted the handles, balancing it carefully as he wheeled it down towards the fence line where a number of horses were lined up in expectation of their food delivery.

Maybe initially he'd offered to take care of Tilly's horses to earn a couple of brownie points, but after doing it for the past couple of days he found himself looking forward to it. There was something relaxing about the chore, despite the sweat he worked up pushing around the heavy wheelbarrow. He always saved the horse in the farthest paddock for last. As he came to a stop now, he smiled at the big head that nodded excitedly in anticipation of the hay he could smell.

This was the horse he'd watched Tilly with on his first visit here. Red. She'd said he had only been there a handful of days then, and Jason could see a change in him now. He wasn't Jason's idea of quiet by any means, but he was at least happy to approach the fence instead of shying away as he had back then.

The horse's brown eyes watched him warily as Jason bent down to lift out the hay. He didn't throw it over the fence as he had with the others, instead he held out a handful, waiting for the horse to sniff at it before cautiously leaning forward to rip a portion of it from Jason's grip.

'Good boy,' Jason murmured as he watched the big animal chew. Red's gaze was fixed on Jason, ready to flee if he sensed any kind of danger. Jason focused on remaining calm and kept his movements slow. He'd never really had much to do with horses, which made the unexplainable pull towards this one even more surprising.

At first, he didn't think much about it. While he worked, he would straighten and stretch and glance over at the paddock. The other horses would graze and go about their business, but there was something about this fella that drew his attention. One day he heard a strange sound and looked up to see Red galloping full tilt across his paddock. Jason had never seen anything quite so moving. He watched the animal move, effortlessly and gracefully, and along his arms goose bumps broke out as the sound of pounding hooves echoed through his body.

After that Jason always took notice of the horse, often finding Red looking over at him. He wasn't sure what it was about this horse, but he felt a weird kind of connection. In

Red's presence at the end of the day like this, he felt more at peace than he could recall ever feeling.

Red was taller than the other horses—big and solid, and with the extra feed since arriving at Tilly's, he'd bulked up considerably. He gave a low snort and tossed his strawberry-blonde mane, pawing the ground. Jason didn't have a great deal of experience reading horse body language, but even he didn't have trouble figuring out this one. Red was irritated. *Just throw me the bloody feed and leave me alone*, is what he would have said if he could speak. That's what Jason was supposed to do—it's what he did with the others, but he was enjoying the time alone with this guy at the end of the day. He wasn't crazy enough to get inside the paddock with him, but out here, on this side of the fence, he felt comfortable enough to get this close.

'All right, here,' Jason said, pulling off another handful of hay. 'Is that good?'

He waited until Red had finished that bit and then dropped the remainder of the hay over the fence. Leaning his arms across the top fence rail, and hitching one foot on the bottom rail, Jason settled in to watch Red eat. Maybe his fascination was because he saw a bit of himself in this horse. He was a loner just like Jason, though this guy's loneliness was forced, with Tilly keeping him away from the mares in the next paddock.

She'd told him that having been a stallion until his gelding, Red was going to be prone to stallion-like behaviour, and would be a little more dangerous until he'd settled in and had some handling. Jason was mindful of the warning, but maybe it was that wildness that resonated inside him—the rebellious way Red trotted along the fence line and called out to the mares. Jason felt like that sometimes too. He needed peace and quiet, and yet lately there were times he yearned for companionship.

But he'd been in this position before with Hayley. Jason had put himself out there and been rejected. In fairness, he'd known she was in love with someone else at the time, so it shouldn't have been a big surprise, but he'd given it a shot despite the odds, and lost. It was different this time with Tilly. It felt different . . . *he* felt different. But she had her own baggage to bring to the table. She had a dead husband. How was he supposed to go up against that? What the hell did he know about relationships? He hadn't had one that lasted more than a few months and that had been years ago, when he had both legs.

A soft snort brought his attention back to the horse before him, and Jason found himself holding his breath as a big nose hovered cautiously, inches away from his arms resting across the top of the rail. Before coming to Ben Tirran, having a horse sniff his arm wouldn't have been high on his list of awe-inspiring moments, but right here, right now, something inexplicable was happening to him. As he stood still and stared into the big brown eyes of the five-hundred–kilo animal in front of him, with nothing but the sound of birds in the trees and a few soft nickers from nearby horses, Jason felt a sense of peace more potent than he had ever known.

In a moment it was over. The big horse, having finished its meal, turned and walked away to graze, leaving Jason to stare after him, wondering what had just happened.

∽

Tilly opened the front door of her sister's townhouse and stood aside for Jess to walk in. 'Home sweet home,' she said, carrying in the overnight bag from the hospital and closing the front door behind them.

The ride home had been nerve-racking, with Tilly constantly looking over to check on her sister, who sat stoically in the passenger seat holding the seatbelt away from her chest, staring straight ahead. The only conversation they shared was after Tilly apologised for about the twentieth time as she drove over a pothole. Jess had gritted her teeth and told her if she said sorry one more time she would get out of the car and walk the rest of the way.

'It's good to be home,' Jess said with a weary sigh.

'What do you feel like doing?' Tilly asked. 'Do you want me to set you up out here in the lounge room, or would you rather lie down in bed?'

'I think I'll have a rest,' Jess said, moving slowly down the long hallway towards her bedroom.

Tilly pulled back the comforter and helped her sister into the opulent-looking king-size bed. She carefully rearranged the pillows, mindful of the tubes still attached to her sister, which would need to be emptied as they drained away the fluid from the surgery.

Jess looked better than she had the day before, immediately after her surgery, but Tilly found it unnerving to see her once vibrant, elegant sister looking so exhausted and frail. It had been a big operation—removing both breasts and then having the reconstructive surgery at the same time—so it was expected that Jess would take a while to recover, but still, Tilly hadn't been prepared for just how brutal the whole process would be.

It wasn't new territory for Tilly to be in, caring for a family member. Her mother had endured multiple surgeries during her illness, so Tilly was prepared for the gruesome aftercare to come. Jess, on the other hand, was not.

From the very first moment they'd brought her from recovery to her room on the ward, she'd been horrified by the prospect of emptying her own drainage tubes.

'How on earth do they expect me to do that?' she'd said to Tilly, staring at the red fluid collecting in the bulb-like end of the drainage tube on her chest.

'It's just part of the process,' Tilly said calmly.

'I don't think I can do it, Tilly.'

'That's what I'm here for. Don't worry about any of that now. Just get some rest,' she'd told her, and thankfully, Jess had been too tired to argue about it, but now they were home the reality was sinking in for both of them.

Jess was no longer self-sufficient, and allowing someone else to do the kinds of things that needed to be done was a huge shock to the system.

The next morning Tilly was up and dressed and drinking a coffee on the front door stoop, just as the sun came up.

*The city's a funny place*, she thought as she sipped her coffee and watched the activity outside. There were a few joggers and lots of people walking dogs. A street sweeper and an ambulance went past. It wasn't the early morning peace she enjoyed at home, but for a city she supposed this was as close to quiet as it got.

She heard movement at the end of the house when she went inside a little while later and finished putting together a breakfast tray to take in to her sister.

She found Jess shuffling from the bathroom back towards her bed and put the tray on the bedside table to help her.

'How are you feeling this morning?'

'How do you think I'm feeling?' Jess muttered, wincing as she tried to wiggle back on the bed.

'Pretty sore, I'd imagine,' Tilly replied, not deterred by her sister's less than cheerful mood. 'You're probably starving since you slept right through dinner last night. I've got some toast and coffee to start with. Do you want me to cook up an omelette or some scrambled eggs?'

'I'm not hungry,' Jess dismissed her listlessly.

'Start with the toast and we'll take it from there,' Tilly said, waiting until Jess was settled back against the pillows before she carefully deposited the tray on her lap.

'Just the coffee will be fine.'

'You have to eat something, Jess.'

'How can I eat anything? I feel sick every time I look down at those stupid tubes.'

'I know they're a bit gross, but they're going to be there for a while, so you're going to have to figure out a way to ignore them or get used to them. In the meantime, you need to eat.'

'Maybe later,' she said, reaching for her coffee cup and giving a small gasp of pain.

'Here, let me pass it to you,' Tilly said, moving forward to lift the cup.

'Damn it, I can't do anything.'

'You just had major surgery,' Tilly reminded her calmly. 'Give yourself some time.'

'This is so frustrating, I feel like a stupid Tyrannosaurus Rex,' she muttered.

Tilly bit back a smile at the image. Now was not the time to point out to her sister that she looked *exactly* like a T-Rex. With limited movement in her arms, keeping them protectively positioned at her sides, it was very hard indeed to do even the most mundane of things. 'After you've finished your coffee, I'll help you have a bath. That'll make you feel a little more human again.'

'I hate this,' Jess said, glaring down into her coffee cup.

'Yeah, well, it is what it is.' *It sure as hell isn't any picnic for me either.* Tilly could think of a thousand things she would rather be doing than bathing her sister, but here they were. 'You'll feel better once you're up and about.'

'I'd rather just stay in bed.'

'The doctor said you should do some of those stretching exercises and go for a walk. We don't have to go far, we could just walk to the end of the street and back. Or I could take you somewhere nice. What about that park under the Harbour Bridge?'

'I don't want to go for a walk. I've got tubes coming out of me—why would I want to go out in public like this?'

'No one would see them if you wore a cardigan. We wouldn't have to walk; we could just take a blanket and sit out in the sun for a little while.'

'I need more painkillers and then I want to go back to sleep.'

Tilly didn't argue with her. Part of her understood Jess's need to hide under a blanket and just feel sorry for herself. Tilly suspected that had she been through this ordeal that would be exactly what she'd be doing too, but she also knew, from nursing her mum, that it was wise to also heed the doctor's advice. She decided to give Jess one more day of moping and then bring out the tough love.

∞

Tilly checked on Jess and helped empty and record the drainage at regular intervals throughout the day as per the instructions. She brought in cups of tea and handed out medication, all without further comment, and she had to admit that the extra rest hadn't done Jess any harm. There was more colour in her cheeks by late afternoon and she didn't argue when Tilly brought in a sandwich and soup for dinner.

The next morning, with Tilly's help, Jess had a bath and washed her hair, before getting out of her pyjamas and into some real clothes to sit out in the lounge room. It had started raining the night before and outside was a gloomy grey—perfect for what Tilly had in mind.

Once Jess was settled on the lounge, Tilly came back into the room with a huge bowl of popcorn and sat it between them, before aiming the remote at the massive TV screen mounted on the wall.

'What movie do you want to watch?' Tilly asked, scrolling through the selection on her sister's streaming service. 'I know, *The Devil Wears Prada*,' she said, searching the long list of movie titles.

'You know, the fashion industry isn't always like it is in the movies,' Jess said dryly.

'Well, what do you want to watch? What's your favourite chick flick?'

'You pick.'

'This is *your* sick day, *you* have to choose,' Tilly said and shared a small smile with her sister.

'I'd almost forgotten about that,' Jess said softly. Sick days were a tradition of sorts in their household growing up. Whenever any of them were home sick from school, their mother always let them pick their favourite movie to watch. It had always been a no-brainer for Tilly—*The Man from Snowy River*—and there had never been any disagreement from her mum. In fact, Tilly suspected she was probably her mother's favourite kid to have home sick in that regard. They had both loved that movie no matter how many times they watched it.

'Well, there is one movie I haven't seen in years,' Jess said, taking the remote from Tilly and scrolling through the movie list.

When she stopped on *PS I Love You*, Tilly felt her heart lurch the tiniest bit, before she summoned a smile. 'Perfect,' she said softly. She hadn't been able to bring herself to watch this movie since losing David. It hit a little too close to home, but she'd always loved it and it had been one of the few things the sisters had in common.

Throughout the movie, the women passed the tissue box back and forth silently, and Tilly sensed it was an opportunity for Jess to release a lot of the pent-up emotions she'd been dealing with over the past few weeks, without judgement.

'So, are you going to tell me about the mystery woman who dobbed you in?' Tilly asked once the movie had ended and they'd decided to watch another one.

Her sister shot her a suspicious glance.

'I know that you must know who it was,' Tilly said.

'Louise,' Jess said with a frustrated sigh.

'She sounded like more than just a concerned friend.'

Jess gave a small shrug and took another handful of popcorn. 'It's complicated.'

'Really? Doesn't seem that complicated to me.'

'What would you know about it?'

'You have feelings for her,' Tilly said matter-of-factly. 'What's so complicated about that?'

'The fact I have feelings for her,' Jess said eventually. 'Why aren't you freaking out about this?' she asked curiously.

'Why would I freak out?'

'Because *I* am,' she said, turning carefully to face Tilly. 'I didn't know I was attracted to women. I mean, I've had boyfriends and I like men,' she said a little stiffly. 'But I've never really found a man I truly felt comfortable with. I thought maybe it was something to do with losing Jim and Dad, I don't know. And then I was so obsessed with fashion and designing I haven't been able to fit any kind of other relationship into my life. I mean, by the time I moved to New York I knew that I was attracted to women and there were a few brief flings, but Lou is the first person who's really understood me. She's important to me.'

'Then what's the problem?'

'I just don't know if I'm capable of a long-term relationship. I mean, she wants it all: kids and a house and soccer games on weekends. I mean honestly, Tilly,' Jess said, eyeing her sister pointedly, 'do I look like the kind of person who would enjoy watching a kids' soccer game?'

Tilly bit her lip a little at the image that came to mind. 'Have you ever tried it?' she said instead. 'Maybe this wasn't what you pictured as a future, but who knows? Maybe you'd enjoy that kind of life?'

Her sister eyed her sceptically.

'I guess what it really comes down to is whether you think Lou is important enough to try something new. If you really see yourself having a future with her, can you accept everything that goes along with it?'

'I don't know.' Jess shrugged helplessly. 'I mean, all this was on the table before I even went to the doctor. It's partly why I decided to have a break back here in Sydney. It scared me. I needed some time and distance away to think. But then with all this—' she waved absently at the tubes on her chest '—I gave her the perfect opportunity to end things, but she hasn't.'

'Well, that says a lot.'

'It says she's stubborn,' Jess muttered.

'She sounded really concerned on the phone.'

'She wanted to fly over, but I didn't want her to.'

'Why not?'

'I don't know. I was frightened, I guess. We had a big fight. I guess I was scared she'd take one look at all this and . . .' Jess dropped her gaze to the rug covering her lap. 'I didn't think I could handle her pity or disgust. I was worried how I was going to look after the surgery, how it would change things.'

'It was a pretty big decision to make,' Tilly agreed softly. 'I can only imagine everything that must be going on inside you right now. I seriously don't know if I could have handled it as well as you have.'

Jess sent her a *Yeah, right* kind of look.

'I mean it, you've made this massive, life-changing decision and gone through a really intensive operation. That's huge. I can't even begin to think how many conflicting emotions you're going through at the moment. I don't know Lou, but I think you need to give her the chance to make up her own mind. I'm willing to bet she cares enough that none of this is going to make any difference to the way she feels about you. She was really worried when we spoke. She didn't want you going through this on your own.'

'I just always thought I had my life together, you know?' Jess said after a few moments. 'I always vowed that after all the back and forth between Mum and Dad when we were growing up, I'd make sure my own life was different. I wouldn't rely on anyone else to make me happy. I'd provide for myself and everything would be reliable and structured.'

Tilly got it. She too hated all the inconsistency their parents' marriage had created, though she was always more than happy to spend whatever time they'd had with their grandparents on the farm. Jess, though, had always been a highly strung kid who thrived on routine, and the kind of lifestyle they'd led as kids was not ideal for a child like that.

'Maybe it's time to rethink some of those things?' Tilly suggested gently.

'Like what?'

'You've done what you set out to do—you've provided for yourself, you've made your name in fashion and you have your own company. You're not in the position Mum and Dad were in. You don't have to depend on anyone else to provide for you. But I think if you believe that a relationship is somehow allowing someone else to control your happiness, then maybe you're looking at it all wrong.'

'From my experience relationships make you vulnerable. I've seen it time and time again. Look at you and David. That almost ruined you.'

'Of course it did,' Tilly said honestly. 'My husband died. We thought we'd have a lifetime together. But that doesn't mean I regret ever finding him in the first place.

'Jess, shutting everyone out of your life just to protect yourself from any kind of pain is sadder than me losing David. At least I have memories and I had a wonderful man by my side for a few years. I can't imagine not having had that in my life. If you don't start to trust people, you'll end up lonely and sad, and that's worse than the risk of being hurt by someone.'

Jess didn't reply immediately, and Tilly wondered if she was about to shut the door on any further discussion, as she usually would if Tilly put forward any kind of opposite opinion.

'It's terrifying . . . the thought of taking such a huge risk,' Jess said instead.

'It will be,' Tilly agreed. 'But it's the only way you're going to find out.'

# Fourteen

Jason grabbed the phone off the counter as he came into the kitchen, relieved he'd managed to catch it before it stopped ringing when he saw the name on the screen.

'Hi,' Tilly said on the other end. 'I didn't interrupt something, did I?'

'No, I was outside getting some firewood. It's freezing tonight.'

'Lucky you got that wall up in time,' she said, and he could hear the grin in her voice. He didn't realise just how much he'd missed seeing that smile until now.

'Not wrong. How're things going down there?'

'Not too bad. Jess is still pretty sore, which is to be expected. She needs a bit of help doing things. I'll probably be here for the next two weeks, or until she gets her drains taken out. It limits what she can do.'

Jason didn't have much experience with that kind of operation, but he'd had his fair share of other kinds to last a lifetime and knew exactly what having drains and tubes hanging out of you felt like.

'Well, don't worry about anything up here. I can keep an eye on the place, and I don't mind feeding the horses.'

'I've asked a friend of mine to drop around now and again to check on them—not that I don't trust you or anything,' Tilly added quickly, and Jason smiled as he pictured her horrified expression. 'Just to have someone with a bit of horse experience make sure there's nothing wrong that you might not notice. Sometimes it's hard to tell if you're not sure what to look for.'

'That's a good idea. I'd feel better if someone was making sure they're okay and I'm doing the right thing.'

'It's not to check up on you,' she told him.

'All good,' he repeated. 'If anything else needs doing, get them to let me know.'

'I'm sure there won't be anything. So, how are the girls treating you at the cafe?'

'I haven't been in since you left.'

'What!' Tilly feigned alarm. 'Paul will probably go broke without you contributing to his daily takings.'

'I only go in there for the service.'

'Yeah, right, and the bacon rolls and coffee,' she added.

'The coffee *is* pretty good,' he agreed.

'Well, I hope you can do without for a couple more weeks.'

'If I get desperate, I might drop in and get takeaway.' He wasn't even kidding. Without her there, he didn't see the point of sitting in a cafe by himself, trying to ignore the looks and hushed conversation around him. Jason knew his arrival in town had caused quite a stir—it annoyed the locals that he was so reluctant to make any real conversation, but he valued his privacy and it really was no one else's business who he was or where he'd come from.

Tilly asked about the progress on his house and the renovations, and they talked for well over an hour before she said she had to go and check on her sister before she went to bed. He instantly missed the sound of her voice in his ear after she hung up.

A thought ran through his head: *What would it be like to have her here, to share their day and general conversation as they went about making dinner together?* He instantly pulled himself up. That was getting just a tad too far ahead for comfort. They'd shared exactly one kiss . . . Well, one real one, the second one was barely long enough to count. It was a relief to have heard her say she hadn't regretted it, but he wasn't sure where they would go from here.

For now, her sister was the main priority, and he respected that completely, but sooner or later Tilly would come home and then they'd have to face it.

Did she want something more? Did he? Was it too soon to throw caution to the wind and dive headfirst into something with Tilly? He had to admit, there'd been nothing serious with Hayley to recover from, only in his own head. So, technically it wasn't like a rebound; only, his heart *had* taken a bit of a beating ... all those niggling thoughts about a future with her had started to sprout before he'd realised it wasn't going to happen, and here he was having them all over again with someone else.

Was he really ready for that?

∽

The next few days passed painfully slowly. He had plenty of work to keep him occupied, but Tilly always seemed to be on his mind, and the thought of waiting two weeks to see her again made time slow down even more.

He often took his lunch down to the far paddock, enjoying the quiet time he spent with Red. The first day he did it, he threw the bread crusts over the fence and saw the horse eye them warily before approaching—but only after Jason stepped away from the fence.

From that day on he made a point of saving his crusts from breakfast to bring along to add to the lunch scraps, and after two days, Red was gingerly taking them from his hand.

He'd tried to touch the big horse on the head each time he fed him, but Red would always shy away, pulling his head just out of reach to avoid contact. Jason had made it his goal to be able to pat him before the end of the week, but after three days of failed attempts, it wasn't looking good. Today, though, when he came down, he immediately noticed something was wrong.

The big horse moved more slowly than normal as he made his way towards the fence.

'Hey, big fella. What's going on?'

Jason moved further along the fence line to get a better look at the animal and immediately saw the problem. Caught in the horse's long red tail was a length of barbed wire, wrapped intricately through the coarse hair and dragging behind him for at least a metre.

Jason swore softly. This was not good. How the hell was he supposed to untangle barbed wire from the tail of a wild horse? He couldn't even pat the damn animal. He thought about leaving Red be and calling the vet to come out and deal with it, but he wasn't sure how soon a vet would be able to get out here. And he had no idea who this friend of Tilly's was who knew about horses, so he couldn't phone them. He didn't want to call Tilly and worry her; though, part of him knew that his reluctance was mostly about not wanting her to think he was completely useless.

Every time the horse moved, the barbed wire bumped his back leg, making him flinch and step nervously. Jason worried that if Red took off at a run the wire would trip him over, or at the very least cut into his leg. He had to do something.

'Okay, boy,' he found himself saying as he nervously slid through the railing of the yard. 'How about I see if I can get you out of that?' He slowly straightened once he was through the rails and took out his pocketknife, locating the scissors. The horse watched him cagily and gave a low snort.

This was going to be painful. Jason knew he would get kicked at some point, but he wasn't sure just how much damage it would do. It didn't occur to him to stop—at this point all he was worried about was getting rid of that wire before it did any serious damage. He slowly reached out and offered a piece of crust to the animal, watching as Red barely even bothered sniffing it before his muzzle gripped it and he took it from Jason, as nimbly as if he had a set of fingers.

'You like that, huh?' Jason said, slowly reaching for more crusts. He threw these to the ground in front of the horse and slowly inched towards the back of the animal while it was distracted.

Red's long tail almost touched the ground and Jason carefully reached over to cut the nearest piece of wire. When he realised he hadn't been kicked, he repeated the action, snipping away at the wire that was tangled through the red horse hair. When Red lifted his head, Jason threw him some more bread before slowly inching closer so he could reach across and use both hands. To his amazement, the big animal didn't move away. As careful as a bomb technician disarming a ticking device, Jason continued slowly snipping and removing the sharp wire until eventually he could unsnag the last piece. It dropped to ground behind the horse's back feet. Jason eyed the barbed wire and thought about leaning down to grab it, but then decided he had already pushed his luck enough for one day and instead threw some bread further away so the horse moved across the yard and Jason could safely retrieve the wire.

He slid back out between the rails and straightened once he was on the other side. He let out a long, grateful breath, still shocked by what had just happened. He'd been centimetres from this horse who hadn't allowed anyone to even touch him before, and he somehow had all his remaining limbs, and a head still attached to his shoulders.

He had survived.

For a long moment he simply stared at the horse on the other side of the fence and felt a rush of excess adrenalin fill his body as he thought about how dangerous his actions had been and what could have gone wrong. It was soon replaced with a powerful sense of wonder. He had just been close enough for this wild animal to kill him, and yet Red hadn't even flinched. The horse had stood still, seemingly content to eat while allowing Jason to help him. He was under no illusion that it was anything other than that—this animal had *allowed it*. Had Red not felt comfortable, he would have simply run. Jason had seen him take off from less threatening situations than this—Tilly had told him these horses relied on their instinctive flight mechanism to survive in the bush and they used it frequently in situations that were unfamiliar to them. Red had *chosen* not to.

For a long time, Jason remained at the fence, his heart rate now back to normal. Something clicked inside him. It was a feeling he had never experienced before, and he couldn't describe it. All he knew was that he and this magnificent wild animal had just shared something amazing; something he would never forget as long as he lived.

## Something Like This

Tilly saw the car parked in front of her house and a flurry of nerves broke out in her stomach at the anticipation of seeing Jason after just over two weeks away. She hadn't told him she was coming back today, and now that she was here, Tilly found herself fighting an embarrassing case of shyness. She took a deep breath, shook her head at her ridiculousness and pushed open the car door to climb out.

It had been a long drive, but she was more than ready to get home, and the thought of going to sleep in her own bed tonight had made the hours pass in eager anticipation.

Jess was doing better than expected and for the first time in a very long while, she seemed calmer. Tilly had been surprised when she'd taken over her own care with a renewed determination, leaving Tilly with pretty much nothing to do.

There were no sounds of building coming from the bunkhouse and when she stuck her head inside, she gaped at the transformation. Jason had been sending her updates of his progress, but she hadn't seen the latest. None of his photos had done the work justice. It looked, to her untrained eye, as though it were complete, and she felt her nerves mix with excitement.

With no sign of Jason there, she headed out to the yards. She had hoped to be home in time to save him having to feed up this afternoon, but it looked like he was already one step ahead of her.

As she passed the first few yards, she saw her animals all happily munching on their hay. She took a minute to stop and say hello and then, as she made her way down, she suddenly froze and her heart flew to her throat in alarm. Jason was *inside* the yard with Red. Her first instinct was to run towards them and yell to him to get out of there, but thankfully common sense stepped in and reminded her that scaring a wild horse like that would be a stupid thing to do.

Walking quickly but trying to keep calm, she approached the yard, and stopped. Not only was Jason inside the fence with the horse, but he was stroking Red's neck. She stood frozen to the spot as Jason glanced up and did a double-take, making the horse give a low nicker, probably at her disruption of Jason's petting.

'What are you doing?' she finally managed to ask, still unsure if she could believe what she was seeing. When she left, this horse had been untouchable, and now . . .

'You're back,' he said, and she saw him smile before registering the uncertainty on her face and taking a small step away from the horse. 'I, ah, Red and I kind of forged an alliance of sorts.'

'I see that.'

'He got tangled in some barbed wire,' he started and immediately Tilly went into panic mode, searching the animal for wounds. 'But I managed to get it untangled. He's fine. It didn't cut him.'

'You untangled him from *barbed wire*?' she repeated numbly.

'Yeah,' he replied as he eyed her a little cautiously. 'It kind of just happened.'

'You got in there with an unhandled horse and untangled him from barbed wire?' she asked again slowly. 'Are you crazy? He could have killed you.'

'Yeah,' he agreed calmly—far too calmly for her liking.

'And you still got in there?'

'Well, I didn't have much choice. I didn't want him to get further tangled up in it.' When she continued to stare at him, he shifted a little before walking towards the fence. 'After that, he kind of warmed to me. I'm sorry, I know you're probably really pissed off at me for interfering with your training routine and everything. I didn't mean to do it. I just reacted without really thinking.'

'You could have been killed,' she said again quietly, her voice shaking. 'You do get that, don't you? You know these aren't normal horses? They haven't had anything to do with people before they came here. They're wild. You can't just go jumping into the yards with them.' She knew she was raising her voice, but images of Jason being kicked or stomped into the ground by a frightened horse kept playing in front of her eyes.

She saw him glance over his shoulder at the horse, who tossed his head at her raised voice, before he slowly slid between the rails and came to her side. Tilly closed her eyes briefly, berating herself. She was supposed to be the professional here and Jason was acting far more sensibly than she was.

'I'm sorry, I didn't mean to yell at you. I just . . . If you'd been hurt . . .' She couldn't even finish the sentence, it was too scary to imagine. Who would have even found him? The man was a hermit! If he'd been injured badly no one would have even realised he was missing.

'I wouldn't have sued you, if that's what you're worried about,' he said stiffly.

'It's not what I was worried about,' she replied, as he started to walk past her to the wheelbarrow. 'If you'd been hurt, I wouldn't be able to forgive myself,' she finished almost defiantly, until he stopped and looked over at her and all bravado fled from his steady look.

She switched her gaze back to the horse happily eating his hay and barely giving them a second glance. Before she left, he was still refusing to come close to the hay while she stood in the yard. This was . . . unbelievable.

'I didn't mean to overstep,' Jason said, looking uncertain. It was a look she hadn't really associated with him before and it snapped her out of the stupor she found herself in.

'It just gave me a fright to see you in there with him at first,' she said, shaking her head. 'You've done really well.'

She saw relief cross his face and then a small shrug that belied the pride she read in his eyes. 'I didn't do much. He just stopped being a pain in the arse and decided it was easier to be nice.'

'So I see.' Tilly still couldn't quite believe it. It shouldn't be this much of a surprise to her; after all, she was about to launch a business that used horses to break through emotional and physical barriers to forge respect and trust, and that appeared to be what had happened here. The only difference was, she would never recommend someone with no experience with horses jump unsupervised into a yard with an unhandled, recently gelded brumby. A million possible scenarios raced through her mind, one horrible event after another, but she forced them away. It was done now. No point in going over everything that could have happened.

'How's your sister?' he asked, picking up the handles of the wheelbarrow as they turned to head back up towards the tack shed.

'She's going to be fine,' Tilly said, letting out a long breath and welcoming the change of topic.

'That's good to hear.'

'Thank you again for your help. I'm not sure what I would have done without you. This was all so unexpected. I didn't have time to organise anything.'

'No worries. I liked hanging out with the horses.'

'You know, I didn't pick you for a horsey kind of guy,' she said, giving him a small smile.

'I didn't either.' Jason shrugged. 'I'm not saying I plan on riding one anytime soon or anything.'

She laughed at his panicked tone. 'Well, if you change your mind, I have a few that would be perfect for you to learn on,' she said.

'Yeah, nah. I don't think so.'

'Oh, come on, Weaver, where's your sense of adventure?'

'I've already lost one leg—I don't plan on breaking the other one,' he told her drolly.

'You only have to worry about that if you fall off. The idea is to stay on and you'll be fine.'

'I think I'll pass on the riding, thanks.'

'That's okay. You can get more from ground work anyway.' She was a big believer in the connection and bond that human and horse could achieve by simply spending time together. Riding was fine, but sometimes it was nice just to be on the same level. Horses had a lot to teach humans, if the latter just took the time to listen.

'You're probably tired after driving most of the day, but do you have any plans for dinner?' he asked once they'd packed away the feeding gear.

'I thought maybe toast with Vegemite would do.'

'I can do better than that,' he told her as they approached the house and his car. 'I'll be back in half an hour with dinner.'

She had been thinking of taking a bath and then going straight to bed, but now that he'd mentioned food, her stomach decided to grumble, reminding her that she'd only had a coffee and a scone at a truck stop since leaving Jessica's that morning. 'Sounds good.'

She decided to forgo her bath and took a shower instead, washing away the weariness of travel and the city, before dressing in comfy jeans and her favourite hand-knitted jumper her mother had made for her. Tilly touched the soft wool and smiled as she remembered her mother holding up the bright red yarn for her opinion.

'What about this one?'

Tilly had shaken her head in despair. 'Mum, seriously, I don't need any more jumpers. I love the ones you made me last year.'

'I know, but I wanted to just . . .' She had paused and Tilly had seen her smile wobble before she'd quickly formed it back into something more cheerful. 'I've got nothing else to do with myself, I may as well knit.'

Tilly had known what her mother had been about to say and kicked herself for not realising sooner. She had just wanted to make one last thing for her daughter.

Tilly's throat had tightened painfully as she'd fought to hold back tears. It wasn't fair. She didn't want to lose her Mum. She'd only just gotten her back. Mustering up all the energy she could find, she had managed a bright smile. 'I love the red, Mum. It'll make a beautiful jumper.'

She pulled it on now, and as always, sent a silent hello to her Mum to let her know she was thinking of her, before heading out to build a fire in the fireplace. There'd been no time to dry her hair and the fire would help take the chill off the room. There was no denying winter was well and truly here.

By the time Jason pulled up outside, the gentle red and yellow glow of the flames made the room feel snug and warm. Tilly hovered over the glass selection, choosing two from the back, ones she'd barely used—another set she'd received as a wedding present. She poured two tall glasses of wine and placed them on the coffee table near the fireplace. It would be nice to eat in front of the fire tonight, she thought, wiping her sweaty palms on her jeans before placing one hand on her stomach to settle the nerves which had suddenly appeared. She'd tried to remind herself this wasn't the first time the man had been over for dinner, but she knew she was kidding herself. It was the first time he'd been over since he'd kissed her. Everything would be different now.

Jason came inside carrying a large black dish with a glass lid, holding the handles with two tea towels. 'Beef stew and dumplings,' he announced as he placed it on her kitchen bench.

'You cooked this?' she asked, staring at the still-bubbling stew inside the pot.

'Yep. I've discovered the slow cooker. I toss everything in before I leave in the morning and by dinner time it's all cooked.'

'I'm very impressed,' she said as Jason served up the meal. 'And yeah, I think this beats Vegemite toast.'

They settled on the floor in the lounge room, the coffee table a makeshift dining area, and as soon as Tilly swallowed the first mouthful she sighed. 'This is amazing.'

'Not bad, huh,' he agreed.

'You are a man of many talents,' she said, shaking her head slightly as she scooped another forkful of the beef so succulent and flavoursome in its rich gravy that it almost melted in her mouth. 'Tamer of brumbies, builder of bunkhouses, cooker of meals.'

'That sounds like a *Game of Thrones* title.'

'It's well deserved. This meal is the best thing I've eaten in a long time.'

'Well, you can thank Barb from West Wyalong,' he said, and grinned when she looked at him with a raised eyebrow. 'I joined a slow-cooker forum. We exchange recipes and whatnot,' he added offhandedly.

Tilly laughed, but then realised he was serious and laughed even harder.

'I'll have you know, those girls can cook a mean chilli con carne, and they don't mind dishing out a bit of sound life advice on the side.'

'I can't even imagine you—big, tough Jason Weaver—sharing recipes with a group of mums and housewives.'

'I wouldn't laugh too hard if I were you. You have the girls to thank for your dinner tonight,' he told her with a haughty tone.

'I'm sorry. You're right, I'm very grateful.'

They continued eating in companionable silence, too hungry to waste time on idle chitchat, until they'd finished their meal and sat back, groaning at how full they both were.

'This is the life,' Jason said as they rested their backs against the couch and stretched their legs out towards the fireplace, drinking their wine. 'Good food, good fire, good company.'

Tilly held her glass up and watched the flames bounce and dance off the crystal in the most mesmerising way. 'Yep, this is living.'

'Do you like to camp?' Jason asked suddenly.

'God no,' Tilly said, shaking her head.

'But you like sitting near a fire?' he protested.

'Yeah, but I prefer it to be inside, and sleeping in a comfy bed, not on the hard ground.'

'You'd love camping. Outside in nature, food cooked on an open fire, sitting around it at night, looking up at the stars.'

'Freezing my butt off. No thanks.'

'You don't know what you're missing.'

'Yeah, I do, and I'm okay with missing it.'

'You know, if I can overcome my distrust of horses and tame Red the wild beast, you might surprise yourself with how much you like to camp.'

'Okay, firstly, you didn't tame him, exactly. He's got quite a way to go before you can call him tamed,' she pointed out. 'And secondly, if I'd been here, you wouldn't have gone in that yard.'

'You would have?' he asked.

'I don't know, to be honest.' She'd thought about what Jason had done, untangling that wire from a horse who had no previous human contact; she wasn't sure how she would have gone about it. Most likely she would have put him in a crush and tried to cut it off while he was trapped, reasonably safely, although she knew what his reaction would be: he would probably have managed to entwine himself even tighter in the barbed wire and cut himself in the process. 'Just promise me you won't go in there anymore without someone else around, okay? He trusts you, which is great, but he's not tame. If you move too fast, try to introduce something he's unsure about, he could still turn on you.'

'So, you don't want me to go near him anymore?' he asked quietly.

'No, I'm not saying that,' Tilly said quickly. 'But there's a method we follow. You've made an awesome start, but you have to go slowly with these animals and be patient.'

'Okay. That's fair enough.'

'Would you like to continue working with him?' she asked, looking over at him.

'I don't know. I mean, I didn't plan on doing as much as I did. I was just helping him, but then he kind of acted like I was supposed to get back in there with him the next day. I know it sounds weird,' he said, shaking his head a little.

'It doesn't sound weird at all.'

'I wasn't really thinking about what I was doing. He seemed content to have me in there, and then when he didn't react when I got close to him, it just kind of happened—I reached out and touched him and he just stood there, eating.'

'Because he knew you were helping him the day before, and you were no longer a threat. It's a great start, and if you want to keep working with him, I'm happy to let you.'

'Isn't he one of your clinic horses? Don't you want to save them for your clients?'

'Red was never really destined for the clinics. He didn't have the attributes I was looking for.'

'Then why did you buy him?'

'I don't know.' She shrugged. 'There was just something about him.'

'I'll think about it,' Jason said after a moment's silence. As he stared into the fire Tilly could almost read his thoughts. He had told her that he had never been an animal kind of guy before, but clearly Red had changed his perspective. She could easily imagine how he had felt in that moment when he'd freed Red from the wire, when Red had allowed him to help.

Beside her she could feel Jason's solid presence. She couldn't remember the last time she'd felt this at ease with another person. As she stared into the dancing flames of the fire, its gentle crackling sounded like a lullaby in the background and Tilly felt herself relaxing as the warmth of the wine spread slowly through her limbs.

Jason wasn't sure how long he dozed for, but the loud pop of the fire had him suddenly awake and searching the room for the source of the noise. A weight on his chest drew his sleep-laden attention to the fact that Tilly's head rested against him, one hand under her cheek and the other draped across his stomach.

He was careful to keep his breathing even so as not to wake her. He couldn't move his arm to check the time and had no idea how long they'd been lying there, but at some point they'd both fallen asleep on the floor and been drawn together, seeking a more comfortable position and warmth.

Ignoring the discomfort of the hard floor beneath the mat they were lying on, he was pretty sure he could happily wake up to this more often. His arm rested on her hip and he could feel her soft curves and gentle breathing against him. He was fighting a losing battle trying to caution his heart from falling too fast for this woman.

He felt her stir and held his breath. He didn't want to break this spell that he'd awoken to find himself in. He knew the moment she realised where she was, because her breath caught and he could almost hear her mind processing her predicament. Slowly she moved to pull away from his chest, and he reluctantly let his hands drop.

'I'm sorry, I must have fallen asleep,' she murmured, her voice raspy but sounding sultry, as she brushed back her hair from her face self-consciously.

'I did too.'

For a long moment they looked at one another and he scarcely dared to move in case he frightened her off. Then, to his relief, she leaned towards him slightly. It was all the encouragement he needed. That first touch of her soft lips against his set off an avalanche of emotion inside him. Ever since their first kiss before she left for Sydney, he'd replayed the moment over and over, long into the lonely nights. He thought he'd remembered it exactly, but now he realised how wrong he'd been. It was so much more.

He lifted a hand to the side of her head and held her steady, his lips searching hers; his heart racing as she answered his unspoken question, moving closer and matching his ardent need with her own.

He let out a low, throaty moan as her hands timidly searched for the hem of his T-shirt to run her fingertips underneath the fabric, over his stomach and up across his chest.

He dropped his hand and encircled her waist, gently lifting her to straddle him, and inched his hands up and under her shirt, feeling the softness of her skin as he moved them across her back without breaking the kiss. He could feel the softness of her chest pushed against his and closed his eyes tightly against the urgent need to swear out loud as she began to move slowly against him. She felt so good, even still fully dressed.

As though reading his mind, she pulled away from his kiss long enough to tug at the hem of his T-shirt and help him pull it over his head before doing the same with her jumper. She leaned down and gently planted kisses along the sensitive skin above his navel, inching her way higher while his hands wrapped around her hips, loving the feel of her skin as he gently squeezed and helped move her slowly back and forth, the friction drawing long, breathless sighs from both of them.

He couldn't think straight, his body craving hers in a way he had never felt before. He'd experienced lust—sure, he was a red-blooded male, after all—only it had never been this powerful. It was more than finding a willing woman who wanted sex; this was his body connecting with hers on some kind of other level.

Her hands moved lower, her nimble fingers finding the button on his jeans and popping it open. Easing away slightly, she slowly inched the zipper down, before hastily doing the same with her own jeans, discarding them in a move so agile that he'd barely had time to blink before it was done. He lifted his hips to help her remove his, only for them to get stuck on his prosthesis, holding up progress, but before he had time to sit up and deal with it, she'd taken matters into her own hands, and manoeuvred herself around them—clearly there wasn't time to waste, and who was he to argue with a woman who knew what she wanted?

# Fifteen

Tilly almost felt as though she were floating above herself, looking down. This was not her normal behaviour. She'd never been this dominating before—never taken charge of a situation so boldly. And yet here she was. One minute they'd been kissing and the next it felt as though fire were running through her veins. She wanted him—desperately, like she'd never wanted anyone or anything before. Yes, it had been a long time since she'd had sex, but she'd never suspected she would go off like a damn firecracker the first time an opportunity arose.

If she could concentrate on anything other than this desire that was currently consuming her, she would be mortified at just how shameless she was, but right now the only thing that mattered was sating this hunger that seemed to have been lying dormant, waiting for the opportunity to roar to life.

In the back of her mind, she'd been thinking about this moment ever since that first kiss on the day she left for Sydney. And there had been times before that when she'd found herself distracted by the fleeting thought of what it would be like, sometimes at the most inconvenient moments, like at the cafe taking his order or clearing away a nearby table. Never had her imagination prepared Tilly for what it would actually be like in real life, though.

She could feel his big hands splayed wide around her hips, helping to guide and move her, the heat of where their bodies joined and the sighs and gasps all mixed together in a heady swirl of desire and need, pushing them further together, headlong into a place neither of them had been in a very long time.

∽

Tilly remained where she'd collapsed, sweaty and sated against Jason's chest as their breathing slowed to normal. She fought the urge to disappear, dreading the awkward *after* conversation. Good Lord, how was she ever going to look at the guy again after this?

Okay, so maybe looking at him wouldn't be too hard—especially now that she knew what was hiding under all that denim.

*Stop it. Just get it over with*, she told herself firmly and slowly pushed herself upright and slid back to the floor, grabbing at her clothes and pulling them on as quickly as possible, not even caring if her jumper was inside out.

Beside her, she felt Jason slowly easing into a sitting position, after pulling back on the jeans she'd help him remove. She closed her eyes briefly, mortified at the memory. She hadn't even allowed him time to take them all the way off before . . .

Jason slid himself higher, until his back was resting against the lounge, and she glanced over at him sharply when she heard a slight noise come from the back of his throat.

'Are you okay? Is it your leg?'

'Nah, the leg's fine, just needs a stretch.'

'I didn't even think about it . . . I could have hurt you—' She stopped abruptly.

'I'm tougher than I look.'

Tilly got to her feet and dragged her fingers through her hair, hoping it didn't look as scarecrow-like as she was imagining. 'I don't do this kind of thing, normally,' she said, the words coming out in a short burst.

'Seemed pretty normal to me,' he joked lightly, but turned serious when he took in her worried pacing. 'Hey, I get it,' he said softly.

'Do you?' she asked doubtfully. 'You're the first man I've been with since my husband died. I don't make a habit of . . . that,' she said, waving a hand back towards the living room floor.

'Are you regretting it?' he asked slowly.

'No,' she said, shaking her head. 'But I just didn't want

you thinking this is some casual thing I do. I'm not like that. I don't really know what came over me tonight.'

'You've been through a tough few weeks.'

Tilly looked up at him quickly. 'I don't think that's a reasonable excuse. I'm pretty sure I wouldn't have done this with just anyone, no matter how rough a time I've had.'

Jason watched her quietly for a few moments, a sober expression on his face. 'I can't say I'm sorry it happened, but I don't want you feeling bad about it.'

'It's not that,' she said, shaking her head quickly. 'It just caught me off guard, I guess. It's a big step for me, to let someone get this close again. I just don't want you to think I do this all the time.'

'I wasn't thinking that,' he told her gently. 'For the record, I didn't make you dinner with this on my mind either.' He grinned. 'Mind you, I'm not complaining.'

Tilly felt a blush creep up her neck and wished she could fake a woman-of-the-world, blasé demeanour. She knew she'd been having feelings that were not in the least way neighbourly towards the man for a while now, but they'd taken a huge step in a direction she wasn't sure she was ready for. She waited for the flood of guilt to flow through her . . . and oddly, found that it wasn't there. There was a touch of something like sadness maybe, a melancholy feeling that seemed to signal an end to something.

'So, what happens now?' she asked, feeling stupid but needing to know where they both stood. If she didn't ask, she would never be able to relax.

He seemed to be as uncertain as she was. Tilly wasn't sure if this was a good or a bad thing.

'I guess we just play it by ear.' He shrugged. 'I'm not in any hurry. Are you?'

'No,' she said slowly.

'Then how about we just take it step by step and see where it goes?'

Well, that sounded sensible. Her spirits rose a little at that. Thank God one of them was capable of being an adult in this situation. 'Okay. Sounds good.'

'Okay,' he agreed with a chuckle. 'Well, I guess I'll see you tomorrow.'

Tilly stood in the doorway long after his tail-lights had disappeared from sight and stared out into the darkness. Lately, life had seemed to be racing at an alarming speed and she had often felt as if she were struggling to keep her head above water. But tonight, for the first time in a very long while, she felt as though she could finally breathe again. For a precious few minutes, Jason had been her life raft. She slowly closed the front door and headed inside to bed. The next few weeks were going to get crazy once more with her regular riding students, as well as the looming deadline to have everything finished in time for her first intake, but somehow it all seemed a little less stressful with the knowledge that Jason would be there beside her.

Tilly waved off the last of her students and took her phone from her pocket. There were two voice messages from Jess, and she immediately listened to them. She'd been trying to call her for the past two days and hadn't managed to catch her. She hoped it was because Jess was at appointments or was busy with work, but she was beginning to have the niggly feeling again that something wasn't quite right.

'Hi, it's me. I know you've been calling but I haven't had time to call you back. I'm fine. Don't worry.' The message ended and Tilly's concern grew as she clicked on the second message.

'Me again. Actually, I'm not fine. I'm . . . I don't know what's wrong with me. I just can't seem to focus on anything. But I *will* be fine. Don't worry about me, okay. There's nothing you can do, I just . . . I don't know, needed to touch base with you or something. Anyway. Bye. I'll call later.'

For a long moment Tilly stared at her phone, a mix of surprise and concern vying for position inside her. Her sister was reaching out—in her own way, of course, but reaching out nevertheless. Clicking on Jess's name in her contacts, she heard the phone ringing and breathed a sigh of relief when it was picked up.

'Jess. Hi. Sorry, I had riding-school lessons.'

'It wasn't important.'

'It was. I'm glad you called. I've been worried about you. What's going on?'

'Nothing. That's just it,' Jess said, and Tilly heard the frustration in her voice. 'I sit down to work and nothing happens. I've lost my focus. I've never lost my focus, Tilly,' she said desperately.

'You're recovering from major surgery, Jess. It's understandable that it's going to take some time to get back on your feet again. Are you still doing your physio?'

'When I can.'

Tilly frowned. 'Physio is important, Jess.' If she was slacking off on her exercises, it would only delay her progress and healing. 'Pack a bag,' Tilly said, crossing the yard to the house with determined steps.

'What? Why?'

'I'm driving down to get you.'

'No.'

'I knew it was too soon to leave you. I can't really afford to be away from the farm at the moment, but I can take care of you up here.'

'You've already done more than enough. You don't need to be stuck with me again.'

'Would you stop? If I didn't want you here, I wouldn't have suggested it. If you're too stubborn to do it for yourself, then think of me. If you don't come up here, I'll only be worrying about you and then *I* won't be able to focus.'

'That's not very ethical of you to use blackmail, you know.'

'It's the truth.'

There was silence on the end of the phone. 'Fine. But I can drive myself.'

'No. You cannot. I'm coming down to pick you up. I'll stay tonight and we'll leave to come back early in the morning.'

'When did you become so bossy?'

'When I realised it was the only way to get through to you. Pack your bag, I'll be there this afternoon.'

∽

Jason's thumb hovered over the call button on his phone and he swore softly once more. He'd headed home last night feeling on top of the bloody world, only to find today that Tilly was doing her best to avoid him. What could possibly have changed in the space of a few hours? He'd come over, a bunch of flowers in hand and wearing a stupid grin, only to find her gone. The horses had all been fed and turned out—he knew she'd had riding lessons earlier, so he'd waited before coming over, but when he got here the house was locked up and there was no sign of Tilly.

He'd figured she'd been called in to the cafe unexpectedly, so again he'd waited, heading back to her place after her shift would normally be finished, but here he was, sitting outside a still-empty house, waiting, hoping she wasn't hiding under a bed or something.

There'd been a missed call earlier and that gave him hope, but so far he hadn't been able to reach her when he'd tried to return the call. Now he was wondering if she'd been phoning to tell him it had all been a horrible mistake and she was too scared to answer his calls.

This was probably how crazy stalkers started out, he thought miserably, but then jumped a little when his phone lit up and started ringing. He hesitated as he read her name on the screen.

'Hi,' he said, trying for cool, calm and collected but fearing his voice may have squeaked like a prepubescent boy.

'I phoned earlier but couldn't get you.'

'Yeah. Sorry. I didn't hear it. I tried calling back a couple of times.' *Couple dozen.* Christ, she'd probably seen all the missed calls and was already at the cop station taking out an AVO on him.

'I've only just pulled up. I'm in Sydney.'

She must be really regretting their evening together to take off down there.

'I got a call from Jess this morning.'

*Jess . . .* He briefly shut his eyes in relief. *Oh, thank God she wasn't running away from him, but hang on . . .* 'Is she okay?'

'There was no emergency,' Tilly said quickly, 'but she's not handling her recovery as well as I'd like, so I came down to pick her up and I'll bring her home for a while. I didn't want to give her time to change her mind, so I left straightaway. I tried to call to tell you, but had to wait until I stopped to try again. Just in case you came over and didn't know where I was.'

'Oh. Yeah. Nah. I've been working flat out all day. I hadn't realised you were gone.' He tried for a casual tone.

'Good. I guess I'm a bit out of practice with the whole "informing someone of my whereabouts" thing.'

'Nah, don't stress. You don't have to tell me where you are twenty-four hours a day. It's not like I'm some weirdo who needs to keep track of you all the time.' He was pretty sure that light-hearted laugh he just tried for definitely sounded creepy.

'Okay, well, I just didn't want you to worry when you couldn't get hold of me. I'll be back tomorrow afternoon. I, ah, wanted to invite you over for dinner, but I'm thinking it might not be such a great idea, with Jess,' she said, sounding nervous.

'No, that's fine. I don't want to get in the way or anything.'

'It's not that, it's just I think she'll be really tired after travelling tomorrow, and it might be better if she doesn't feel as though she has to stay up and be sociable.'

'All good. I think it's best if you get her settled.'

'Yeah.' She sounded relieved and he felt better for the first time all day. Although pretty stupid. 'I was looking forward to seeing you today,' she added, dragging his thoughts away from where they'd been.

'I was too.'

There was a small pause on the other end of the line. 'Well, I better get on with it. I just wanted to let you know where I was. I'll talk to you tomorrow.'

'Drive safe. I'll see you when you're home.'

Jason dropped his head and let out a long breath. He felt like he'd just been through some kind of emotional boxing match and it took a minute to sort it all out. Tilly hadn't been under her bed hiding from him. She hadn't been avoiding his calls. She'd wanted to see him today. Letting out a shaky chuckle, he called himself a bunch of unflattering names as he turned on the ignition and headed for home. Was this thing really worth putting himself through this kind of ridiculousness? Flashes of the night before replayed in his mind and instantly put things back into perspective. Hell, yes, it was.

# Sixteen

'Home sweet home,' Tilly said, dropping her sister's huge suitcase by the door of the guest bedroom. 'I'm not sure you've packed enough clothes, though, Jess, considering the social mecca that Ben Tirran is, and all.'

'For your information, it's not full of all *my* clothes. I brought along a heap of samples. I thought I might meet up with that woman who has the blog in town and give her an exclusive look at the new line.'

'Wow. That's nice of you.'

'Yeah, well, give back and all that jazz.' Jess fluttered a hand in the air.

'It might be wasted on a small-time blogger from Ben Tirran,' Tilly warned.

'Oh, I checked her out. She's not that small-time.'

'Really?' Tilly asked doubtfully.

'Social media has a world audience, Tilly. It doesn't matter whether you live in New York or Ben Tirran—the internet is universal. You can run anything from anywhere nowadays.'

'Huh,' Tilly mused. *Who would have thought?* 'Well, how about you have a rest for a bit before dinner. You've been sitting in the car for ages.'

She'd been a little worried by how drawn her sister had looked when she'd arrived in Sydney, and was glad she'd decided to bring her home. Tilly felt better knowing she could keep an eye on her here. It was nothing that a little home-cooked food and a bossy younger sister couldn't fix.

'I think I might,' Jess said, crossing to the bed. 'Tilly?'

Tilly stopped and turn back to face her sister.

'Thank you.'

Tilly smiled. 'You're welcome. I'm glad you're here. Get some rest.'

Later, as she chopped veggies in the kitchen and threw them into the pot on the stove for soup, she found her mind wandering back over the same thoughts she'd been consumed with on her trip down yesterday. Jason. She missed him. Maybe she shouldn't have asked him not to come over tonight after all. Jess needed the rest, she knew that, but equally, Tilly needed to see him again. How did someone become so important to you after such a short time? She put the soup on the stove and went outside to tend to the animals before dinner. Tomorrow she would make sure she saw him. One way or another.

∽

'I hope you don't mind, Jess, but I've invited a friend over for dinner tonight. If you don't feel up to visitors, I can set you up in your room, but you're more than welcome to join us.'

'A friend? Would this happen to be a certain neighbour by any chance?'

'Yes, as a matter of fact. It's Jason.'

'I thought there was something going on there,' Jess said, eyeing Tilly thoughtfully.

'Before you say anything disapproving, I really like him, and no, it's not serious.'

'Then what is it?'

'I don't know. It's only new. It's too early to be rushing into anything. I just like him and I like spending time with him.' She glanced over at her sister, who remained silent. 'Speaking of . . .' Tilly said pointedly, 'how are things going with Louise?'

Jess's expression lost its previous interest and she suddenly began concentrating extra hard on the exercises Tilly was overseeing. 'I don't know. I haven't spoken to her.'

'At all?' Tilly gaped at her sister.

'There hasn't been time.'

'Well, I can see why, with all the physio you *haven't* been doing, there wouldn't be a spare moment to make a quick phone call, would there?' Tilly said sarcastically and saw her sister look up at her defensively. 'Come on, Jess, we talked about this. You care about Lou and she obviously cares about you. What's going on?'

'I don't know,' Jess said, standing up from the bed carefully and walking across to the window. 'I thought with time, once I started to heal, I'd be able to cope with all this. But, I just don't know, I still don't feel like myself. Everything's strange and sore and ugly. If I can't stand looking at my scars, how can I expect anyone else to?'

'Because if you care about someone, you don't see the scars. You see the person.'

'How do you know that? You don't have any,' Jess said bitterly.

'No. But Jason does,' Tilly said softly. She hesitated for a minute before continuing. It felt a bit like betraying his trust, but this was her sister and it was important. 'Jason lost part of his leg years ago and wears a prosthesis.'

'I had no idea,' Jess said, staring at her wide-eyed.

'Well, it's not something he advertises and it's hard to notice if you're not looking for it. The point is,' Tilly said, getting back on track, 'I know that he had similar hang-ups to you—different of course, but still similar. I know that he still feels a bit awkward when we're together. Actually, we haven't really talked about it, to be honest.' She remembered that initial moment of discomfort the other morning when he'd been getting dressed. At the time she'd been too preoccupied with her own embarrassment about him seeing *her* body, she hadn't even thought about how he might be feeling. 'But, speaking as the person on the other end, as Lou would be . . . the scars don't matter. It doesn't stop me wanting to be with him.' *All the time*, she added silently.

'And I'm keeping you from him,' Jess said, with a twist of her lips.

'No. *You* are my main priority at the moment and you are always welcome here. You're family, and family comes first.'

'If I'm not going to be in the way, I'd like to join you for dinner tonight. After all, I *am* your big sister, so I guess it's up to me to find out what his intentions are.'

Tilly couldn't help a small smile. She knew exactly what his intentions were, and they were just as impure as hers.

∽

Jason arrived at Tilly's feeling nervous. He wasn't sure if it was because Tilly had given him a rundown of her sister's previous conversation and he was half-expecting an inquisition, or that he was just eager to see Tilly again. Either way he gripped the two bunches of flowers tighter than was necessary as he headed for the front door.

His mouth dried up when Tilly opened the door and smiled at him, and for a moment, he simply stared at her. How had he forgotten how bloody gorgeous she was? Christ, he'd missed her. More than a grown man probably should. It had been two days, but it felt like a lifetime.

'Flowers?' she asked, searching his eyes with a curious kind of smile.

It was enough to jolt him from his momentary stupor. 'Oh yeah. For you, and your sister,' he added, stepping into the house and spotting Jess as she walked into the room.

'So far so good,' Jess murmured, giving him an amused grin.

'Nice to see you,' he said, releasing the flowers as Tilly took them to the kitchen. He wasn't sure what to expect when he saw Jess again, after her operation, but she looked good. She moved a little slower and seemed tired, but on the whole she didn't look as bad as he was expecting after such an intensive surgery.

'You two take a seat and I'll just check on dinner and be back out in a sec,' Tilly said, sending them a nervous look before disappearing.

'I think she's worried I'm going to give you the third degree,' Jess said dryly.

'I'm not sure what she's worried I'll do,' he countered.

'I can't say I'm entirely surprised by the two of you. I knew she was a little distracted when she was down with me after the operation.'

'Ah, yeah. Well, it's all kind of new. I wasn't exactly planning on . . . Let's just say I think it's caught us both by surprise.'

'I don't think I have to tell you this, but I will anyway seeing as I'm the only family Tilly's got left. She's been through a lot over the past few years. I don't want to see her hurt again.'

Jason gave a slow nod and a quick smile. 'I have no intention of hurting your sister. She's pretty special.'

'Yes, she is.'

Jason knew that the two women had a bit of a rocky past, but clearly they'd reached an understanding or two during the past few weeks. He suspected Jess was a woman of many layers, and under the sophisticated exterior she put up hid a woman who was more than a little vulnerable.

Once they sat down to eat the initial tension eased, and Jason found himself listening avidly as Jess told stories about a younger, horse-obsessed Tilly who would sit for hours cutting out photos of horses from magazines and sticking them in a scrapbook, and would follow their grandfather around the property like a miniature shadow. Then the conversation shifted to tales of the mischief Tilly and Jim constantly got up to.

'Tilly used to take Jim to the lolly shop in town when we were kids because he'd always manage to sweet talk the grumpy old woman who owned it into giving us a few extras in the bag—using our little brother for extortion.'

'Well, I wasn't stupid.' Tilly shrugged. 'He could charm the paint off the wall, that one.'

Jess started giggling and Jason couldn't help but stare. The woman he met weeks ago in the cafe, cool and somewhat reserved, was very different to the one he was seeing now.

'Remember when you made him busk on the street corner on his recorder for money? And you told everyone you were his manager?'

'Dad said I couldn't have a dog unless I paid for it myself,' she explained to Jason, with a grin of her own. 'What can I say, the kid had a talent. He was cute and he could wrap everyone around his little finger with just a smile. We made a fortune that day.'

'Oh my God, and what about when you were six and you told him he was holding up a sign to sell lemonade but you were actually selling him!'

'You tried to sell your sibling?' Jason asked, raising a doubtful eyebrow.

'At the time, I needed a pony more than I needed a brother,' Tilly said, with a small wince. 'In my defence, that was much earlier, before I realised how useful he could be in other areas.'

Jess shook her head, still chuckling. 'Mum came out and saw this four-year-old sitting on the footpath holding up a For Sale sign and freaked.'

He chuckled at the stories, and despite the occasional dark warning Tilly sent her older sister, he saw that she was enjoying the trip down memory lane as much as Jess was.

He really liked hearing what Tilly had been like as a kid and a little more about their family. For a moment he paused as it sunk in that everyone they had mentioned was now gone. It was just the two of them left.

After dessert, Jess excused herself to go to bed and Jason helped Tilly clean up. As Tilly turned from the sink, Jason stepped in front of her and slid his hands around her waist to pull her against him. 'You have no idea how hard it's been to not touch you all night,' he said against her mouth as they broke apart from a long, hungry kiss.

'I have some idea,' she said, lifting an eyebrow and moving her thigh against his groin suggestively.

'Don't toy with me, woman,' he all but growled against her neck, grinning at the throaty chuckle she gave him.

'I wouldn't dream of it,' she said, her brown eyes smiling up at him.

Jason froze, staring down at her. He was prepared for a low-key dinner and had braced himself for the fact he probably wouldn't be staying over, but if he were reading this situation correctly, and he believed he might just be, Tilly had other plans.

'Follow me,' she said, sliding out of his arms and beckoning him with a glint in her eye.

They went outside and into the dark, Tilly's hand holding his tightly as she led the way purposely forward. When they reached the shed he'd recently converted into sleeping quarters for guests, he felt relief and desire flood through him in levels he had never experienced before. *Halle-freakin-lujah.*

They didn't waste time talking, removing their clothes with complete disregard for zips and buttons. The first touch of her skin against his sent his brain into overdrive. How could he miss something he hadn't even had in his life long enough to miss? But he had missed her. He went to move when Tilly sat up and reached for the button of his jeans, but she pushed him back and swatted his hands away.

'I'll have to help. You won't get them over my leg,' he started, then felt an attack of nerves.

'I can do it,' she protested, and he reluctantly allowed her to continue.

His breath caught when her hands brushed his thighs as she worked the denim down his legs. When Tilly reached the top of his prosthesis he froze, catching her eye and holding her steady gaze.

Slowly, she removed his jeans and when he reached down to remove the prosthesis, she stopped him. 'Show me how,' she said.

Jason tried to keep his face calm, but inside he was a mess of emotions. He'd never allowed anyone to do anything this personal, and it *was* just that—personal. Logically he knew that if they were going to move forward, she would at some stage be part of everything, including seeing him without his leg, but it was tough holding open that door that exposed him.

Slowly, he went through the process of removing the prosthesis, her hands over his as she followed his movements. He let it drop to the floor and tried not to feel anxious as he lay back and watched Tilly lower her gaze to his thigh and the stump he'd spent the past few years not drawing attention to.

He held his breath as she reached out and gently ran her hands up both of his thighs. As her hands skimmed the edge of the stump, his leg instinctively twitched, but unperturbed she continued to lightly caress his thigh, slowly working her way further up his body until she straddled his lap and leaned down to kiss him.

The need to feel her against him hit with a swiftness that surprised them both, as he deftly he swapped their positions and went about showing her how much he'd missed her.

As the cool night air touched their sweaty bodies afterward, Jason could feel his heart rate gradually returning to normal.

'I missed you,' he said, kissing the top of her head where she was nestled snugly against him. 'I was worried I'd scared you off.'

She lifted her head slightly to look at him. 'Really?'

'Well, only for a minute. The timing was a bit iffy. You were nowhere to be found the day after we—' He stopped and then changed tack. 'I just wasn't sure if maybe you were avoiding me.'

Her eyes softened and she gave him a small smile. 'I figured I was only going to be gone overnight. I was just really worried about Jess and I didn't stop to think about letting you know until it was too late. Then I couldn't text you till I stopped again.'

He sounded like a whiny kid. 'I get why you went down. I'm glad you brought Jess home for a while. It's hard trying to cope after a big operation like that.'

'I think it's the mental side of things she's struggling with at the moment. She's dealing with more emotions than she was expecting. It's kind of sideswiped her.'

'She'll get there. She's lucky she's got you.'

Tilly laid her head back on his chest and he ran his fingers through her hair.

'Did you mind what happened earlier . . . with your leg?' she asked quietly, and he detected a note of uncertainty.

'No. I didn't want to push you into having to deal with it until you felt ready.'

'I've been feeling a bit like it's the elephant in the room with us. We've never really talked about it.'

'I wasn't sure you wanted to.'

'The thing is, I don't,' she said, then pushed herself up again to look at him. 'I mean, it's not that I don't want to *talk about it*, it's that I don't see it as something that gets in the way. I was thinking about something Jess said earlier about how she was worried people will see her differently now, and I thought of you. I don't think of you as someone who's lost a leg. I *know* you have, and I know that it came with a lot of pain and it changed your life, but I see it as part of *you*. Part of who you are. I don't want you to ever feel as though you have to hide it from me—hide *anything* from me.'

Her words caught him square in the chest. Part of him had been waiting for her to suddenly realise she couldn't deal with a man who wasn't . . . complete. He hadn't realised how worried he'd been though until now—when the relief rushed over him like a tidal wave.

'Your sister's going to be fine. She just has to find the right person who'll come along and see her for who she is.' *Like I did with you,* he added silently.

Her soft smile tugged at the corners of her mouth and when she leaned forward to plant butterfly kisses along his chest, he sucked in a long breath, too distracted to think about anything else for a long time.

∽

Tilly made a point of asking Jess to help her with the horses each afternoon. Tilly did all the lifting but Jess walked with her along the yards at feed time and helped throw the hay out. It gave Jess the exercise she needed, and it was becoming one of Tilly's favourite parts of the day.

She noticed Jess tended to linger around one of the mares, the one with the young foal at foot, each time they came down here. Every day the little foal had been getting more curious.

'Why don't you try holding out some hay?'

Jess glanced over at her, looking unsure, but pulled apart a handful of the hay and timidly stuck it through the rails.

'You hang out here for a while and I'll finish throwing out the rest of this to the others.'

Tilly filled up water troughs and spread out the hay to the remaining animals before making her way back up to where she'd left Jess with the mare and foal. To her amazement, as she reached them, she found her sister gently stroking the foal's neck.

A slow, satisfied grin spread across Tilly's face as she looked on quietly, unwilling to end the precious moment. As far as she knew, Jess was the first person to touch the young foal. Jess turned her head towards her and the joy on her sister's face made Tilly grin back, blinking quickly to rid herself of the sudden sting of tears that followed.

# Seventeen

From the very beginning, Tilly had her plan firmly in place. The cafe job had provided the income she needed to live off while the renovations were completed, and had also provided her with a nice little buffer for the initial months ahead once she opened the business. However, the time was always going to come for her to leave the cafe and stand on her own two feet—and that time had all of a sudden arrived.

'I can't believe this is your last day,' Allie said, shaking her head sadly.

In her absence Paul had put on a trainee—a very serious-looking woman named Sharon—who was apparently working out, which made Tilly feel a little less guilty about leaving.

'I know. It's all becoming very real,' Tilly responded.

'You've been working so hard to get your new business up and running. I just know it's going to be a huge success, Tilly,' Allie said, giving her a hug.

'I hope so,' Tilly breathed. 'Worst-case scenario, I'll be working back here full-time.' She grinned weakly. Although, now that Paul had hired Sharon, finding another decent-paying job in Ben Tirran might be a bit of a problem.

'Nope. You're on to bigger and better things from now on,' Allie said confidently.

'Speaking of better things, did I see you getting dropped off this morning by a certain mail courier?'

Tilly grinned as Allie started fidgeting with the hem of her apron. 'We've been seeing each other now and again,' she admitted somewhat shyly.

'When did this start happening?'

'While you were away with your sister,' she said reluctantly. 'I was going to tell you, but I figured you've had a lot on your plate.'

'That's great news,' Tilly said, smiling at her friend. 'I'm happy for you.'

'Well, it's not really an official *thing* yet,' Allie added quickly. 'But so far, it seems to be going well. The boys really like him.'

'I know you think you're pretty clever branchin' out on your own and everything,' Paul said from the doorway, 'but you still have one shift left, so maybe we could get some customers served?'

'All right, keep your pants on,' Tilly told him with a roll of her eyes. 'I'm coming.'

She walked out into the cafe and stopped in her tracks as a crowd of people greeted her.

'Surprise!'

Tilly stared at the smiling faces of Vera, Janice and Ted as well as so many other regular customers and burst into tears.

Around her came an instant chorus of *Oh no's* and *Aw's* and she quickly pulled herself together. 'I wasn't expecting a farewell party,' she said, sending Paul an accusing glare.

'We wanted to make sure you left,' he grunted, but he gave her a wink and placed a large cake in front of her with *Good Luck* written across it. 'I guess we'll miss you around here,' he added.

'Oh guys,' Tilly said, overwhelmed by the unexpected gesture.

'The cake's on the house but not the coffee and tea, so get out there and take some orders,' he instructed, waving his finger to the packed cafe and milling well-wishers.

It now made sense why all three waitresses were on this morning, and they were soon kept busy delivering beverages and handing out cake. Tilly stopped short when she spotted her sister, dressed casually but with a touch of her old elegance. It was a relief to see her looking happy as she mingled with her new best buddy, the blogger woman.

It was a wonderfully crazy morning, and the shift seemed to fly by, with the morning crowd departing but replaced by the lunchtime patrons, and she was pretty sure by the end of the day she must have spoken to every single resident of Ben Tirran. By the time she arrived home late that afternoon, she was emotionally drained.

'How was the party?' Jason asked as he arrived at her place shortly after she got home.

'How'd you know?'

'I bumped into Allie yesterday down the street and she invited me.'

'I didn't see you there,' she said, confused.

'I figured it was something you and your regulars should do.'

'You were one of my regulars not so long ago,' she pointed out, sliding into his arms.

'Yeah, but I reckon I've moved up the ranks since then.' He smiled.

'I can't believe you didn't tell me.'

'It was a surprise. I was sworn to secrecy.'

'Just for future reference, I hate surprises,' she warned, but then she smiled. 'It was very sweet of them, though. I certainly hadn't expected Paul to get so sentimental.'

'So, how are *you*?' Jason asked, looking down at her.

It was scary how in tune with her this man could be in such a short amount of time. 'It's been a little bit tough actually,' she admitted. 'I don't think I really thought about how much I'd miss that place in this whole grand plan of mine. I'm going to miss seeing them every day.'

'You can still see everyone. You're not leaving town,' he pointed out.

'I know. But it'll be different.' Tilly lowered her head onto his chest and closed her eyes for a few moments, enjoying the comfort of standing close to him.

'In light of your recent announcement regarding surprises ... I just want to point out that I planned this one before I knew how much you disliked them.'

'What have you done ... ?' She looked at him, already full of dread.

'It's okay, I think you'll like it,' he said, taking her hand and leading her outside.

She followed him down the hill towards the recently converted bunkhouse and yards and stopped short.

In front of the round yard stood a small yet substantial grandstand.

'Jason,' she gasped. 'How did you even know ... ?' Her original budget hadn't included the type of seating she'd wished for. After pricing a grandstand-type arrangement, she'd discovered how expensive they were and decided plastic seats would have to do for now.

He shrugged, looking a little embarrassed. 'You mentioned the other day it was something that would be handy down the track for demonstrations. I had a heap of timber from my place and was able to get the rest from a demolition place really cheap. So, I figured I'd whack one together. It's not huge, but we can add on to it down the track if you need a bigger one.'

'It's amazing,' she said, walking forward and climbing the three rows of timber seating, then turning to look down at him with a wide smile. 'You're amazing,' she added. 'Thank you, Jason.'

'You're welcome.'

Tilly stepped back down and moved towards him, stunned by his thoughtfulness. When she'd mentioned the need for some seating the other day, it had just been in passing, only a thought, but the fact he'd been listening and then had taken it upon himself to make it a reality meant more than he could imagine. Over the past week since she'd been home, they had fallen into a new routine of spending almost every waking moment together, apart from the hours she worked at the cafe. She couldn't get enough of him and already she was beginning to forget what her life had been like before Jason Weaver became a part of it.

'It's the start of a new era for you,' he said quietly. 'Are you ready?'

'I hope so, because suddenly I feel like I've just jumped out of a plane and I'm not sure if I have a parachute.'

'You don't need one. You'll see. You've got this.' He grinned and Tilly felt her heart momentarily stop at the familiar words. She summoned a semi-confident smile for him. Like it or not, she was in it now. She *had* to be ready.

# Eighteen

It had been a little over two weeks since Jess had come to Brumby Creek, and Tilly was happy with her sister's progress. She'd been eating and doing her exercises, and their relationship had definitely changed for the better. Tilly enjoyed spending the evenings chatting long into the night and reminiscing about the past. They'd managed to move on from the sad times that had previously bonded them, almost as though confronting it all had finally released them. Now they were free to remember the good times—and there *had* been good times, lots of them, and it was nice to be able to relive them with her sister.

Jess, encouraged by the trust the foal had shown a few days earlier, had been spending quite a bit of each day down with the mother and foal duo. She would take a chair and set up on the outside of the yards to sketch.

'I'm really enjoying it,' she'd announced to Tilly one evening. 'For the first time in ages, I feel inspired and exhilarated again.'

'But you're a designer, you're always sketching,' Tilly said.

'Designs, yes, but I used to draw everything as a kid, remember? Mum would call me in to help with something, and I'd be outside somewhere capturing everyday life—like the neighbour mowing his yard in budgie smugglers.'

Tilly chuckled. She *did* remember that, it had been as detailed as a photograph . . . almost too detailed for the subject matter, Tilly recalled with a grimace. She could still see the neighbour's huge hairy belly spilling out over the bright yellow Speedos.

'I haven't drawn just for the love of it since back then. I think, losing Dad . . . all that side of me just shrank away somewhere.'

Tilly carefully flipped through her sister's sketch pad and marvelled at the beautiful images. Jess had caught the mare and foal when the foal had been feeding from its mother and it looked so real, Tilly could almost feel the soft fluffy coat of the foal as she looked at it. She turned the page and froze as she found a drawing of her and Denny that Jess had somehow managed to catch. Tilly felt her throat tighten as she stared at the image. It was beautiful.

'You should draw more often. Dad was right. He always said you had talent. These are amazing, Jess. Just stunning.'

'Thank you,' Jess said, sounding humbler than Tilly had ever heard her.

The two women shared a watery smile and Tilly quickly wiped her eyes, handing the pad back to her sister and getting back to making dinner.

But underneath the new, lighter side of Jess, there was still something sad lingering, and Tilly knew what it was. They talked about Louise a lot. Tilly knew her sister was still very much in love, but her fears of rejection after her surgery ran deep.

'Have you thought anymore about the kids and family thing?' she asked Jess one afternoon.

'There doesn't really seem much point.'

'Put aside what your fears are telling you about your scars and the operation, and let's discuss the other things that are worrying you. Have you thought about it any more?'

'It's all I think about,' Jess admitted miserably. 'I've had a lot of time on my hands lately,' she added dryly.

'And?'

Jess shrugged and stood up, walking across to the verandah rail. 'I can't see the original image I used to have about us as a couple. Now all I see is kids and a house and weekend barbecues with neighbours, who look like they stepped out of a bad sixties sitcom.'

Tilly smiled at her sister's overactive imagination. 'And you hate this version of your life?'

'No. That's just it. I like it,' she said, shaking her head as if mystified.

'Well, isn't that good?' Tilly asked cautiously.

'I don't know.'

'Have you spoken with Lou lately?'

'She's called to see how I am.'

'And?' *Seriously, how hard was it to get information out of this woman?*

'She says she's looking forward to me coming back.'

'Are *you* looking forward to going back?'

'Yes. But, at the same time, I'm not sure. I know we spoke about things the other day and I get what you're saying . . . I just don't know if I'm ready to face up to the fact that she might not feel the same about me anymore.'

'I know it must be scary. But I still think you're not giving this woman enough credit. For your own peace of mind I think you need to face it and find out once and for all.'

After a moment, Jess gave a resigned sigh. 'You're probably right. I just need a little more time.'

Tilly understood why her sister was so worried, but deep down she was concerned that the longer Jess delayed, the harder it would be to do it. The next day she bit her lip thoughtfully as she stared at her phone. The number on the screen was still saved in her phone from the night Louise had rung to tell her about Jess's surgery. She pressed the button and ignored the little voice inside that called her a traitor, concentrating instead on the sound of the phone ringing in her ear.

'Hello, is that Louise?' she asked when the line was answered. 'This is Tilly—Jessica's sister. I think there's something you should know.'

A week later, Tilly had breakfast on the table early, her insides jumping at every sound. She was a nervous wreck and she only had herself to blame. 'Breakfast!' she called out to Jess.

'Why are we having breakfast so early today?' Jess grumbled, smothering a yawn as she sat at the table.

'Because I have a big day ahead and I thought you should probably get up and get dressed.'

'Why? What's happening today?'

'Nothing much, but you know, you've been in your PJs till close to noon most days and I've got meetings today with the council and stuff. I just thought you might like to be dressed in case I'm not in the house when they arrive.'

'Are you all right?' Jess asked, watching Tilly with a strange look.

'I'm just trying to tie up all the loose ends before the first clinic. It's only a few weeks away, you know.' And that wasn't a lie. She *was* anxious and stressing that everything wouldn't be done in time.

'Okay. Calm down. It'll be fine.'

'Well, I just wanted to make sure you were up and about before I went down to the horses. Don't forget to get dressed. In something nice,' she added.

'Why?'

'I want to make a good impression on them. Don't just get back into new pyjamas.'

'Okay, okay. I'll dress to impress.'

Tilly left the house and pushed away the heavy cloak of guilt that threatened to weigh her down. *It's for her own good,* she told herself firmly. Jess just needed a bit of a push so she could move forward.

'Morning,' Jason said, arriving a few minutes later. 'Your sister came out and seemed disappointed when she saw it was only me. Apparently you've got a meeting with someone? I thought we were working with Red this morning?'

'We are. And *I* don't have a meeting. *Jess* has. Any minute now actually,' she said, looking nervously up at the house.

'Who's coming and why do you look so worried?'

'I may have done something . . .' she hedged.

'What have you done, Tilly?' Jason asked reluctantly.

Just then a car pulled up outside the house and a woman dressed in a brightly coloured, flowy skirt and top got out. Her long, wavy brown hair was pulled back by a bright yellow scarf and she looked at the house for a moment before closing her door and walking up the path.

'Who's that?' Jason asked, looking down at Tilly curiously.

'That would be the woman my sister may or may not have a future with after this visit.'

At Jason's confused look, Tilly sighed. 'Before the operation, Jess and Louise were pretty serious, and Louise dropped a bombshell about wanting a family. Jess got cold feet and came back to Sydney to think things over, and then the lump and operation thing happened. Louise was the woman who called to tell me that Jess was having the operation.'

'I see,' Jason said slowly. 'And why do you look so guilty?' he asked, and at her small wince, his eyes narrowed suspiciously. 'Jess *did* know she was arriving . . . didn't she?'

'Not exactly,' she said guiltily. 'Don't look at me like that. All I did was call her. We got talking and I mentioned how confused and anxious Jess has been about everything.'

'So you invited her here without telling Jess?'

'She offered to come.' Tilly shrugged. 'Look, I sussed her out first. She loves Jess. She's frustrated because Jess is being Jess and started shutting her out of everything when life suddenly got scary. They need to sit down and talk.'

Jason eyed her doubtfully and gave an unamused chuckle. 'I can't see Jess thanking you for sticking your nose in her business.'

'Well, hopefully they'll be too busy working out their relationship to worry about me.' The fact Louise decided to fly all the way over from New York to try to sort things out was a good start. Surely if she wasn't committed, she wouldn't have put herself through that.

Tilly pushed her sister's visitor out of her mind and focused on Jason and the big red horse in the round yard. They'd been working him for a few weeks now, and Tilly was more than happy with the progress of both horse and man.

'Keep pushing him around the yard,' she called as she watched Jason lunge the horse around him in a wide circle. 'Wait for his head to drop.' They'd been working on joining up for the last couple of sessions and already Tilly could see a huge difference in both Jason and Red.

'Wait for that inside ear to turn onto you,' she said, reminding him what signals to look for. In the wild, the lead mare ran the herd. By lunging, they were teaching Red that Jason was his lead mare. Seeing as a horse was most comfortable when he was in his mob, sending him away, around the yard, was recreating what happened in the wild by a lead mare to gain respect from a misbehaving or challenging rival.

To regain a position within the mob, the horse on the outside would have to surrender its dominance to the lead mare in order to be let back in. In the same way, Jason was now waiting for Red to submit, which he might do by lowering his head, as though grazing, and to lick his lips and chew. This was also a signal that a horse was thinking about things, which was always a good sign in training.

She watched as Jason caught the signals and Red slowed to a stop, facing up to him. Jason turned his back on the horse, and Red took a tentative step forward. 'Okay, now slowly walk away,' Tilly called. She watched as Red followed Jason across the centre of the yard.

'Great work,' she said, grinning proudly as she watched Jason turn to the horse and stroke his face.

They'd come such a long way together, and Tilly finally knew Red's purpose. He wasn't for her; he was for Jason. She could see the bond between man and horse strengthening every day.

After they'd finished, Tilly glanced once more up at the house and tried not to worry. There hadn't been any sound—no yelling or crying—but they'd been in there a long time and she desperately wanted to know if they'd managed to patch things up.

'We should go to my place for a while and give them some space,' Jason said, seeing where her gaze had landed.

'Yeah. I guess so. Do you think they're okay in there?'

'I think it's too late to worry about that now. They'll either sort it out or they won't.'

Which was true enough.

When they reached the house, Tilly looked up as her sister called out to her from the front verandah.

'This is Louise,' Jess said, introducing the woman who stepped out beside her.

'Oh. Hello,' Tilly said, with what she hoped sounded like surprise, although she didn't have to fake the curious interest.

'Tilly, it's nice to meet you. At last.'

'Likewise,' Tilly replied, unsure how to gauge the situation.

'If you don't mind, I'm thinking I'll head back to the city,' Jess said. 'Lou's offered me a ride and it'll save you taking me back next week.'

Tilly noticed for the first time that her sister's suitcase was sitting by the front door, just behind her. When she'd invited Lou up here, she hadn't expected that Lou would be stealing her sister away quite so quickly, but she was relieved that Jess seemed happy. 'Oh. Sure. If that's what you want.'

'We've got some things to work out, and I'm feeling a lot better. I guess I just needed some sister time to get me back on my feet.'

Tilly swallowed hard against the tightening of her throat. 'Anytime you need it, you know where I am.'

She hugged Jess and squeezed her eyes shut tightly against the sting of threatening tears.

'I know what you did,' Jess whispered, before pulling back to look her in the eye. 'Thank you.'

Tilly managed a relieved smile before Louise stepped forward. 'I'll make sure she's taking care of herself,' she said, placing a hand on Tilly's arm. 'Thank you for looking out for her.'

'Thanks for coming,' Tilly said, and the two women shared a small grin.

'I've got it,' Jason said, moving around them as Jess bent to pick up her bag.

'You take good care of my sister,' Tilly heard Jess say to Jason as they headed towards the car.

'I intend to,' he replied, and Tilly's gaze flew to his. He was watching her with a look that momentarily distracted her from the unexpected emotion of saying goodbye to her sister.

'Let me know how it all goes,' Tilly said as she waited for Jess to open her door.

'I will—I think we might be able to work things out. We'll see.'

As Tilly stood beside Jason and waved them off, there was a brief, empty feeling of goodbye, but it was swiftly followed by a lighter, happier emotion. She'd managed to reconnect with her sister, and better yet, her meddling seemed to have pushed Jess in the right direction to move forward.

# Nineteen

Tilly looked up as the minivan drove up the driveway. The *Healing Hooves Horse Therapy* sign was hung on the front gate and everything was ready to go.

This was it. Her first official day. The boys arriving were all part of a program for troubled teens—it was the last stop for many of them before juvenile detention or prison. She'd been prepared by the coordinator at various meetings in the lead up to the program's commencement that these kids came with many challenges. So she was under no illusion that this was going to be some polite, school excursion class. This was a last chance for these kids. Inside she was a mix of nervous excitement, with a flurry of uncertainty. What if this didn't work? What if she couldn't connect with these kids? The thoughts began to circle unchecked inside her head before David's calming voice once more rose above the din.

*You don't have to connect with the kids—the horses do. And they will. Let them work their magic.*

He was right. This wasn't about her. It was about the horses. She might be having doubts about her own abilities right now, but she believed in the magic of the horse bond, and instantly her nerves settled.

Tilly walked across to the tall man who climbed from the driver's seat of the van and shook his hand with a smile. She'd met Glen on her last interview with the organisation, and he hadn't been anything like what she'd expected. Instead of someone a little hard and world weary, he was tall and fair-haired, with a wide, kind smile and quite a youthful appearance.

'Great to see you again, Tilly. Are you ready to meet the kids?'

'Sure am,' she said and hoped she looked a lot more positive than she was feeling. *They're just a bunch of kids. You've got this,* she told herself.

Five teenage boys climbed from the minivan with varying degrees of reluctance, and Tilly felt her smile slip a little when none of them made any attempt at eye contact. A few kicked at the dirt beneath their sneakers and gave their surroundings only the barest of glances, while another slouched against the side of the van, arms crossed and wearing a scowl that clearly indicated he was not here willingly.

'Righto, let's get to it,' Glen said, giving a clap and rubbing his hands together. What the boys lacked in enthusiasm, Glen was clearly making up for. 'Introductions,' he continued, moving towards the closest boy. 'This strapping lad right here is Tyler. That's Jayden, Elijah, Noah and the tough guy pulling off a fantastic impression of James Dean is Ethan.'

Tilly smiled again and at least got a flicker of a glance from most of them, but the boy still leaning against the van refused to acknowledge anyone. Glen continued on unfazed, so she tried not to take it personally.

'This is Tilly, and while we're here, on her property, she's the boss. I don't want to have to remind you about what we spoke about on the bus,' he said, lowering his tone slightly as he looked at each of the kids pointedly. 'I want you all to listen to what she's got to say and then we'll go over the rules once more before we start.'

'Hi, and welcome,' Tilly started, feeling her hands shake a little. 'This is a pretty big day for me—you guys are the very first class to go through our program. My husband and I started planning this program about five years ago; he was a police officer and did a lot of work with kids and I've worked with horses and therapy, so we decided to combine the two things and came up with Healing Hooves. I really hope you guys get something positive out of your week here.'

'What happened to your husband?' a voice spoke up in the silence that followed her greeting. Tilly looked over at the kid leaning against the bus.

'I'm sorry?' she replied uncertainly.

'You said he was a police officer and he isn't here doin' the talkin', so what happened to him?'

'Ethan,' Glen warned, before Tilly spoke up.

'No, it's okay,' she said calmly. 'My husband died. But I decided to continue with our program because I know that he really believed in giving kids a second chance.'

'How'd he die?' Ethan asked, unperturbed, momentarily surprising Tilly with his blunt question.

'He was killed breaking up a fight,' she said, holding the kid's strangely unemotional gaze.

'Okay, how about we unload the van,' Glen cut in, breaking any further line of questioning.

'I'll show you to the bunkhouse and then we can go and meet the horses,' Tilly said, glad of the distraction but feeling a little shaky at the unexpected questions.

Behind her there were grumbles and some muttered swearing as the boys dragged themselves to the rear of the van and collected their belongings. Was she sweating? They were just kids, she reminded herself again. *You get in a round yard with a five-hundred-kilo wild horse. You can handle a bunch of teenage kids.*

Horses were one thing; kids were something altogether different. This was David's area of expertise. He was supposed to be here handling this part, hers was the round yard and horses. *Stop it. It is what it is. Now, pull yourself together.*

∽

Tilly was stroking Denny's neck when she heard the group approach the arena.

'Quiet down.' Glen's voice rose over the din of insults and pushing she hoped was good-natured, normal teenage behaviour as the boys reached the grandstand next to the rails where she stood.

'Now that you're all settled in, I guess it's time to introduce you to some of the horses you'll be working with,' Tilly said, feeling a lot more confident here in the yards. 'How many of you have had any experience with a horse before?' she asked, waiting for a show of hands and discovering none. 'That's okay, it means you guys will be on equal footing with the horses. They haven't had much experience with humans before either.' She gave Denny a final pat before walking closer to the rails. 'So, the horses we'll be working with are Guy Fawkes Heritage Horses. They're a very special breed of horse because they come from the wild. Sometimes they're referred to as brumbies. Does anyone know anything about brumbies?' she asked and tried to ignore the sea of blank faces before her. 'No one?' she asked again. 'Well, then, I guess you guys are in for a treat, because that means I get to tell you all about them.'

That, at least, drew a response even though it wasn't a particularly encouraging one.

'Okay, so there were no horses in Australia before the arrival of the First Fleet. As the settlers began to spread out across the country, they brought their horses and other livestock with them. Most of the country was thick bushland, and occasionally horses would escape or wander off, and over time living in the bush, they grew bigger and stronger and developed incredible stamina. The settlers would catch the wild horses and break them in. Then the government started buying the horses to use for the military. You might remember hearing about the Australian Light Horses in World War One?' she asked, looking around at the bored faces of the kids before her. *Okay, don't panic. The history lesson isn't cutting it, just wrap it up.* 'These horses we're using here are direct descendants of those horses,' she continued, 'which makes them very special.'

'Can we ride them?' one of the boys asked from the back and Tilly sent him a relieved smile. Maybe there was some hope after all. 'Not the ones you'll be working with. Those horses are all too young to be broken in. They haven't even been handled yet. There won't be enough time to get to the breaking-in stage this week.'

'I reckon I could ride one,' another of the boys said, leaning back in his seat cockily.

A chorus of not very polite responses followed and Glen had to step in yet again.

'Riding these brumbies isn't on the agenda, but I do have riding-school horses we can use. It takes patience and hard work to earn the trust of a horse, especially one that's lived its whole life in the bush. And that's the whole point of this program, to show you that you can do something really special.'

'How are we supposed to do that if we don't even know what we're doin'?' a smaller kid down the front asked.

'What was your name again?' she asked.

'Noah,' he said, almost reluctantly.

'Well, Noah, because I'm going to show you. You don't have to have any experience with horses, you just have to listen, to me and to the horses. Okay, so let me show you a few things on Denny here. I've had him for about fourteen years now so he's had lots of training. This other boy I want to show you, though, is a lot less experienced.' She looped Denny's reins around the post and crossed to where she'd had Rommie tied up waiting. 'This guy has only been off park a couple of months.'

'Off park?' one of the other boys asked, and she felt her spirits lifting slightly at the show of interest.

'That's the term we use for horses that have recently been trapped in the national park and get rehomed.' She continued to stroke Rommie's neck. 'He hasn't been broken in, so he can't be ridden yet, but already I can touch him and halter him, and he knows how to do things like lift his feet and load onto a horse float, and he's done lots of ground work, which is what you guys will be doing with your horses.' She led Rommie out further into the arena and demonstrated a few of the basic ground-work techniques.

'This is what you guys will be doing,' she said, after working Rommie in a wide circle and having him face up and stand still as she approached, patting his face. She came back to the rails. 'We only have a week, so I'm not expecting you guys to get further than this, but we hope to get most of these horses to a point where they can be touched. It doesn't seem like a big deal, but once you meet the horses you'll be working with, you'll understand just how hugely important that first touch really is.

'Not everyone will get there, and that's not necessarily because you didn't do everything right, it's because these animals are all different, they have their own personalities, just like you all do. But if you take this thing seriously, and you really try hard, there shouldn't be any reason you can't get to this point with your horse.'

Tilly took the boys over to the yards where they would spend the majority of their days for the next week. The set-up, with segmented yards opening onto a larger space, allowed her to move each animal from their individual yard into the larger one she would use to work them in.

She opened the gate and moved the first of the horses into the yard, warning the boys not to climb up on the rails. 'This is Rosie. She's about eleven months old,' she said, watching the young filly as she nervously moved around the yard, eyeing the audience warily. The little bay trotted to the furthest corner, ready to flee at the first sudden movement.

'She's been off park now for about a month and although she's used to seeing people around, and she's settled in a bit, she hasn't been handled. As you can see,' Tilly said, taking a step towards the filly, who immediately fled to the opposite side of the yard, 'she still has that flight instinct. Horses are a prey animal. Which means their instinct is to always be aware of anything around that might be about to try to eat them. In the bush, wild dogs are about the only predator they have, but that instinct is just as strong in them now as it was in their ancestors. Our job is to teach her that she doesn't have to be scared of us—that we're not going to hurt her. We have to build trust, and that can take time,' Tilly said. 'Everything new to her is going to seem really scary, but as soon as she figures out that something new doesn't hurt her, she'll accept whatever it is. So, when we do something as simple as stop moving towards her,' Tilly continued, taking a step and then moving back again, 'it shows her that if she stops, we don't chase her. We call this putting on and taking off the pressure. We use this in our ground work too. If she runs, we put pressure on her by moving towards her or waving our arms around, but when she stops running, we stop whatever we're doing and that eventually sinks into her head—that it's better for her to stop than to run.'

As Tilly spoke, she looked around at the faces at the fence and was relieved to see that while there wasn't any wide-eyed amazement, there was definitely some interest and it spurred her on.

She continued to demonstrate some of the basic things the boys would be doing over the first few days, which included feeding and cleaning out the yards where their individual horses were being kept for the week. The hands-on approach was part of the training, giving the kids one-on-one time with the animals so they could get used to each other.

Most of the kids accepted her instruction willingly enough, even if with a lack of enthusiasm, but she saw almost immediately there was a definite spark once they were introduced to their horses.

'Just remember, slow, gentle movements,' she reminded them as she allowed the first boy, Tyler, to go into the yard with his horse. The others were instructed to remain outside the rails. 'For now, we just want them to get used to us. Don't approach them, just let them suss you out in their own time. Some might take longer than others.'

'What do I do?' Tyler asked warily.

'You're doing it,' she said calmly. 'We're just going to hang out in here with her. She'll go on eating, but she'll be watching us, and once she realises we're not in here to hurt her, that she can eat and we're not going to do anything, then she'll begin to relax. You can slowly walk around a bit, put your hands in and out of your pockets. Turn your back on her, walk in circles . . . just do whatever you feel comfortable doing, but make your movements slow and gentle.'

She moved on to the next boy, and eventually she had all five in with their animals.

'So far so good,' Glen said, coming to stand beside her at the rails as they watched the row of yards and boys.

'Yeah,' Tilly said with a smile. 'I'm happy with their progress so far. They seem keen enough; well, most of them,' she added as her gaze fell on Ethan, who had decided to lean back against the rails with his eyes closed for a sleep.

Glen followed the direction she was looking in and gave a small grunt. 'Ethan's a bit of challenge.'

'I get the feeling he's not as on board with this whole thing as the others?'

'That's probably my fault. I fought to get him included in the program. I've tried just about everything else with him and this is pretty much the last hope. He's not as tough as he makes out—I've seen glimpses of what he could be.' Tilly heard the almost wistful tone in the social worker's voice and it struck a chord inside her. David had come up against a few kids who'd presented him with the same kind of frustration. She remembered him saying, 'If I could just get past all that pent-up anger they use to keep everyone away . . .' Ethan would have been a prime candidate for David to work with.

'I guess I'm just stubborn when it comes to these kids. I don't give up easily on them, but occasionally, there's one who you just don't know if you're going to reach in time.'

Tilly had listened to David telling her the same thing in the past. If these kids just had a chance, had the opportunity to make smarter choices, they could change the direction they were heading and make a life for themselves. Too many times he'd seen kids fall into the same trap their parents and other family members had fallen into. It was a vicious cycle that had to be broken.

'I think the biggest hurdle is having someone who cares,' Tilly said to Glen, 'and he definitely has that in you. The rest will be up to him.' She nodded towards the horses. 'I've seen them work miracles before, and there's no reason why they can't do it here.'

'Then let's hope for a miracle, because at this point I think that's what it's going to take.'

# Twenty

At the end of the lesson, Tilly walked along the row of yards and handed out rakes, making sure each boy had a wheelbarrow. She came to a stop before the last yard where Ethan was slouched against the rails with his arms crossed defiantly.

'Here you go,' she said, holding out a rake, but the boy simply remained where he was. 'You'll find raking up the horse poo a little easier with one of these than your hands,' she suggested dryly.

'I ain't doin' that,' he said, lifting his dark eyes to hers insolently.

'Everyone has to do it. It's part of taking care of your horse. I've explained all this, what you need to do at the end of each day.'

'Nuh. Not doin' it.'

*Okay, no need to panic, you knew there'd most likely be some resistance . . . just stay calm.*

'It's a way to help create a bond between you and the horse,' Tilly tried again.

'I'm not cleaning up some stupid horse's crap,' the boy said slowly, straightening up and revealing just how much taller he was than her. 'You do it,' he said, pushing the rake towards her.

'Ethan!' Glen's voice cut in from behind them, drawing the boy's attention from her momentarily.

'I'm not doin' it,' he said, raising his voice at the man who had now planted himself between them.

'We spoke about this, Ethan. Either you do as you're told or you're on that bus and headed back,' Glen answered, and for a moment Tilly didn't recognise him. She'd only heard the gently spoken Glen up until now, and this version was surprisingly authoritative.

For a moment the kid didn't budge, just glared at the taller man. Then, eventually, he snatched the rake back from Tilly, catching her off guard and almost pulling her along with it. He yelled a string of swear words Tilly wasn't sure she'd heard before and went to jump the railings into the yard.

'Hey!' Tilly snapped to attention. 'You use the gate. And you're not going in there if you're going to yell.'

'Then make up your mind, do you want me to shovel shit or not?'

'I'm not letting you anywhere near my horses if you're going to yell. So, calm down, and then you can go in,' she said, keeping her own voice low and calm, despite the fact she wanted to yell back at the surly little jerk.

Ethan let loose another barrage of curse words, but at least this time they weren't yelled and he swung open the gate, allowing the metal chain to rattle loudly against the post as he threw it over the latch.

Tilly gritted her teeth as the young colt skittered away to the furthest corner of the yard, startled by the loud noise.

Ethan took his frustration out on raking up the horse manure into one big pile, his anger making his movements jerky and abrupt as he continued to mutter under his breath enough swear words to have used up a whole cake of soap if her grandparents were here to hear it. Sweating and slightly out of breath, he finished the raking and turned to glare at Tilly and Glen expectantly. 'There. Happy?'

'Good job. Now take the shovel and scoop it all into the wheelbarrow,' Tilly said, biting back a smile.

'We were expecting Ethan to resist a bit more than the others,' Glen said quietly from beside her.

'That's okay. We can work with resistance,' she said, watching the kid shovel manure with far more force than was warranted. 'As long as horse or human isn't ever put in danger,' she added. At this point she was more concerned about horse than human. She would throw herself bodily in front of the kid if he ever threatened her horses. Letting out a small breath as Glen walked away, she told herself to be patient. Slowly, slowly.

Jason watched the kid strut away from the case worker, and realised his fist was clenched by his side and made a conscious effort to release it. He'd been on his way to the yards the minute he saw the teen try to stand over Tilly. The little shit was lucky the tall guy had stepped in when he had. If Jason had got there before him, the kid would be wearing that smirk on the other side of his face.

Jason had a bad feeling about this whole thing. He'd been a pretty wild kid himself at one point, and had been given the option of joining the army before he ended up in serious trouble. That was back when the army used to straighten you out. He knew first-hand how volatile a teenage boy could be, and while Tilly had assured him they were supervised and the program vetted the kids who were selected, he wasn't comfortable with the idea at all. They were still teenage boys—and delinquents at that. He didn't care how much screening anyone did, teenage boys were full of hormones and hostility and could explode at any moment.

'Hey,' Tilly said, eyeing him curiously as she came up to the fence where he'd been standing. 'I didn't see you arrive.'

He stepped back and waited as she slid through the rails and slipped into his arms. 'I just got here. How's it going down there?'

'It's a bit rocky, but I think it's going as well as can be expected.'

'That one's going to be a problem,' he said, nodding towards the kid he'd been watching a few moments earlier.

Tilly turned her head to follow his gaze and gave a small grunt. 'Well, there was always bound to be a few who try to push the boundaries.' She shrugged. 'I knew we weren't dealing with a church group.'

'I don't want you anywhere alone with him,' Jason said, watching as the kid knocked the hat off one teen and shoulder-barged another.

'There's very little chance I would be. My role's only out in the round yards with them,' she said, turning back to frown at him. 'What's the matter?'

'I saw how he was. He could hurt you if he wanted to.'

He saw a flicker of something pass over her expression and wasn't sure if it was annoyance or fear. He suspected it was the former when her frown deepened. 'Do you honestly think I walked into this whole thing unprepared for what these kids were like?'

'No, but—'

'You know how hard I've worked to get this place up and running. Why would you expect at the first taste of some kid being a little jerk I'd suddenly rethink everything I was doing?'

'I didn't say you had to rethink anything, I'm just saying I don't like the way that kid was acting.'

'This is what it is. There are kids who have issues; that's why they're here—to connect with the horses.'

'And that's all fine and dandy, as long as you don't get hurt along the way.'

'So, what do you suggest? I hire a bodyguard to stand over them?'

'You don't need a bodyguard. You have me.'

'Okay, Kevin Costner, you put your entire life on hold to come here every day and keep watch.'

'I plan to.' He shrugged.

'Fine. Waste your time, it's your life,' she said, then turned to put away the rakes and shovels.

'I will.'

'Good,' she shot back, without looking at him.

Wordlessly he helped pack away the equipment and feed the rest of the horses. If she thought he was joking she was in for a rude shock.

∞

Tilly knew that Jason was only being protective and reacting to what he considered a threat. Of course she'd felt a small quiver of fear ripple through her today when Ethan stepped towards her the way he had, but his insolent attitude had made her angry, and that countered any momentary fear.

Possibly Jason's over-cautious worrying had hit a nerve, and maybe she'd taken her insecurities out on him. Deep down, despite being prepared for a tough fight, she'd been hoping for something different. A miraculous moment where all the kids suddenly connected with the horses and were happy to be there. The reality was something else entirely. They weren't instantly enthralled; in fact, she was fairly sure most of them would rather be anywhere else *but* here, and yet, she knew to expect anything more was naive.

Having Jason point out another negative thing about her day had just topped her mood right off. She wasn't stupid, she knew her limits—yes, she was sure most of these boys were stronger than her, pretty much all of them were taller, but she also knew from past experience with the kids David had worked with, that most of their talk and bravado was just bluff. In their world they couldn't afford to be seen as soft, so they talked tough and they acted tough, but she knew they were selected for the program because they were the ones who the social workers saw something saveable in.

That was what had sold her on this whole program to start with: the passion shown by the social workers. They wanted to break the cycle of crime and drugs and destruction these kids were headed for. They wanted to see them make something of their lives, just like David had been trying to do.

Tilly knew if he were here right now, he would just shake his head and chuckle. 'If these were horses, you wouldn't be taking it personally,' he'd say. And he'd be right. There were days when horses could be frustratingly unresponsive, and even go backwards in progress, but she never considered it a disappointment or failure. She knew it just took some more time and patience. God, it hurt that even now, the man could be so reasonable and wise.

Mind you, if a horse had shown her disrespect or insolence the way Ethan had today, she would have lunged the crap out of it until it'd found its manners . . . But she didn't suppose Glen would be on board with that idea. More's the pity.

Day two went much the same way as the day before, but there was morning feed to do before the boys had their breakfast. That piece of news was met with as much enthusiasm as Tilly had expected.

When they trickled down to the tack shed to collect the hay, most were looking as excited by the prospect as a trip to the dentist. 'Come on, the sooner you feed the horses, the sooner you get fed,' she said cheerfully.

The yards didn't need raking this morning thanks mainly to the fact that Tilly turned the horses out into the paddocks the night before, and had brought them back in earlier this morning. 'It could be worse, you could be shovelling still-warm manure first thing in the morning,' she added with an extra cheery grin as the last of the boys filed past her to gather their allotted hay and put it in their wheelbarrows.

She forced the smile to stay in place as she met Ethan's sullen expression. As he drew level with her, she held his gaze steadily. 'I hope we'll have a better day today,' she said calmly and saw his expression turn more into a sneer. Only when he'd walked past did she let out a long sigh and allow her shoulders to relax. Her gaze fell on a long lunge rope and her fingers itched to grab it as she reconsidered her previous plan to run the insolence out of him. *Patience and time*. The words floated through her mind and she rotated her head from side to side to ease the tension in her neck. While the boys headed back to the bunkhouse to cook breakfast—another part of the program that was designed to teach them life skills and encourage a bit of team building, Tilly prepared the horses for the day ahead.

The main focus of the day was to get the boys in with the horses. 'We're going to start teaching them about facing up,' she told the boys later that morning. 'As the trainer, you need to have the horse's attention in order to teach them anything, so we have to make sure they learn how to listen.'

She walked them through a demonstration where the horses were encouraged to move around the outside of the yard, until they stopped and faced her. 'Once we get them used to this, it makes it easier to start communicating.'

Tilly needed to work with each boy one-on-one, which made for a long morning. By the time she got to Ethan she was exhausted.

'Who's that?' he asked when she reached his yard.

Tilly glanced over her shoulder to see Jason leaning against the rails of the main fence, watching them.

'Don't worry about who that is, you just need to focus on your horse.'

'Is he your boyfriend?' Ethan continued belligerently.

'Yes. He is. Now, are you ready?'

'Why's he just standin' there like that?'

'He's watching how you train this horse. Can we get started?'

'Is he jealous or somethin'?' the kid went on, unfazed by her attempts to change the subject.

'What?'

'Is he the jealous kind—you know, won't let you talk to anyone . . . that kinda thing?'

'No. He's just on a break and wants to see how the program's run,' she said firmly.

'What's wrong with him?'

'There's nothing *wrong* with him,' Tilly snapped.

'He's got a limp. Noticed it the other day.'

'He used to be in the army and he got injured.'

'Yeah?' For the first time since he arrived at Brumby Creek, Tilly saw a spark of interest light up Ethan's eyes.

'Let's get this guy moving,' she said, taking a step away from the gate.

'What kind of injury was it?'

'A bad one. Now, will you please concentrate?'

'Was it real bad? Like, has he got a big scar?'

'He lost half his leg, okay? Now, if you don't want to do this, we can get Glen over here and he can find you something a lot less fun to do,' she snapped.

'All right, calm your knickers, darlin',' Ethan muttered with an infuriatingly condescending tone that far belied his sixteen years.

*Count. To. Ten.*

'Step towards the horse and get him moving,' she instructed firmly.

'Okay guys, that's lunch,' Glen called, as he walked along the outside of the yards.

'Aww,' Ethan said, with fake sincerity. 'Lunchtime.' He turned away and headed out the gate without a backwards glance.

'I know he can be frustrating,' Glen said, coming up beside her, 'but he'll come around.'

'The others seem to be enjoying it a bit more today,' Tilly said with forced brightness.

'They are. I'm seeing a lot of interest.'

Tilly wished she could say the same for Ethan, but still, in terms of percentages she supposed she was doing okay. There was still this afternoon's session to go. She wasn't giving up yet.

# Twenty-one

Jason groaned out loud and dropped his head.

'Come on, I said we'd go down there for a while,' Tilly said, tugging his hand.

As a reward for a great afternoon, the boys were given permission to play computer games after dinner, and the promise of access to technology seemed to improve morale no end.

Jason had just come in from feeding Red and was feeling relaxed and content, until Tilly dropped her bombshell. The last thing he felt like doing tonight was hanging out with a bunch of bratty teenagers. He and Tilly had just finished dinner and he was looking forward to a quiet night in. Just the two of them. He'd been itching to get his hands on her all afternoon.

'Can't we just stay here? I haven't seen you all day,' he groaned.

'Haven't seen me? You've been *here* all day.'

'Yeah, but we've barely had two minutes alone.'

'I know, and I'm sorry it's been so hectic, but it's only for a few more days, then things will settle down again for a bit,' she said, touching his face gently, which made him feel like a whiny pain in the arse.

Jason caught her hand, brought the palm of it to his mouth and kissed it. 'No, *I'm* sorry. I just miss having you all to myself.'

'I know. It sucks, but soon you'll have me around so often you'll be begging to have some time away from me,' she said as he pulled her onto his lap.

'That,' he said, kissing her, 'is very unlikely. I can't get enough of you.' Tilly had become his favourite new distraction. He knew they were taking things slowly, day by day to see where it led them, but each day he only found himself wanting her more. He hated dragging himself away to work on his own place, but thankfully he was finding a lot of things to take care of around here to keep him nearby.

'I just haven't felt like I'm connecting with these kids,' Tilly said with a tinge of uncertainty in her tone. 'Maybe if I spend a bit of time with them away from the horse stuff, they'll let their guards down around me a bit more.'

'They're just ruffling their feathers, trying to be cool. They'll warm up eventually.'

Jason hadn't been joking when he'd told her he'd be keeping an eye on that kid Ethan. She might be able to dismiss the threat of something going wrong, but he couldn't. He still didn't trust the little prick, and the last thing he wanted to do was spend more time around him tonight when this was *their* time to be alone. But then, how was he supposed to say no to Tilly when she was looking at him like that?

'Fine. But we're not staying long,' he said, trying for an indifferent tone but knowing he sounded like a grumpy old bastard.

It had been hard getting much done through the day. In between glaring at that punk Ethan, he had occasionally been distracted by Tilly moving around the yards. He loved the way her jeans hugged her hips and legs, and each time she slid through the rails he felt a twitch of anticipation. Unfortunately, his libido took a dose of cold water when he realised he wasn't the only one fascinated by her arse.

He'd caught more than one of the boys staring at her through the day and found himself becoming increasingly irritated. Jason recalled well how rampant teenage hormones worked, and he took a small amount of satisfaction from intercepting a couple of eyes, sending them a none-too-subtle death stare that soon had them scurrying away. All except one. *Ethan.* That little shit had been pushing Jason's buttons from a distance ever since he'd laid eyes on him.

The smug grin he always wore and the way he tried to stand over Tilly whenever he thought he could get away with it did Jason's head in.

Ethan reminded him of a kid he went to school with. Karl Jenkins had been a smart arse too. He got his kicks out of being a bully and he'd made Jason's life a living hell for years. He was two years older than Jason and considerably bigger and stronger. The humiliation of being pushed around and picked on in front of kids at school still burned a hole of shame inside him.

He saw in Ethan the same cocky self-assured swagger, and it instantly set off his alarm bells. The kid needed landing on his arse to wake him up. But no matter how badly Jason wanted to flatten him, he knew he couldn't, so he gritted his teeth and did his best to ignore him.

As they walked into the bunkhouse, he found the kids crowded around the TV, yelling out instructions to the ones immersed in their combat game. On the screen a battle was underway—teams of animated, buffed-up military men strutted around cutting down other equally buffed-up enemies as explosions went off and semi-realistic blood splattered the screen. He bit back a sarcastic scoff. Like any of these kids had the first idea what real life combat was like.

Yep, this was fun, he thought as he greeted Glen, and Tilly made the introductions.

'So, you're a builder?' Glen said, making conversation.

'Yep,' Jason replied. He wasn't sure why, but this guy annoyed him too. Part of him knew he sounded like an arsehole, but seriously, Tilly should be proud of him for at least trying to be polite. Normally, he'd never be in a room with any of these people by choice. Glen the social worker and Jason the ex-soldier were about as opposite personalities as you could get.

'I believe you were responsible for getting all this built?' Glen continued. 'My grandfather used to be a builder. You've done a great job in here.'

Okay, so maybe he wasn't as big a tosser as Jason had first assumed. 'Thanks, yeah, I'm happy with how well it came up.'

Thankfully an argument broke out between two of the boys and Glen wandered off to intervene, saving Jason from any further small talk.

He exchanged a glance with Tilly and her smile gave him a warm, lovesick kind of satisfaction. He wasn't sure how he was supposed to keep up with all these weird emotions flowing through him.

During a break as players swapped consoles, Ethan came over to them, flopping down on the bean bag nearby.

'So, how'd ya lose your leg, anyway?'

Jason felt Tilly's eyes on him and fought back his initial reaction to follow through on teaching the kid a lesson. 'Roadside bomb,' he said calmly.

'Yeah? Cool,' Ethan hooted. *The little bastard actually laughed.* Something snapped inside Jason at the kid's excited expression. The TV had been turned up and sounds of exploding bombs and gunfire almost drowned out conversation. It was all a game to them, he thought, feeling hollow in his gut. He took out his phone and scrolled through some images until he located the ones he wanted.

'Yeah. It was pretty awesome,' he said dryly. 'Check it out.' He held the phone up to the kid and felt a stab of gleeful satisfaction as he saw his expression change.

'This was just after; you can still see the smoke haze,' he continued, without needing to look down at the image that he sometimes still saw in nightmares. 'Check out this one. See that little kid in the street? Look, it blew her in half . . . That's her mother, she's just sitting there, in shock, holding her little girl's hand,' he said, watching the boy's face lose colour as his eyes widened at the images.

'And check this one out, that's me. Well, most of me, they couldn't actually find my leg, but you can see where it used to be.' He caught the phone as Ethan tried to push it away.

'You're fuckin' sick, man,' he said, his face pale.

'Come on, you were just crowing about how awesome it was to blow shit up and use that machine gun a minute ago with your mates . . . What's wrong?' Jason taunted. 'Reality a bit harsher than you were expecting? Animated blood a bit easier to feel tough around?'

'Jason,' Tilly spoke up from beside him. 'That's enough,' she said quietly.

He'd just wanted to shut the little smart arse up, but opening those photos and seeing these kids laugh about senseless violence dug up long buried pain.

'Come on, let's head up to the house,' she said, waiting for him to follow her.

Slowly he turned away, holding Ethan's wary gaze just a little longer, refusing to soften his angry glare.

They walked back to the house in silence, the red glow of anger slowly fading into just plain old regular irritation. Jason was angry at himself for letting the little prick get under his skin in the first place, and now he felt bad because he couldn't quite gauge Tilly's mood. She had every right to be pissed off at him and he wouldn't blame her if she kicked him out and told him never to come back again. He'd overstepped the mark big time.

He followed her inside and into the kitchen. The familiar smell of the house—a mix of fresh sheets and the baking she'd done earlier for the kids still lingered—wrapped around him and sent him back to his childhood, memories of his mother's cooking floating to the surface of his mind.

'Do you want coffee, or something stronger?' Tilly asked, interrupting his brief reverie.

'No, I'm fine,' he said, shaking his head. 'Look, I'm sorry.'

'No, *I'm* sorry,' she surprised him by saying. 'Ethan was way out of line and the whole situation was . . . Well, it was a train wreck waiting to happen.' She managed a small smile that looked more like a wince. 'I shouldn't have put you in that situation. I don't know these kids well enough to know how they'd behave. I just thought they'd like another male around. Glen said most of them don't have many male role models in their life.'

'I didn't mean to lose it like that.'

'I think Ethan knows how to push all the right buttons in people to get a reaction,' she said, then chewed her lip for a moment before continuing. 'Can I ask why you have those photos on your phone? It's just . . . I was a little surprised that you had them.'

Jason shrugged awkwardly. He hadn't really considered it before. It wasn't like he made a habit of showing people, but he supposed it might seem a little weird. 'I remember bits of that day, but not a lot. I don't remember the first few days in hospital, I was pretty out of it,' he said a little hesitantly. 'I don't know, I guess I reached a point where I had so many conflicting emotions running around inside me.' He looked over at her, searching her eyes for some kind of hint she understood. Tilly held his gaze with a patient expectancy that told him she was trying to understand and it spurred him on to explain further.

'There were so many things I suddenly didn't have any control over—losing my leg, being stuck in a hospital away from the rest of my unit surrounded by strangers. I knew there was a photojournalist on the ground with us that day, and I got my mates to track him down. I was hoping he'd shot some photos and that I could maybe see how things unfolded.' He frowned slightly, unsure if he was making any sense. 'The things I remembered were kind of flashes of images, and clips of voices here and there. I just wanted to see if maybe I could piece together more of it if I saw some of the photos he took. Turns out he'd snapped the whole thing. He'd held an exhibition, using a lot of the photos from that mission. It was pretty full on—beats the hell out of me why anyone would want to go to an exhibition showing all that, but apparently, they did. So, he sent me the photos.'

'Did it help?'

'Kind of,' he said quietly. 'I still don't remember all of it, but yeah, I think it helped somehow. Maybe I was in a bit of denial too. It sounds stupid, but a part of me didn't want to believe my leg was that bad, that they could have saved it. I think I was using anger to block out how serious it really was. But there wasn't any way they could have saved it. Seeing the evidence for myself made me face the reality that I had to accept it. After that I was able to move on a bit better.'

'I can't imagine how horrible that whole thing must have been for you,' she said, sliding in close to him.

He put his arm over her shoulders and drew her tightly against him. 'I was pretty lucky, all things considered. There were guys there who lost more than half a leg.' He fought back the images that instantly came to mind of men with bandages holding their partially missing faces together; others with multiple limbs missing. Then there were the ones who hadn't even made it to hospital. In the grand scheme of things, he'd got off pretty damn lightly. He could still walk, and he'd managed to pull himself together and get his life reasonably back on track. There were so many others with both physical injuries and those that were harder to spot—the wounds that were invisible, but just as debilitating—who weren't coping or who'd given up trying. He knew too many of those, and it tore him up inside to think of them now.

'Thank you for not giving up,' she said quietly, turning her head to look up at him, and the words hit him squarely in the chest. 'We'd have never met if you had.'

The words he wanted to say in return wouldn't form, so instead he did the next best thing and kissed her. Everything he'd been through until this point seemed to unravel inside his head like a film running on fast forward—all the pain, heartache and suffering, along with the good times, met and mixed in a crazy dance until it unwound itself right at this very moment and hit him like a tonne of bricks.

He was in love with Tilly Hollis.

Everything that had happened in his life had led him right here to this precise moment in time. She was what he'd been waiting for—what he'd been fighting for. She was the reason he'd never given up. Shaking, he pulled back and looked deep into her eyes.

'What's wrong?' she asked, searching his eyes.

'Nothing.' He smiled down at her. 'Everything's just right.'

He watched as her concern relaxed and then sobered. 'I really am sorry about tonight.'

'I'll apologise to the kid and Glen tomorrow,' he said, shaking his head.

'You don't have to.'

'I don't want to stuff up anything here for you with the program. Traumatising one of the little bastards probably wasn't included in the brochure.'

'I'm sure there was no lasting damage done.'

'Can we talk about something else . . . and by talk, I mean *not* talk,' he said, kissing her, but this time there was an underlying hunger. All he wanted to do was lose himself in her. She had the ability to take away all the memories and the pain, and right now that's what he needed. Just her.

∽

Tilly woke slowly, savouring the warmth of her bed and the comforting heaviness of Jason's arm across her hip.

A few months ago she wouldn't have imagined waking up with a man in her bed again. She missed that aspect of marriage—the companionship, and having someone to talk to in the dark. Being on her own hadn't worried her, but times like this certainly brought home how quiet this place had got. She felt Jason stir behind her, and gently remove his arm.

Tilly felt the weight of the mattress shift slightly and she turned over, watching him from snuggled under the covers, as he sat up, leaning over to pull his prosthesis on.

Her movement caught his eye and he glanced down at her with an almost embarrassed smile. 'I was trying to be quiet so you could sleep in a bit,' Jason said, standing up to gather his clothes and pull them on.

'I was already awake. I'll get some coffee,' she said, moving to sit up.

'That's what I was going to do.'

'Well, you can help me in that case,' Tilly said, about to slide out from under the blankets before remembering she was dressed only in her underwear and a thin T-shirt she'd grabbed from the bedroom floor on her way to the bathroom through the night. 'Actually, I'll meet you out there.'

Jason threw her a lopsided grin and lifted an eyebrow. 'It's a bit late to worry about me seeing you naked.'

She sent him a stern look.

'Fine, I'll go and put the kettle on. You get dressed in peace.'

She heard him walk down her hallway and rolled her eyes. It was stupid to be suddenly worried about him seeing her undressed—she wasn't even sure where this shyness came from, only that in some ways all this was still so new.

Dressed and feeling more in control, Tilly walked out to the kitchen and stood by the doorway watching Jason at the sink for a moment.

It felt strange to have a man in her house again. She let her eyes roam across his broad shoulders covered by a faded old T-shirt and down to narrow hips and strong thighs, faithfully outlined in soft jeans. *He's so . . .* She sighed silently, and thoughts of the night before went through her mind. She was getting far too used to this man being part of her life. She felt like a hypocrite after telling him she wanted to take things slowly, when all she wanted to do was jump his bones and tell him to move in. *Whoa. Okay, so maybe that's going too far,* she told herself, and pulled the brakes on abruptly. It was just her under-used hormones rebelling. For a long time they'd been suppressed and quite frankly, too sad to be put to any good use, but now, having had a taste of freedom, they were suddenly eager to be unleashed.

Jason turned around holding two mugs and saw her standing there, and they shared a smile before taking the coffee outside onto the verandah to sit down.

'Everything okay?' he asked, looking over at Tilly as he sat with one arm behind her on the swing chair, while his other hand cradled his mug.

'Yep.' She smiled, resting her head back against his arm contentedly. 'Everything's perfect.'

# Twenty-two

'Good morning, Tilly. Can I have a word?' Glen said when he came down to the yards.

'Sure. What's up?'

'It's about last night,' he said, looking down at the ground.

Tilly felt a tinge of unease at his serious look.

'Ethan was pretty upset.'

'I can understand that,' she said slowly, 'and Jason's sorry that he let Ethan get to him like that.'

'The thing is, Tilly, I've been finding Jason's presence a little distracting. The boys are picking up on his, well, to be honest, pretty obvious disapproval of them.'

Tilly eyed the man warily, unsure where this was heading. *Just stay calm.*

'You know that we're already fighting an uphill battle with these kids as it is. They don't need any more negativity in their life—especially here. I'm afraid that his presence is hindering the program.'

*Hindering?* 'With all due respect, Glen, these kids haven't exactly been acting like angels either. Ethan in particular was going above and beyond to get a reaction out of Jason last night.'

'Agreed, but reacting to things like that only makes the situation worse. He's the adult.'

'Last night was a social occasion—I admit, Jason's actions weren't appropriate, but he wasn't there in a professional capacity, so it's not fair to judge him for how he reacted under those circumstances.'

'That's the problem. He isn't technically part of this program, and I'm afraid if we're to go ahead with this in future, who's here will play a big part in whether or not we continue.'

'So, I have to have approval for someone to be on my own property?'

'In relation to this program, yes,' Glen said bluntly.

Tilly frowned as she felt all her plans for the future begin to slip away.

'These kids are my first concern, Tilly. I'm sorry, but I don't think Jason being here is a good idea.'

'You want me to tell him he can't be here?'

'Not in connection with this program. What you do after hours in the privacy of your own home is your business, but through the day, I think it would be wise not to have him within the vicinity of the boys. It's too much of a distraction.'

Tilly managed a tight smile as he apologised before excusing himself to get back to the boys, and her earlier bliss of this morning disappeared.

⁓

'Good job, Jayden,' Tilly said from inside the yards later that morning as the teen stood almost within touching distance of Gallipoli, the horse he was working with. So far almost all of the boys had progressed from day one. She saw far more interest from them today and her spirits had lifted enormously. Maybe this wasn't going to be a huge failure after all.

'Now slowly move towards her a little more,' she said calmly.

The teen took a step and instantly the young horse took off to run around the yard.

'Okay, now move to cut her off and as soon as she stops, you stop. Remember, pressure on, and then pressure off is the reward.'

It took a few more attempts to block the horse's circle work, but eventually she stopped and planted her feet nervously, her focus on the young boy in the centre of the yard.

'Good,' Tilly said quietly, although inside she was jumping excitedly. It was a small step, but it was *a step*, and when she caught the grin on Jayden's face, she felt her heart catch a little and thought about David. She could imagine him standing at the rails grinning right back at them.

After a few more minutes, she finished up with Jayden and moved on to the yard next door.

'How's it going in here?' she asked Ethan, already knowing exactly how it was going, or rather more to the point, not going. From the corner of her eye she'd been watching him sulk by the rails, barely even attempting to make contact with Sinai, who watched him from the far side of the yard.

When all she got was a sullen stare, Tilly took a breath and reminded herself to count to ten. 'Okay, let see what's going on. Move towards him slowly.'

For a moment she thought he was going to ignore her, but after a loud, hard-done-by sigh, the kid eventually pushed himself away from where he'd been slumped and stomped towards the centre of the yard. At the sudden movement, Sinai ran, and Ethan let out a barrage of swearing that did nothing but send the young colt into a fresh wave of panic.

'This is fucked!' he yelled, stomping back towards the gate.

Tilly followed him, but placed herself in front of the gate, preventing him from leaving the yard. 'I think it's time for you and me to have a bit of a chat about what is and what *isn't* acceptable,' she said, struggling to keep her temper under control. 'Firstly, what part of "slowly" didn't you understand? The whole purpose of this is to gain the horse's trust. How did you think he was going to react to you stomping across towards him? You scared him.'

'Everyone else got a quiet one, I got stuck with this piece of shit.'

'Everyone else has been listening to what I've been telling them. None of these horses are quiet. They react to what they see and feel around them. If you're going to behave like an immature child who throws a temper tantrum and swears because he can't use real words, then I don't blame Sinai for wanting to stay as far away from you as he can,' she snapped.

She saw Glen approach wearing a concerned expression, and once more forced herself to take a slow breath. She knew these kids needed careful handling, and it wasn't her job to reprimand them, but it was extremely hard to keep her mouth shut and only stick to the training talk when this kid was being a proper little pain in the arse.

'The problem isn't with the horse,' she said calmly. 'It's with what you're projecting. Let's try it again. Remember, when we move, we do it slowly,' she said, taking a small step forward and looking to him. The wait was agonisingly long, but eventually with a long eye roll and a disgusted glare, he followed.

'Better,' she said. 'When we move again, he'll probably take off, and that's okay, but we need to move with him until he decides to stop and then we take a step away to give him his space.'

As predicted, the colt launched into a canter, kicking up dust, sticking to the side of the rails as it searched for a way to escape the scary humans in the centre. Tilly and Ethan followed, moving around with the horse until finally it skidded to a stop, panting as it watched them warily. 'Now step back,' Tilly said. 'And another step back, slowly

'. . . That's good. See how he didn't immediately run away? Okay, now let's step towards him again.'

Together they took a step, and Sinai's ears flicked and he tossed his head, before he once again ran.

They moved their feet in a circle as they followed the horse round and round, until he eventually stopped running once more and they rewarded him by stepping away.

'So, we just run in circles all day?' Ethan said irritably. 'What's the point of that?'

'*He* runs in circles for as long as it takes *him* to figure out that running isn't working. When he works out that stopping makes life a lot more comfortable, then we know he's getting it.'

'How long will that be?'

She shrugged. 'As long as it takes.'

'What if he never gets it?'

'Then it's up to you to help him. They pick up on what you're feeling. If he senses anger or aggression, he's not going to trust you. Why would he? He'd rather stay safe. You need to dial down that aggression and start to concentrate on how you can make that horse trust you,' she said firmly. 'Spend the rest of the time before lunch working on what we just did. Remember to step back when he stops, to reward him.'

Tilly closed the gate gently and faced Glen. 'I know, I'm sorry, I shouldn't have spoken to him like that,' she said immediately, but stopped when she saw he was no longer frowning.

'It seemed to work,' he said, nodding towards the yard she'd just come out of. Inside, Ethan had just come to a stop and had taken a step away.

Tilly studied the horse and smiled. 'See how he's chewing?' she said. 'That's good. It's a sign he's thinking about things, which was exactly what we wanted him to be doing. He's not jumping out of his skin at the slightest movement.

'That's probably a good place to stop things for lunch,' she added, without taking her eyes from the boy and horse in front of her. It seemed a shame that it had taken until the end of the session before Ethan had begun to make any headway, but as her Pop had always told her, it was best to end on a good note so the lesson was a positive one.

'Good work, Ethan,' she said as Glen called out to tell the boys to wrap it up for lunch.

'He still doesn't like me,' the boy responded as he walked towards the gate.

'He doesn't know you yet. But he trusts you a bit more now than he did earlier.'

'How can you tell?' he asked, eyeing the horse doubtfully.

'Look how much closer you ended up being. It might not look like much, but it's a big step.' She saw Ethan processing that with a somewhat surprised look on his face. 'We can practise a bit more this afternoon after your session with Glen, if you like?'

He gave a nonchalant shrug as he walked past.

*Small steps*, she told herself firmly. *Small steps*.

Tilly entered the house with a heavy heart that afternoon. Despite how well things had gone today, the fact she had to bring up Glen's concerns with Jason sapped all her joy.

She stopped when she saw Jason was in the kitchen cooking.

'Hi, hope you're hungry, I've made enough to feed an army here,' he said, carrying a large pot from the stove top to the bench.

'Wow, this was unexpected,' she said, crossing to take a seat at the bench. 'Smells great.'

He busied himself serving out two bowls of the fragrant stew and despite the unpleasant topic she had to bring up, Tilly's mouth was watering.

'So, how'd it go today?' he asked.

'This is so good,' she said, scooping up another spoonful and trying to avoid the conversation for as long as possible. At his curious look, she finished her mouthful before answering. 'Today went really well. Ethan had a positive session. I think we're making progress.'

'I wouldn't get your hopes up where that kid's concerned,' Jason muttered under his breath. 'He'll always be a problem.'

Tilly wasn't sure if it was just because she'd been on edge since Glen had spoken with her this morning, but his remark irritated her. He *was* negative. She knew he'd had every right last night to be angry about Ethan's callous comments, but still, she was trying to show a bit of excitement for the fact a troubled kid she'd been having doubts about had made real progress.

'That's the reason he's here,' she said a little tersely, 'to change that.'

'If you ask me, they should have sent him home the day he got here.'

Tilly tried to concentrate on her food and stay calm. 'I was really proud of him today.'

'Proud of him?'

'Yes,' she said, looking up irritably. 'I think he's finally getting the hang of it.'

'After what happened last night, you're *proud* of him?'

Tilly's hand paused, holding her fork halfway to her mouth. 'Last night has nothing to do with today and the program.'

'It has everything to do with it! You're wasting your time on a kid who has no intention of changing.'

Tilly stared at him, her anger growing. 'How do you know that?'

'Anyone with two eyes can see it. He's a cocky little bastard who gets his kicks out of causing trouble.'

'He's had a tough life, and none of them are angels.'

'Everyone's had a tough life. It doesn't give you the right to become a bloody delinquent. It's a choice,' he said, pushing away his plate and leaning back in his chair.

'Sometimes these kids need help making the *right* choice, Jason. It's not always that black and white.'

'The problem with kids today is that there're too many do-gooders giving them excuses, instead of a kick up the backside.'

'And that's your way of dealing with them? More violence?'

'You're beginning to sound like Glen. It's not violence. It's discipline. Tough love,' he added.

'Glen's trained to deal with kids like that, and quite frankly, I can see why they try to stay away from the whole tough-love thing. That's probably what these kids have grown up with a little too much of.'

'I can guarantee if they'd had a bit more tough love they wouldn't be here now.'

Tilly pushed aside her own plate, her appetite well and truly lost. 'That's not fair, Jason. Not every kid had the good fortune to grow up with at least one dependable parent the way we did. That's why we wanted to create a program like this. Some kids need a second chance.'

'*We*, meaning you and your husband,' he said, holding her gaze levelly. 'I didn't know David, and I'm sure he was decent guy, but sometimes it doesn't do a kid any favours to tiptoe around things.'

Tilly felt her breathing change at the mention of her husband's name in a tone that held more than a hint of dismissive disapproval, and realised her hand was shaking. She lowered her gaze to the table in front of her and tried to get her rioting emotions under control. 'He *was* a decent guy and he believed in what we were doing.'

She saw Jason clench his jaw silently before saying in a calmer voice, 'I didn't mean to sound as though I was putting him down.'

'Well, it did sound that way. And it feels as though you're putting me down too.'

'You know that's not what I meant,' he said irritably, a frown marring his face.

'I'm not sure I do. I came in here, excited by my day and how much progress we'd made, and you've managed to ruin it with your negativity.'

'Come on, Tilly, you're overreacting,' he said, then stopped when he saw her face.

'Overreacting?' she said quietly.

'Okay, bad choice of words maybe,' he started again.

'You know, Glen came to see me today about what happened last night. I was angry that he was pretty much blaming you for what happened, and I defended you,' she said, watching as his frown deepened.

'And what exactly did Glen have to say?'

'He suggested you shouldn't be around here during the day while the program is underway because you're having a negative effect on the boys.'

'What the hell!' Jason exploded.

'I thought it was a bit over the top too, until now. He's right, Jason. You stand at the rails and glare at those kids all day. I've been putting it down to you just being overprotective, but Glen might be right; it's intimidating and it's not helping.'

Jason gave a harsh snort. 'Glen knows shit.'

'That right there is the problem,' she said quietly.

'So, what? I'm not allowed here because Glen thinks I'm a bad influence?'

'Pretty much,' she agreed.

'You can't be serious.' When she didn't comment straight-away, he stood up abruptly and stared down at her. 'This is bullshit, Tilly.'

She would have smiled if it had been any other time, because he sounded *exactly* like Ethan. 'I don't have much choice. Glen basically told me that they'd rethink sending any further groups out here if I didn't do something.'

'So, Glen gets to tell you who you can have here?'

'He does when it comes to the program,' she said quietly.

'And that's what you want?'

'It's not what *I want*, Jason,' Tilly said desperately, 'but this is my business we're talking about. You *are* sending out disapproving vibes and I can see how the boys would find it off-putting,' she said.

'Because they're staring at your arse!' he said, raising his voice. 'You reckon I don't know what they're all thinking? I told you I don't trust them.'

'It's not working,' she said sadly. 'Look, you can still come here for dinner and we can work with Red. But during the program hours, I don't think you should be here.'

'Is that what you want?' he asked again tightly.

'No, it's not what I want . . . but you don't seem to be interested in what I'm trying to achieve with these kids, and I have to put this business first.'

'Before your happiness?' he countered.

'You don't understand,' she said, taking her bowl to the sink then turning around to face him. 'This isn't just my dream. I'm doing it for David as well. For so long this has been a huge part of my life. Now that it's finally happening, I can't afford to risk losing it.'

'And I'm not David,' he surmised. 'That's what this really comes down to, isn't it? *He* wouldn't be making the kids uncomfortable.'

Jason's statement hit her like a physical blow, momentarily stealing her breath. 'It's not about comparing you to him. I understand that this was never something you signed up for.'

'And yet, that's what it is. I'm competing with a ghost,' he said, holding her hurt gaze defiantly for a few moments before walking towards the door.

She should have called him back, but she didn't. She simply stood in shock, watching him leave.

## Twenty-three

Jason swore and hit the steering wheel. How had everything suddenly gone so wrong? This morning they were talking about a future, and now it was over.

Who the hell did this Glen fella think he was, dictating who was allowed to be here and who wasn't? Jason knew this was a knee-jerk reaction from the night before, that the guy thought he'd been out of line with Ethan. But this was going too far.

He started the car and headed home. As he unlocked his door and stepped into the cold darkness, for the first time since he arrived, it didn't feel like home.

Swearing again, he tossed his keys on the bench and went outside to get some kindling to light a fire. That's all this place needed, a fire. Then it would feel better. But half an hour later, seated before a roaring fire with a beer, he still felt like crap and his mood had only sunk lower.

Jason hadn't meant to throw her dead husband's memory in her face, but Tilly had brought him up first. That innocent 'we' she'd slipped in there had struck home. *We,* meaning David and her . . . The man she'd loved and lost. The man she'd built her dream with . . . The man who wasn't . . . *him.* Jason glowered at the fire harder. He sighed irritably before conceding what he hadn't wanted to acknowledge before—he felt inadequate. The more he learned about David, the more he realised what a bloody saint the guy had been. He was a cop. He volunteered with troubled kids. He even died a hero. How the hell could anyone compete with that? Especially a crippled, worn-out war veteran.

Tilly wanted him to be something he wasn't. Glen was the kind of guy she should be with—the touchy-feely, new-age kind of guy. The opposite of Jason. When he'd joined the army he'd learned the hard way, just like everyone else who'd gone through basic. There was no coddling in the army, and say what you will about tough love, it worked. The army had given him skills he depended on to this day. Discipline. Hard work. Perseverance. The ability to pull your head in when you were told. Respect. Things that were sorely lacking in most kids today, especially the kids in that group. He'd seen his share of bad arses go into basic and he'd watched as a few of them tried to hold out, but ultimately the only thing they responded to was discipline. They turned out, in most cases, to be some of the best soldiers.

Maybe he *had* come on a little strong the other night with the kid. He did feel a bit bad about that—but there was a lot to be said for shock value. It had shut the little prick up quick smart. Of course, it had also resulted in getting Jason turfed out of Tilly's life, so maybe he should have thought it through a tad more. Hindsight was a fine thing.

He leaned forward and tossed another piece of timber onto the fire, stoking it before leaning back in his chair.

This whole thing had a déjà vu feel about it. It had been stupid to get his hopes up yet again over a woman. When would he bloody learn?

∽

Tilly forced herself to focus on her work. Things were moving ahead, and the boys were finally starting to engage with the horses. Two had already got that precious first touch on their animals, and the others were well on their way to making meaningful connections.

However, it was Ethan who surprised her the most. For the first time since he arrived, he followed instruction and didn't talk back once during the morning session.

'So, where's ya boyfriend today?' he asked as they were cleaning up that afternoon.

'He had some things to do,' Tilly said, which was true. Jason had been neglecting his own house renovations for the past few weeks and was most likely making up for lost time. She'd been trying not to think about him too much since he hadn't been answering her calls.

'I heard he got told to leave,' Ethan said, eyeing her curiously.

'Jason wasn't part of the program. He was doing some work for me, that's all.'

'So, Glen didn't tell him to go?'

Tilly shot a quick glance across at the boy and saw he was watching her intently. 'Glen didn't agree with what Jason did the other night,' she said slowly. She didn't want to lie to the kid, but she didn't particularly want to get into all this with him either.

'So, he had to leave because of me?'

'Well, not just that. Look, it doesn't matter, you just need to concentrate on working with your horse. The rest isn't important.'

Ethan continued to rake the manure in silence, but it was short-lived. 'He was pretty bad-arse, wasn't he?' he said after a few moments. 'In his army days.'

Tilly wasn't exactly sure what to say to that, but for the first time since she'd met him, Ethan didn't seem to be acting like an obnoxious brat.

'I mean, he went through some pretty heavy stuff.'

'I guess so,' she said, watching him uncertainly.

'I kinda respect that. I mean, he didn't just use some weird psychological bullshit on me the way Glen and the other case workers do. He didn't treat me like a kid. He showed me something most other adults wouldn't. He was actually kinda cool.'

'Well, I think it was more of an automatic reaction. He probably shouldn't have done it.'

'Glen shouldn't have sent him away.'

'He was only doing what he thought was best for you guys.'

'Is he coming back?'

Tilly felt herself flounder slightly at the question. 'I don't know,' she finally said, forcing away the lump in her throat. 'I can finish up here if you want to head back to the bunkhouse,' she said.

'I don't mind. I thought, maybe, if you needed a hand I can help . . . if you want,' he said with a shrug and a tone that didn't quite sound as nonchalant as he might have intended. 'Movin' the horses and stuff.'

*Interesting.* She didn't dare get her hopes up, but it almost sounded like this kid wanted to have more contact with the horses.

Glen walked towards them, watching Ethan closely, but as he approached, Ethan was quick to jump on an opportunity.

'Tilly needs some help puttin' the horses out. I said I'd do it.'

Glen eyed Ethan thoughtfully before turning to her. 'Is that okay?'

'Yeah. I guess.' Tilly wasn't altogether sure where this new enthusiasm was coming from, but she didn't want to turn down the opportunity for someone to spend more time with the horses if that's what they wanted. 'Empty the wheelbarrow first, though,' she instructed, and Glen swapped a slightly amused glance with her when there was no protest.

'I don't know what you did to him, but this is the most engaged I've ever seen him,' Glen said as they watched him leave.

'I didn't do anything,' she said, equally as dumbfounded.

'I'll be nearby if there's any problem,' he said as Ethan came back.

Tilly gave Ethan instructions, sending him out to open the gates as she moved horses between the yards and out to the larger paddock where they would feed and spend the night.

'So, where's that Jason fella live when he's not here?' Ethan asked as they closed the final gate and watched the horses.

'Up the road a bit. He's renovating an old house,' Tilly said a little cautiously. For a kid who'd seemed to have taken an instant dislike to him, he seemed suddenly focused on Jason. 'You know, it's not your fault he isn't here. If that's what you're worried about.'

'I'm not,' he said, sounding almost offended. 'I don't care if he's here or not.'

'Okay, then,' Tilly said calmly. *Geez, talk about touchy.* 'It's almost dinner time, you better get back now or you'll miss out. Thanks for the help,' she added.

'Yeah.' He threw the word over his shoulder, trudging up the hill to the bunkhouse where she could already smell the mouth-watering scent of barbecued onions sizzling.

Well, that was the strangest few minutes she'd had lately. The kid was like a yoyo. One minute he was being annoying, the next helpful. What would tomorrow bring?

A loud knock at the front door woke Tilly. Sitting up in bed in the pitch dark, she glanced over at the bedside clock and saw it was eleven-fifteen. The knocking continued as she made her way, blurry-eyed, to answer it, opening the door to a frantic-looking Glen.

'Ethan's gone,' he announced without preamble.

The fogginess of sleep instantly evaporated. 'What?'

'I did a check just a minute ago and he's not in his bed.'

'Maybe he's with the horses,' she said, grabbing her gumboots by the door and pulling them on. 'I'll go down and check.' She took the torch from the hallway table and together they headed down towards the yards.

Jason stared up into the clear vastness of the night sky. He'd come out after dinner only meaning to sit for a few minutes before having an early night, but it had been so peaceful he'd got a surprise to realise how late it was.

Footsteps of someone approaching from the darkness launched him from the chair faster than he'd thought he was capable of doing at his age. Automatic reactions apparently didn't dim after you'd left the army. His gaze narrowed as a figure emerged.

'What the hell are you doing here?' Jason demanded.

'Nothin'. I was sick of bein' cooped up. Came for a walk,' Ethan snapped back at him, as though it were completely normal for him to be out strolling in the middle of nowhere late at night.

'How the hell do you know where I live?'

'Took a guess. Tilly said you were renovating. This dump looked like it needed fixin' up.'

He was too surprised by the kid's sudden appearance to be offended by his comment. 'You aren't supposed to be here. Don't you have some kind of curfew?'

'I heard you got kicked off Tilly's place,' Ethan countered. 'That had to suck,' he added, taking a seat on the step.

The last thing Jason needed was this kid coming here to gloat. 'Get up. I'm taking you back before they call the cops out to look for you.'

'They won't. You got another beer?' Ethan asked calmly.

'No. Now get up.'

'Aw, come on. I just came here to chill for a bit. One beer?'

'Are you trying to get me in trouble? Again?' Jason asked sarcastically.

Ethan scowled up at him. 'I didn't get you in trouble the first time. I never said nothin' about getting you sent away.'

'And yet I was. Get up.'

'Look, I came here to say sorry, all right?' Ethan yelled as Jason took a step towards him. He lowered his voice. 'I shouldn't have been such a dick about your leg.'

Jason stopped and stared at the kid. He hadn't been expecting an apology and from the look on the kid's face he probably wasn't used to giving them. 'Yeah, well, I probably overreacted. I didn't mean to freak you out with the photos.'

'I wasn't freaked out,' the teen said quickly, before looking at Jason sheepishly. 'I just wasn't . . . expectin' it, that's all.'

Jason gave the kid a measured look before slowly lowering himself back into his chair. He wasn't sure what the game was here, but he got the feeling there was something different about the kid tonight.

For a long moment neither of them spoke.

'So,' Ethan said, finally breaking the silence, 'you were in the army?'

'Yep.'

'For how long?'

'Since I left school, till a couple years ago.'

'Was it cool . . . you know, other than losin' your leg and everything? Did you like it?'

'Yeah. I did.'

Ethan nodded but seemed at a loss to think of anything else to say.

'Is that something you want to do?'

'Join the army?' Ethan said, managing to sound both surprised and maybe a little unsure.

'Yeah. Why not? You don't have a criminal record yet, do you?'

'No,' Ethan said quickly, but with a definite edge of defensiveness.

'Well, then, you wouldn't have that against you. There're worse jobs out there.'

'I don't know anything about the army. I mean, I wouldn't know what to do . . . how to join.'

Jason heard the uncertainty in the kid's voice and it lowered his guard a little. Was he really starting to feel sorry for him? 'You'd have to work hard to get accepted—train,' he said.

'Train? Before you even get accepted?'

'Yeah. You have to be able to pass a fitness test and medicals . . . aptitude tests.'

'Yeah. Nah. That doesn't sound like me,' Ethan said, shaking his head.

'Why? Are you somehow above everyone else?' Jason asked, lifting an eyebrow.

'Nah,' Ethan protested gruffly. 'It just . . . it just sounds too hard.'

'Well, with that attitude you probably wouldn't make it into the army anyway.' Jason shrugged.

'I could so,' Ethan retorted with a glare.

'Not if you think just *applying* is too hard.'

'Yeah, well, maybe I will then,' he snapped.

'Okay. I'll come and talk to that social worker of yours tomorrow.'

'What? Why?'

'If you want to join the army, you should do something about it. How old are you?'

'I'll be seventeen in a couple of months.'

'Well, you should start looking into it now. Won't hurt to ask Glen to help you take the first steps. But you can start training now so you're ready.'

'Do you reckon you could, you know, show me what stuff I need to do?'

'I don't know. Maybe. But you'd have to be fair dinkum about it. No more fooling around and being a jerk to everyone.'

'I can't make promises,' Ethan said, and Jason saw a return of the cockiness.

'Then I'm not wasting my time on you,' Jason said.

'I'm kiddin'. Geez. Lighten up.'

'Yeah, well, it's late. Get up, I'm taking you back.'

Thankfully, Ethan didn't protest this time, and as Jason slid into the driver's seat all he could think about was what kind of reception he was in for.

'They won't even know I'm gone. I've done this heaps of times before.'

As they drove up the driveway to Brumby Creek, Ethan groaned and Jason's mouth formed a tight line at the house lit up ahead of them.

'Oh yeah. Pretty sure you outwitted them this time.' Jason pulled up and saw Tilly, dressed in pyjamas and gumboots, turn around to watch their approach. Standing beside her was the lanky Glen, looking frazzled and none too pleased.

'Still think leaving was a good idea?' Jason asked Ethan.

They climbed out of the car and immediately Glen walked towards them, his usually serene face a mask of irritation. 'You're heading back to the city tomorrow. I've had enough of your behaviour. This was your third strike.'

'But I—'

'Save it, Ethan.'

'Look, mate,' Jason said, turning to Glen when Ethan looked across at him almost desperately. 'This is partly my fault—' he began, before being cut off abruptly.

'Yes, it is,' Glen snapped. 'You've also potentially ruined Tilly's chance of getting any further groups or funding out here, so I hope you're pleased with yourself.'

'Now hang on,' Jason started, frowning as he saw the devastation on Tilly's face.

'Get back to the bunkhouse now, Ethan. We'll deal with this on the way back tomorrow.'

'Wait,' Jason growled, putting his hand on Ethan's arm as he went to storm past. 'Just hang on a sec.'

'Take your hand off him,' Glen said, stepping towards Jason.

'Calm down, mate,' Jason said, lifting his hand off the teen's arm.

'Do *not* tell me to calm down.'

'He didn't do nothin'. It was my fault,' Ethan cut in.

'You left the bunkhouse without permission. That's running away. You broke the rules. You're going home.'

'I went to say sorry for getting him into trouble. I wasn't runnin' away.'

'The kid's telling the truth. He did come over to apologise, even though I was the one who was too hard on him the other night. He wanted to know more about the army and he's keen to look into joining when he's old enough.'

Glen paused, his gaze narrowing slightly on Ethan's face. 'Is that true?'

'Yeah,' Ethan replied grudgingly. 'I figured he'd know what I had to do. And it's not like I could wait and ask him next time he was here, 'cause you sent him away,' he added pointedly.

For a minute they all stood there waiting to see what the social worker would do, and Jason breathed a small sigh of relief when Glen took a step back and gave a long sigh. 'You'll be on clean-up duty for the remainder of the stay and no Xbox for leaving the bunkhouse,' he said eventually. 'But I'll consider the returning-you-home bit after I've had time to think it over some more. Now get to bed.'

Ethan, clearly knowing when not to push his luck, jogged off towards the bunkhouse and disappeared inside.

'You should have called immediately for me to come and pick him up. That kid . . . all those kids are my responsibility,' Glen continued testily, turning back to face Jason.

'Like I said, he came to apologise and then he started asking about a career in the army. Call me stupid, but considering these kids were about to head for detention centres and a life of crime, I thought his initiating an interest in a legitimate career was probably worth investing a few minutes of conversation in,' Jason said, turning away. 'You're welcome, by the way, and don't worry, I'm leaving.'

'Jason, wait.' Tilly spoke for the first time since he'd arrived. 'Glen, I think you owe Jason an apology.'

She sounded angry, and Jason paused, almost relishing the fact that, for once, it didn't seem to be aimed at him.

He watched as Glen stared at Tilly before seeming to square his shoulders and clear his throat.

'I guess I do.' He switched his gaze across to Jason before sighing again. 'I may have been a little harsh earlier,' Glen admitted.

'Will the program be safe for Tilly to keep hold of here?' Jason pressed.

'Under the circumstances, it seems like it's worked better than we anticipated. I reacted from a mixture of fear and relief, possibly a bit of suppressed anger too,' Glen said with a slightly guilty smile. 'Ethan knows how to push buttons.'

'No one's going to argue with you there,' Jason muttered.

'Well, goodnight. I'll leave you to it,' Glen said to Tilly, before sending a brief glance towards Jason. 'Thanks for bringing him back.'

They watched him walk away in silence, before Jason shuffled his feet, suddenly feeling more awkward than he had in a very long time.

'I should probably let you get back to bed,' he finally said, breaking the silence between them. Then he wished he hadn't mentioned the word 'bed' when images of last time he'd been in her bed went through his mind.

'I'm sorry,' Tilly said abruptly.

'About what?' he said, looking down into her worried face.

'That I didn't fight harder to tell Glen he was wrong about saying you couldn't be here. I let my panic that I could lose all this override my common sense.' She closed her eyes briefly before opening them and focusing on him steadily. 'I should have talked more, let things cool down a bit. I don't know,' she said with a helpless gesture, 'I should have done something, but instead I let you walk away.'

'I didn't go too far,' he said softly, then sobered. 'I probably could have been a little less pigheaded. I shouldn't have brought up your husband like I did. I get that this was a dream you two had long before I came on the scene, and you were right to be scared by the thought of losing it. And I *have* been acting like a dick lately. I should have known better than to let a kid get the better of my temper the way he did. I haven't been very helpful around here.'

'I felt miserable all day,' she admitted sadly.

'Yeah, me too.'

He saw Tilly bite at the inside of her lip and realised how much he'd missed just being around her—even though it had only been a day. It was more than just missing her, though. If he was feeling this miserable after being out of her life for twenty-four hours, how the hell would he cope with forever? In that moment he decided he wasn't giving up. He wasn't going to walk away from this woman.

'Tilly, I understand that my attitude was what messed this thing up in the first place and I'm sorry for that. I want to fix it. If staying away for now is the only solution, then I'll stay away, but I want to prove to you that I'm not the same irrational, jealous idiot I was acting like before.'

For a minute he wasn't sure Tilly was going to respond.

'It's been a huge learning curve for me as well,' she said quietly. 'I've been feeling so incompetent. I wasn't ever supposed to be doing this on my own. David was supposed to be here to deal with the attitude and the whole delinquent-teen thing. He knew how to talk to them, what to say to defuse a situation. I was only ever supposed to do the horse handling. So, I've been a little preoccupied with fighting my own sense of inadequacy.'

'You've been doing a great job with those kids.'

'I seriously don't feel like I have been,' she said, looking up at him with big soulful eyes.

'Hey, I was the one up there watching, remember. In between shooting looks that could kill, I saw the way they've been listening to you. When you praise them for doing something right, they light up like bloody Christmas decorations. I've seen the change in those kids over the last few days, and good ol' Glen sure as hell hasn't been the one responsible for it. It's all you.'

Tilly's soft smile tugged at his weary, cynical heartstrings and he reached out a hand to touch her face. 'Go get some sleep. I'll call you tomorrow.'

As Jason drove the short distance back to his house, his mind was on Tilly and the strange warm feeling inside his chest. It wasn't lust or satisfaction or the afterglow of spending the night with someone . . . It was love.

## Twenty-four

Tilly woke at her usual time, despite the late hour she'd finally got back to bed, and dragged herself to the kitchen to make coffee. 'First, coffee, then we do the things,' she muttered, then smiled to herself as she thought about her old work T-shirts. She wondered briefly how they were going at the cafe. She missed her workmates—even grumpy Paul. Still, she had more than enough on her mind to take away the moment of longing that had surfaced for her old, simpler life.

It was the penultimate day—the last full day of horsemanship. All but one of the boys had managed to get a touch on their horse—Ethan. He was going to be her focus today. She had already decided that if it looked like it wasn't going to happen, she would bring in Denny, and Ethan could do some more advanced ground work with him to give him a sense of achievement, but ideally she wouldn't need to. She wanted Ethan, along with the other boys, to experience for himself that magical moment of gaining the trust of a wild animal.

As soon as she walked into the yards, she knew today was going to be something special. For starters, all the horses had been brought in ... and there, grinning like the Cheshire cat waiting for her, was Ethan.

'I know, you're probably gonna yell at me for doin' stuff with the horses without you, but I wanted to do something to say sorry for all the crap that happened last night.'

Okay, so that took the initial wind out of her sails and silenced the safety speech she'd been about to give. *It's the second-last day ... Count to ten and move on.*

'Good job,' she managed instead, surprising even Ethan.

'Ethan!'

They both turned to see Glen storming down the hill towards them.

'Please don't tell me you came out here without telling him where you were?' Tilly groaned.

There was no time for Ethan to reply, and just by looking at his guilty expression she knew there was no point in trying.

'What are you doing?' Glen said, frowning as his gaze switched between the two of them uncertainly.

'I thought Ethan might like to give me a hand this morning getting the horses in, since he kept me up late last night and I was a bit behind schedule,' Tilly said casually, hoping Glen didn't see through her lie.

'Oh. Well, it should have gone through me first, but I guess under the circumstances...'

'You didn't think I'd nicked off again, did ya, Glen? Man, you *really* have trust issues, huh?'

'Ethan, how about you make sure the water troughs are full?' Tilly cut in, sending him a look that suggested he quit while he was still ahead. 'Sorry, Glen. Late night and all that,' she added lightly.

'Yes, well, I'd better get back to the others before they all revolt.'

'See you down here soon.'

Tilly shook her head as she glanced over at the teen going about the chores as though he were born to it, instead of having been introduced to the concept in the past week.

'*You* have to learn a very important lesson, mister,' she said sternly. 'You need to stop antagonising people for your enjoyment. If you're serious about joining the army, you're going to need Glen to help you. I don't think you appreciate just how much.'

She saw him give a small wince, before nodding. 'Yeah, I guess.'

'I mean it, Ethan. That man is on your side. He's not the enemy. He's the kind of person who would move heaven and earth to help out one of his kids,' she said, holding the boy's eye sternly. 'He has a lot of red tape to deal with, but the fact he fought so hard to get you on this program in the first place should tell you that he won't give up on you ... as long as you don't give up on him. I think you owe him a lot more respect than you've been showing.'

'Yeah. I know.'

Tilly watched him stare down into the water trough as it filled. She smiled at the sight. Most of her best thinking happened while doing this task. There was something soothing about watching the water level of a trough rise slowly. It could be very therapeutic.

A movement drew her gaze and she murmured Ethan's name. 'Very slowly, turn your head,' she said calmly—far more calmly than she was feeling.

Ethan did as he was told, and Tilly saw his eyes widen as he found the little colt had moved towards him and was timidly lifting his nose in the air.

'Don't try to touch him yet. See what he does.'

For a few moments Sinai nodded his head uncertainly and inched forward, until he nudged the hem of Ethan's T-shirt.

It never ceased to amaze Tilly how these animals picked up on emotions. For the better part of the last week Ethan had been carrying so much anger and frustration around with him, and his horse felt it, but today, finally, the boy seemed to be calmer and the little colt sensed it straightaway.

'Slowly put your hand out,' Tilly said, and felt her throat tighten as she saw the muzzle lightly touch the teenager's hand. She shared a grin with Ethan when he looked up at her, his smile—the first genuine one she'd seen from him—lighting up his face. Tilly fought hard to blink away the sting of happy tears that had rapidly begun to fill her eyes. Damn it, she was not going to cry. Instead she bit down hard on the inside of her cheek and gave him a wide grin.

This was it. This was what it felt like to achieve your dream. It might only last a split second, and maybe once these kids left here their life might go back to their version of normal, but for that split-second this kid just realised he was capable of doing amazing things.

'Good job,' Tilly said softly.

∽

Ethan's day went from strength to strength. After that first touch, he and the colt forged ahead. By morning tea, he had a halter slipped over his head and by lunchtime he was leading Sinai around the yard.

After lunch, when the boys all came back down to the yards, Tilly was waiting with her riding horses lined up and ready.

'Since you all did so well today, I figured it was time we did some riding. Anyone keen?' She saw the boys' eyes light up and there were a few shouts of excitement—very different to the bored, unresponsive kids who'd shown up here on day one.

Tilly took them through the basics and made everyone do a few circuits of the round yard before she was confident they were comfortable in the saddle, then led the way on her own horse to the open paddocks beyond.

They rode through the top grazing paddocks and down towards the gate that gave her access to the rear of the national park, where they crossed the gently bubbling Brumby Creek: the place her grandfather had named the property after. Tilly often used the trails through here with her riding students and for her own relaxation; there was nothing like a ride through the bush to clear your head and make you feel like you were a thousand miles from anywhere.

Behind her she heard the boys following. Their joking and teasing had taken on a different tone to the way it had been at beginning of the program, and Tilly felt quiet pride in how the past week had brought the boys closer together.

There was much protesting and complaining when she announced it was time to turn back and head home, but she suspected that this hour-long ride for kids who'd never ridden before would probably mean they'd be hurting enough by tonight, and be glad they weren't riding any longer today.

They helped unsaddle the horses, and Tilly showed the boys how to wash down and groom them before they went back to tend to the other horses and do the afternoon feed.

'Why couldn't he have been this good on day one?' Ethan said, after saying goodnight to his now affectionate little brumby as the afternoon session came to a close.

'Because the whole point of this is earning trust and building confidence. Nothing worthwhile comes easy,' Tilly said. 'You wouldn't have got this much pride from a job well done if he'd let you do that on day one.'

'I suppose so. I'm gonna miss him.'

'I think he's going to miss you too,' Tilly said, feeling a little sad that Ethan's journey at Brumby Creek had all but ended.

'You're lucky you get to work with them all the time,' he said as they walked towards the bunkhouse later.

'I guess I am. But that's because I worked hard to make this dream happen. You'll have something that makes you just as happy one day if you do the same. I promise.'

As they reached the top of the hill, Tilly stopped at the sight of a familiar four-wheel drive parked in front of her house. Jason and Glen seemed to be deep in discussion and hadn't noticed them walk up.

'Hi,' Tilly said, eyeing them cautiously.

'I was just about to come and get you,' Glen said to Ethan.

'I didn't do nothin',' Ethan said automatically. 'Tell him, Tilly, I've been with you all day.'

Tilly opened her mouth to verify it but Glen gave a brief chuckle. 'Calm down, you aren't in trouble . . . I know, it's a shock to me too,' he added dryly as he took in the boy's wary look. 'Jason came to put an idea forward, and if you agree, I think we can make it work.'

Tilly looked over at Jason expectantly, who seemed a tad uncomfortable under the spotlight.

'Jason's willing to give you a job, as his offsider while you wait until you can apply for the army. Like a traineeship.'

Tilly's eyes widened, but not quite as much as Ethan's.

'You'd have to pull your weight,' Jason jumped in quickly. 'I've picked up a few jobs around here and I could use an extra set of hands. I figured if you're serious about the army, I could help you work out a training schedule and get you prepared for your application.'

'For real?' Ethan asked, staring at Jason as though waiting for some kind of punchline.

'For real,' Jason said.

Ethan kept looking from person to person, as he tried to absorb the enormity of the offer.

'You can take some time to think it over,' Tilly said gently.

'No! I mean, I don't need to think it over. I'll do it.'

'It still needs to be approved and we have a lot of forms to fill out and processes to go through,' Glen said, playing the voice of reason, 'but I can't see why it couldn't work in theory.'

'Oh mad. Wait till I tell the others,' Ethan said, turning to jog back to the bunkhouse.

'You understand this isn't my decision,' Glen said, turning back to Jason. 'I have to run this past my boss, but Ethan's in his aunt's care and I think she'll be happy about the idea of him starting a job and moving out. He's been a bit of a handful for her.'

'I understand,' Jason said, reaching out to shake the other man's hand. 'Much appreciated.'

Tilly stared at him, speechless for a moment after Glen left them. 'Why? What on earth made you do that?'

'I've had time to think. You were right. These kids have been dealt a shitty card in life so far. Watching you these past few months, building this thing up and then working with the kids . . . it was an inspiration. *You're* an inspiration,' he added. 'I wanted to help somehow and this seemed like an area I could do some good in.'

'I had no idea you were planning on expanding your building business.'

'Apparently Bob Peterson is planning to retire. That fall made him reconsider going back to work, so I've had a few enquiries lately. I can't do it by myself. Who knows, maybe I can offer apprenticeships down the track if we get a kid through here who's so inclined.' He shrugged.

'We?' she said, with a small smile.

'That's what I'm hoping,' he told her quietly. 'Tilly, I know what I want.'

'And what's that?'

'You,' Jason said simply. 'I moved here thinking I'd get away from everything for a while. Fix up an old house, maybe even sell it and move on and do it all over again. I didn't expect to walk into a cafe one day and find the person I want to be with forever. I love you.'

Tilly held her breath. She waited to feel something—guilt? Grief maybe? But there was none of that, only a warm, happy glow. David was moving aside, and her heart felt suddenly free to move on. 'I love you too,' she said honestly, and saw him smile. 'I guess it was a good thing you learned how to say please and thank you, back on that first day then.' She grinned, stepping closer to him.

'You certainly put me in my place quick smart.'

'Yeah. I think we can find something useful for you to do around here,' Tilly agreed, sliding into his open arms.

# Epilogue

Tilly stood at the fence and watched Jason in the centre of the round yard, demonstrating on the big red gelding to a group of three men and a woman how to face up.

After the session finished, he came towards her and smiled as he pulled at the edge of his hat, making her grin spread wider. *Ah, that never gets old,* she thought, and wondered if those butterfly feelings that she felt when she saw this man would ever stop.

'How did it go?' she asked when he reached her.

'Pretty well for the first day,' he said, glancing over as the group headed back to the bunkhouse to get ready for dinner. This group was Jason's department. He'd come a long way in many things, but especially with horses.

He and Red had a bond that had only grown stronger over the past year.

Seeing the difference that handling could make in troubled kids' lives, Jason had been keen to extend the program to others—primarily, returned service men and women who were struggling. Tilly had been more than happy to let him take an active role in the business—especially when he'd researched the program and found such a huge need among his fellow veterans. This was only the second clinic they'd hosted, but following the popularity and referrals from the first one, they now had a waiting list for more sessions to be scheduled through the year.

It had been just over twelve months since Healing Hooves Horse Therapy had officially opened its doors, and they'd had every clinic booked. Tilly had a wall in her office dedicated to photos of the kids who'd kept in touch and often sent her updates on their progress, and every time she pinned another photo to the wall she felt a swell of pride. Maybe there weren't hundreds of kids up there yet, but the growing number of successes meant they'd managed to make a tiny difference in a few lives, and for those few, that meant everything.

Tilly let herself into the yard, preparing to lend a hand with the clean-up. 'I just got off the phone with Jess,' she said, frowning as Jason stepped in and took the shovel from her hand.

'How is she?'

'Great. She called to say they're coming over next month.'

'That's awesome,' he said, swiftly intercepting when she reached for the rake. 'I can't wait to meet Jack.'

A lot had happened over the past twelve months for everyone, but none more so than for Jess. Tilly's initial fears that Jess was withdrawing after her surgery were thankfully alleviated after Louise's visit. Jess's new clothing line and her company were thriving. Two months after her return to the States, she called to announce that she and Louise had eloped and were married.

Things were definitely looking up for her sister, and Tilly couldn't be happier. The sisters talked regularly and there was a new, stronger bond between them. Finally, after all these years, she had her sister back. And not only that, but six weeks ago, thanks to the miracle of IVF, Louise gave birth to their baby boy.

'Me too. I've really missed Jess; I can't wait to see them all. What do you reckon about having a get-together when they're here? It'd be a great excuse to see everyone. It seems like forever since I've seen Allie, and I'd love for Jess to finally meet Ethan.'

Allie and Tommy had tied the knot only a few months earlier and moved to Armidale. Although it was only an hour and a half away, Tilly hadn't had an opportunity to visit her friend. In fact, the last time she'd seen her was for the girls' night out and farewell she and Allie had thrown for Josie, who'd announced out of the blue one day she'd secured a job in Canada. Trust Josie to take 'broaden your horizons' quite literally and go to the other side of the world.

Ethan had become part of their family almost as soon as he'd started working for Jason. He was like a different kid once he had a purpose in life. Jason set him a training routine and by the time he was eligible to apply for the army he blitzed his tests. The day they learned Ethan had been accepted had been a huge celebration and no one had been prouder than Jason. It was after Ethan left for basic training that Tilly suggested Jason help out a bit more with the horses. He would never admit it, but she knew he missed Ethan terribly.

'I guess a party would also be a good opportunity to make our little announcement too,' Jason said, sliding his hands gently down to her belly.

'I guess so.' Tilly smiled. He still hadn't lost that strange look of wonder with a healthy dash of terror he'd had since she'd told him three weeks ago. 'It's going to be fine,' she said yet again, placing her hands over his.

'Yeah, I know. I just . . . I don't want to stuff this up,' he said, and it almost broke her heart each time he mentioned his deepest fear.

'We're in this together, remember? You think I have any idea what to do with a baby? But you know what? I'm not worried about it because I know that I have you and we'll figure it out as we go.'

They stood close together, looking out over the paddock of grazing brumbies, and Tilly felt her heart swell. Life really couldn't get any better than this. She had everything she could ever want: a man who loved her, a baby on the way, a wedding to plan in the near future and a business that allowed her to work with the horses she adored every day, in order to help people.

She sometimes still felt David around the place. Tilly knew he would always be watching over them, wearing his *I told you, you could do it* smile. She would always miss him, but she'd learned that letting go of someone didn't mean you couldn't still love them and think about them. It just meant that you were allowing yourself to go on living.

'It was my lucky day when I walked into that cafe,' Jason said, breaking the peaceful silence that had fallen upon them.

'Oh, I don't know . . . play your cards right, mister, and it *still* might be your lucky day.' She grinned as they headed back to the little house waiting for them at the top of the hill.

# Acknowledgements

Thank you to Kaaleena Potter, Oliver Elson and Caryn Hargrave. Thanks to Erica for all her horsey wisdom and always knowing how to pick a Karly horse when a new lot of horses come in . . . and also knowing when to tell Karly she doesn't need any more horses . . . Just one more?

If you follow me on Facebook, you're probably already familiar with my addiction to Guy Fawkes Heritage Horses. I currently own four of them.

I'm certain fate drew me to them. In 2017, while researching information for *If Wishes Were Horses*, I contacted the Guy Fawkes Heritage Horse Association located in Ebor, in the New England region of New South Wales.

I was amazed by these incredible wild horses that are descendants of the animals used in World War One by our troops and in even earlier conflicts in India. Their hardiness and endurance—their life of constant movement, travelling huge distances in search of food and water, in pockets of rugged terrain where they're still found all over Australia today—was incredible.

In 2000, National Parks and Wildlife culled six hundred horses in the Guy Fawkes National Park and as a result of public outrage, a group of amazing volunteers stepped forward and created what is now known as the Guy Fawkes Heritage Horse Association. This group receives horses captured by the national parks and rehomes them, eliminating the need for the ineffective and inhumane act of culling.

These horses are now a registered breed of their own and excel in all areas of equine discipline from show jumping to camp drafting, pony club and everything in between. Horses are bought and transported to all corners of the country and are in increasing demand because of their hardy breeding and unequalled temperament.

If you'd like to help this amazing organisation, head over to their web page http://guyfawkesheritagehorse.com where you can become a member, without buying a horse, making sure culling of these magnificent animals of heritage and incredible value never becomes an issue again.